Rhiannon Lucy Cosslett is a writer and editor for the *Guardian*. In 2012 she co-founded *The Vagenda*, a feminist blog which was published in book form by Vintage. In 2014 Rhiannon was short-listed for a press award for young journalist of the year. As a freelancer she has written for publications as wide ranging as *Elle*, *Stylist*, the *New Statesman*, *The Independent* and *Time*. She has extensive radio experience, having appeared on Radio 4's *Woman's Hour* and the *Today* programme. She was born in Islington, grew up in Wales, spent time living in France and Italy, and has now returned to her birthplace. This is her first novel.

The Tyranny
of Lost Things

Rhiannon Lucy Cosslett

Leabharlanna Poiblí Chathair Baile Átha Cliath

Dublin City Public Libraries

SANDSTONE PRESS

First published in Great Britain by
Sandstone Press Ltd
Dochcarty Road
Dingwall
Ross-shire
IV15 9UG
Scotland

www.sandstonepress.com

The publisher acknowledges subsidy from Creative Scotland
towards publication of this volume.

ISBN: 978-1-912240-14-2
ISBNe: 978-1-912240-15-9

Cover design by David Wardle
Typeset by Iolaire Typography Ltd, Newtonmore
Printed and bound by Totem, Poland

Acknowledgements

Many thanks to all those who championed this book and helped to bring it into the world, especially Diana Beaumont, my agent, Moira Forsyth, my editor, and everyone at Sandstone Press. You have all been so enthusiastic and supportive and I so appreciate it. Also I owe a huge debt to my early readers Holly, Sarah, Natalie, Kate, Ed, Siân and Simone not only for their thoughtful comments and suggestions but also for their tolerance of my neurotic cross-examination afterwards. Jessica, thank you for your support and your guidance on the ins and outs of the publishing industry. My friends in the writing group at Shakespeare & Co in 2005-2006 made me believe that one day I might just be able to do this – thank you. I am also grateful to my parents, who are thankfully nothing like the parents in this book and have always showered me with love and encouraged me to write. And most of all, to Tim, my husband, for all you've done, including all the times you have allowed me to use "I have a book to finish" as an excuse, and for the few small things that you graciously let me borrow.

For all of the flatmates, especially the one I married.

'Contrary to popular belief, the past was not more eventful than the present.'

– George Orwell

Landing, in the small hours. The boy man who brought me vanished somewhere, to take or to pick up can't remember which. Lean against the woodchip, bobbles grazing the softness of my exposed back. Cheap ass party dress, polyester static sticking. Sweat on the back of my neck from other bodies, familiar strangers glimpsed in cloisters and plaster corridors; arts and humanities, history, languages. Their conversations rambling, pretentious: T. S. Eliot capitalism electro ketamine Derrida, chunky jumpers and trilling voices. Music shakes the stairs, a spiral curl like the wet ends of my hair, stained carpets rumble. Hot smoke.

Then, from nothing, volume set to low. But mouths and limbs keep moving, a silent film on getting wasted. Then, high-pitched whining. Sharp skull dig of almost separate pain. The edges where I end liquesce. Tingling fingertips grab the banister, solid. Sudden, paralysing fear. Nausea. A child tap dancing on my chest, banging out every beat. The tightness of suffocation.

Sit on the floor that's what Mum always says. Are you ok? Is she ok I think she needs a doctor. Her eyes are rolling lie her down is there a medic here, no we never invite those twats. What did she take was it some of Johnny's stuff where is he go find him. Oh Christ she's being sick now.

Another drunk girl at a party.

I'm not her, I'm not. This is terror. I am dying, plunging down the black hole in the middle of the snail shell of the stairs. Drowning in its well of ink. On and on and on for miles and miles, like Alice into her underworld. I dreamed it, the nee naw nee naw of sirens come too late. I know how it ends. I'm ready for it. The sharp intake of breath like a heart patient shocked back to life. The solid, inevitable crunch of ground. The splintering of bone shattering to a fine, dusty powder. Dissolving, like salt.

Bones

Beach bucket, red plastic, 16 cm x 16 cm x 16 cm,
castle-shaped. Made in China c.1994.
Assorted rabbit bones (28).

The scream, if that's what you could call it, sounded like a cat dying. Or, to be correct: it sounded like the idea of a cat dying (when our cat died, ancient and dribbling, it bolted silently behind the horsehair sofa and would not come out). It was a horrible sound, too protracted to be foxes mating, a noise any Londoner is familiar with. It echoed through the still summer dawn, bouncing and ululating across the half-stuccoed terraces that stand gravely, like balding wedding cakes, along what is, apart from our crumbling black sheep of a building, a very respectable middle-class street. Longhope Crescent was populated by retired newspaper editors, Marxist university professors and one former Labour Party leader – not the kind of people who make such noises, normally. It certainly wasn't an animal, I was sure about that, but as I came to in a strange bed on my first morning in that house, my mind groping for clarity like fingers in the dark, it occurred to me sleepily that I had heard such a noise before, a long time ago.

The kitchen, later that first morning. I was making a pot of coffee and Josh, my new flatmate, was putting on his trainers, about to run out the door to work. He was – I would learn later – habitually late, waiting until the last possible moment to roll out of bed and often not even showering before he went. Apparently it's quite difficult to get sacked from local government, even if you have poor personal hygiene. Especially if you're in the union.

I hadn't seen him since I had moved into the house on Longhope Crescent the afternoon before, but from the stumbling sounds and muffled swearing coming from the hall in the early hours, I gathered it had been a late one. Hungover and in the process of removing a pallid, not-quite-cooked potato waffle from the toaster, he didn't seem in the mood to talk. But the strange howling sound had unnerved me, though not as much as the answer he gave me did.

'Did you hear that, this morning? What the hell was it?'

'It's her downstairs,' he said. 'Sometimes her dad comes over and shags her.'

I gawked at him. His accent – northern, scratchy – made the statement sound even more uninterested than his casual delivery, but I suspect he enjoyed shocking me.

'She's had a hard life, let's put it that way,' he said, and went.

At this point, having just moved in, I had not met any of our neighbours. I knew that they were not 'like us', being, we were told by the agency who managed our flat, local authority tenants (if that sounds snobbish, it's not meant to be, I'm merely stating the facts). Upstairs was a Womanist lesbian with a vegetarian cat who complained about the smell of bacon wafting through the kitchen door (Josh said we were not to give the cat, which he nicknamed Chairman Meow, tuna lest it be sick in the hall again and cause another row) and downstairs was 'The Screamer'. Our privately rented flat was sandwiched between them and let out for a sum much closer to the market rate, but it had retained something of the institutional ambience that the housing association had created in the years since it had taken over the property – woodchip wallpaper and strip lighting, a Victorian conversion butchered and divided, all false ceilings and that clear, checked glass in the doors that looks like the transparent paper pages of a maths book. Fire door, keep shut. Like I said, a terrible conversion, a tragedy, really. If aesthetics are important to you. If you can afford for them to be, which I can't.

That the house was a shadow of its former self was a fact that I had almost shared with Josh when he showed me around as a prospective tenant. He walked me from room to room, not realising that I not only knew the building better than he did, but that the house had been a central part of my identity for so long that his attempt to explain it to me seemed presumptuous. Longhope made me. He was only its custodian, until such time as I saw fit to return.

It was nothing like I remembered. The patch of concrete out front on which I'd played hopscotch was miniscule; the hall was not cavernous and majestic but shabby, the air dead and musty, as though it had been shut up from the moment Stella and I fled it. The wallpaper was a horror of magnolia woodchip, durable enough to withstand the building's conveyor belt of tenants. Nor was the house the same as when I saw it in my frequent claustrophobic dreams, and in some ways I was affronted. I had experienced a similar feeling when, as a teenager and after much nagging, my godmother had taken me for a drive past the old place in her car. 'They've changed the curtains,' I said, insulted. In my childish way I had genuinely and innocently wanted that house to be kept as a perpetual mausoleum to my presence there, and was outraged when I saw this was not the case – I had cried for the entire drive back. 'I shouldn't have taken you,' she said, then. 'Some things are best left alone.'

I cried this time, too, though after Josh had shut the door. And all because the bathroom suite was no longer blue and there was a pound shop power shower. When he took me on the tour, I had almost mentioned this fact before checking myself in case I ruined my chances of being accepted. Because who does that? Stakes out a house they lived in long ago? A crazy person, no one you would want to live with.

How clearly I could remember sitting in that blue bath as a little girl, the sting of cheap soap between my legs and in my eyes, my mother tutting and rinsing – a present from Grandma, and God knows how old – war soap. I did not want him to know my reasons for wanting to go back. I knew that being honest about my childhood there would only create unease between us. We are taught from a young age that to live is to be in a state of constant forward momentum. It's viewed as suspect to dwell on the past; to move back into it, suitcases in hand, is pure insanity. But I needed to feel that I existed somewhere.

Besides, the reasons for my presence were too nebulous to be articulated. All I had to go on were the furtive, guilty whisperings of my mother Stella, whose departure from the house when I was little had coincided with a break-down, and who would clam up or worse, go into a frenzy, every time I probed too deeply, until eventually I learned to avoid the topic, and never mentioned the appearance of the house in my dreams, in which I patrolled the building moving from room to room in the wake of whatever it was I sought. I was in pursuit of someone, or something, that remained elusive. Some scrap, some clipping of a memory long dulled, and I reached out for it, but like a child grasping for its mother's skirts as she is leaving, I found myself alone, abandoned in the hallway as I stared at my empty palm in realisation that I had clutched only air. Above, the chandelier swung and creaked, as I stood waiting for Stella's inevitable scream to perforate the dead air. 'Don't look! Don't look!' She dragged me away, a bundle in her arms as the sirens started.

After these dreams, I woke in a terrified state, startling and gasping for oxygen as though coming up to the surface of the sea. I did not know the reasons for these nightmares. For months I had felt that somehow the house represented unfinished business. The urge to return strengthened as the dreams became more frequent and my sleep more disrupted. This was during the autumn term of 2010, in the second year of my degree in archaeology and museum studies. During my waking hours, I felt constantly restless, as though every cell in my body was buzzing at a higher frequency. A sense of dislocation, which I now know to be the depersonalisation that is so often associated with trauma, pursued me everywhere I went. And then there was the episode at the party. I had been standing on the landing surrounded by people, smoke and noise, and all of a sudden had the horrifying sensation that a part of me was being ripped away, and that I no longer knew who I was. Even after they had picked me up off the carpet and taken me home and put me to bed, to sleep longer and more deeply than I had in years, it seemed to me that normal service had not resumed. I had been splintered into my component parts and I did not know how to reassemble them. And so I went back to Longhope, the only place that had ever felt unshakeable to me, until one awful day it hadn't.

In any case, explaining the episode, and these vague urges to return to the house of my young childhood, wouldn't have changed much as far as my new flatmates' initial impressions of me were concerned. Later, when we began to speak with more honesty, Josh told me that he had had reservations about me, as a flatmate.

'I thought you might be a potential weirdo,' he said. 'But Lou liked you, so that was that.'

'Why did you think I was a weirdo?' I said. It became a joke eventually, but at the time I was hurt. I had made such concentrated attempts at nonchalance.

'It just all seemed a bit strange – someone of your age, a student. I assumed you'd be in a student house, and wondered why you didn't seem to have any friends to live with. I said to Lou – be careful of her.'

What did he think? That I would attack them? That my sleepless nights, spent sitting in the living room wrapped in a blanket, clutching a mug of herbal tea so hot it burned my hands, were signs of a dangerous instability?

'I have friends,' I said, with a degree of defensiveness. But the truth was, I didn't have many. The student part wasn't strictly true, either.

As I unpacked that first, bright day in early summer, I found my teenage years in the pockets of an old denim jacket, a jacket my father had bought me sometime in the late nineties, when they were briefly fashionable. 'You'll wear this for life,' he had said at the time, in his Tesco jeans and his Paris '68 T-shirt and his cherry red Doc Martens (as if he'd know). In fact, the trend had been fleeting and was only just seeing a resurgence. The 'creatives' of East London had decided at some point that year (2011) that looking as though you were raised on a New Jersey turnpike was the last word in cool. I had always vaguely aspired to hipsterdom, hence the jacket's presence now, but I lacked the angular, androgynous face and figure, and despite a diet consisting mainly of toast, cigarettes and instant coffee, my fleshy thighs remained stubbornly together, rubbing when I walked. Ninety-nine per cent of succeeding as a hipster seemed to involve being thin, and I wasn't. I craved that effortless spindly lightness that men seemed to like (these days I wonder instead about those men, who seem to like girls that are fragile and breakable, and take up less of their space). Still, the jacket fitted better at twenty-four than it had at eighteen.

So, emptying those pockets, my Proustian madeleine was a denim scrunchie and an old newsagent's receipt for *Just Seventeen*. It was discarded chocolate wrappers, from when I used to have a bar every day on the way home from school, before my weight became a source of shame and worry, and those tiny plastic butterfly clips in pastel colours, run through with glitter. There were the audition guidelines for a school play, the main part in which I had desperately wanted, and had not got, largely because of what I had been unable to accept was a mediocre singing voice. Instead I was a chorus girl in a fur coat and pin curls. 'You actually look pretty', a girl in my class had said to me, 'when you wear make-up.' I have worn it every day since.

Looking at the contents spread out on the dusty carpet, the tastes of my childhood came right back to me. I remembered the fluorescent green, acidic tanginess of Hubba Bubba and how it makes your tongue contract. The saccharine peachiness of Campinos from the vending machine. Home, meanwhile, tasted like the lentil stew that my mother had perfected in the London house and had

7

continued to experiment with long after we moved away. We ate a lot of lentil stew. I can still feel the mealiness of it sticking to the inside of my mouth. It was just about the only thing she could make, and she only made it when she wasn't in one of her 'blue' periods. Most of the time it was I who cooked, following vague instructions mumbled from beneath her duvet. Or else we ate sandwiches.

Lunch tasted of free school meals, the phrase so often used by newspapers as a marker of deprivation. 'Seventy per cent of the pupils are on free school meals,' they'll report, but to us it just meant that your dad didn't live with you. (I don't think Bryn ever sent us much money.) They used to have these bacon burgers – imagine, in this superfood-preoccupied era, such a thing as a burger made of reformed bacon. I loved them, not because they tasted of actual bacon, but because they tasted of pretend bacon, like crisps, or in the same way a banana milkshake tastes like an alien chemist trying to replicate the distilled essence of a banana: banana extra, banana concentrate, with added banana. A pretentious acquaintance had a nostalgic dinner party once, when we were students, and only just discovering that there were things to be nostalgic about. We all sat down and consumed huge quantities of mini pizzas and potato smiley faces and Spaghetti Hoops and Angel Delight, and I'd scoured the aisles of Iceland looking for those fondly remembered, umami-ish bacon burgers, but no luck. They have probably been banned. So I came empty handed, and felt uncomfortable at the canteen memories that were less novelty than daily reality for a child whose mother was governed by mysterious forces that swept in like storms to galvanise and then disable her.

The smells are less tangible. I know in theory what it should smell like, a nineties childhood: Impulse body spray and Matey bubble bath, and too much Lynx (clinging to the skins and clothes of boys who wanted us to want them while at the same time hating and fearing us and our strange bodies) but I can't raise any of these memories. The only smell I recall is the one which, all summer, emanated from the utility room. We'd spent a day at the beach – a secret beach, I had called it, because along with my mum's friend Susan and her daughter we had driven for miles through windy country lanes, eventually parking next to a bank of sand dunes. From there we had walked for what seemed like miles, across the dunes, until we reached a stretch of unblemished sand. I can still see it now: the sea sparkling in the sun as I ran towards it, seven.

But the smell wasn't the sea, not quite. On the long trudge back to the car across the dunes that hundreds of rabbits had made their home, Sue's daughter lagged behind, pausing to pick things up and dropping them in her bright red bucket. It wasn't until we got home that we realised she'd been collecting bones. The bucket was full to the brim with little rabbit bones, bleached white by the sun but browning at the edges. There was even a skull, beaky and bird-like without its distinctive ears. Later, after tea, Susan's daughter got in the car and forgot them, leaving them to rot over August in the utility room, producing a smell that I could only describe as decaying seawater. So there it is: my childhood smells like a bucketful of rabbit bones. It's not ideal. Strange, though: I cried when my mother threw these precious found objects away.

'Do you ever feel an overwhelming sense of sadness that you'll never be a child again?' I once asked Lou, after I had been at Longhope Crescent for a month or so and had got to know her better. I was thinking of the denim jacket, which I was wearing, and how, instead of making me look fondly back on my teenage years like someone older, wiser, thinner, it just made me feel sad for the things I had lost.

'Sometimes,' said Lou, smoking a fag out of the window. 'It's normal, though, isn't it?'

'Is it?' I said. 'I thought there was something quite feeble about it.'

'Like how?'

'Like sometimes, when I was a teenager, and even now when I'm being particularly negative, I sort of wish I could just check into a hospital, maybe a psychiatric ward, maybe for exhaustion, and just be looked after for a bit, or possibly forever. Then I wouldn't have to think any more, and people would feel sorry for me, and visit. It's pathetic.'

Lou looked at me. 'I'd say that's pretty normal, darling. Maybe you're having a quarter-life crisis.' She waved her hand at a pile of newspaper supplements lying haphazardly on the kitchen table. 'Aspiration-fuelled anxiety. Call up the papers, they'd be all over it. The "lost generation", that's us. Or what was it one of them said? The "fuck it" generation. Fucked. We're fucked.' She said this almost jubilantly, carefully enunciating every letter of the word with pleasure, but mixed with a hint of derision that implied that to have any kind of crisis whatsoever was unbecoming.

'Ha.' I walked over to the window.

'It's the boomers, of course, bringing us up to think we're such special fucking snowflakes. And they sneer at us. We were raised by people who were never hugged as children. Our grandparents' generation were practically Victorians. Why else did they have the sexual revolution, the summer of love? They wanted the affection they never had as kids, ergo they were all nailing each other. The boomers are a generation of casualties.'

'I was hugged as a child,' I said.

'Of course you were. We all were. Probably too much. That's the point, isn't it? They didn't want to make the same mistakes that their parents did, so they smothered us with love and attention and told us we could be whatever we wanted to be. And now they say we're entitled and idealistic and they resent us. They resent us for having the love that they never had, even though they were the ones giving it. Well, I resent *them*.'

She put her fag out, as I did a rapid mental audit of how much I had told her during those first, fast-talking coked up nights in the kitchen, when she told the story of her childhood and I skimmed the surface of mine. That my parents were self-styled bohemians, that we had lived in a commune, though not that it was in this house, and that they had divorced. Nothing, as far as I remember, about all the pain that had played out within these very walls, Stella's removed sadness as a result of it, the wounds it had left on me. 'Where did you go after the commune?' Lou had asked. 'Everywhere,' I said. 'Stella never settled.' I told her nothing about how we had left, had tried to be a family, only for my mother to flee back to Longhope, taking me with her for those few short months that ended in horror. I didn't even know where to begin to talk about that summer.

'Spare me the pop psychology,' I said. But Lou's talk of Victorian parenting brought to mind my stern, sullen grandfather, a man I had met perhaps twice, and one time barely counted because he had come to try to persuade Stella to 'rejoin society' as he saw it, and my mother hadn't let him past the doorstep.

'Sometimes I think you girls are obsessed with your parents,' said Josh, from the doorway. 'It's all you ever talk about. Why not live your own lives?'

They made it impossible, I wanted to say. Or at least, mine did. The myth of their wild youth muffled everything else, and because of that I barely know myself. Beyond the walls of this house, and all it stands for, I am a curious outlander. The only clues are to be found here. Instead I said nothing.

'How can we not be?' said Lou. 'They played us their music, endlessly. They reminisce fondly about *Astral Weeks*, and get maudlin over Polaroid photographs. They watch BBC4 documentaries about the sixties and every other weekend is the anniversary of something, some momentous, history-changing occasion: John Lennon taking a dump, or whatever. And they're surprised when we fetishise vinyl and put little nostalgic filters on our photos? Is it any wonder we talk about them? It's the last time anything was tangible. All our shit is in a cloud.'

'It's ridiculous,' said Josh. 'You say you hate it, but you love it. You know all the words to all eight minutes of 'American Pie'. I've seen you in the kitchen, dancing to the Stones, looking at pictures of your mum from her modelling days and going on and on about how your dad once got off with Nico, as though back then it was so great and there were no power cuts or unemployment or bombed-out bloody buildings all over the shop. Things are better now.'

He sat down at the table. They often had arguments like this, in which Lou would argue flamboyantly and dramatically while Josh would play the part of the no-nonsense, straight-talking northerner. He seemed to consider it his task to rile her up and calm her down

12

again, while he acted as a vessel for her class-based frustrations and her vague sense of embarrassment at her own privilege.

'Things are better now? Things are better now? They had it so bloody good, Josh, with their free education and their massive houses that cost a piece of piss and are worth millions now...'

'My parents bought their council house,' Josh said, or tried to, but was drowned out.

'Even the drugs were better back then. That weed I picked up last week was shocking. You smoked it; you know what I'm saying. No one laughs when they're high anymore, have you noticed that? I hate them. I hate them for doing everything first, and for free, and then destroying it for us. I hate them but I want to be them. Don't you?'

Throughout this exchange Lou had been waving her hands about and the kimono that she used as a smoking outfit (and which, of course, like almost everything else she owned that wasn't digital, had once belonged to her mother) had fallen open to reveal the cream perk of her breasts. But Josh was still looking at her face. It was taking some effort.

'It's obvious you want to be them. I mean, look at you Lucia,' he said. 'That hair.'

Lou lit another cigarette. 'You think things are better now?' she inhaled. 'When everything is a version of something else? Every fashion trend is recycled, and every song is sampled? And every plot's already been done a thousand times?'

'I just think you live in the past to avoid having to think about what's going on now,' said Josh. 'And that's also why you dress like a grandma.'

'Harmony?' she said. 'Aren't you going to back me on

13

this?' They both looked at me, but who was I to mock the idea of living in the past? Josh was right, to an extent. I revelled in the lives that they had led.

I stayed silent. My parents met at a CND rally. They were everything Josh talked about, and more besides. Their nostalgia weighed more than my own ever had.

Summer 1984

I know from the moment I meet the house that this is where I want to be. I like how grand and looming it is, compared to the squat, grey buildings at home. I am too tall for those houses. The air in them doesn't circulate. Cooking smells and fag smoke linger in the net curtains, our drawn faces reflected in too many mirrors, put up years ago to give the illusion of space.

When we arrive, we are shown to a room in the top of the house, by a slight blonde-haired woman, older than me, who introduces herself as Coral and is trying to hide her pity in welcome flustering. She's dressed in the sort of way that would get you looks, where I'm from. The beads and bangles jangle in an offbeat rhythm as she moves her hands expressively, directing us towards bathrooms and towels and the hot water tank. Though it's June, as she talks and talks all I can think of is a scalding bath. The chill of hunger seems to have entered my bones.

The other doors are all open, hinting at helter-skelter lives within. Bare floorboards, piles of books, the few pieces of furniture draped in colourful clothes, mattresses on the floor. From somewhere upstairs I hear strains of *London Calling*, an LP I heard once at a friend's party, brought along by a boyfriend from Newcastle. We don't normally listen to that kind of thing. Truth be told, we haven't listened to much in recent months.

I can tell that Mark is on edge because of the way he has squared his shoulders. He's hiding how uncomfortable he is with cockiness, like he always does. He thinks it gives him authority but it just reminds me of the spiky lad he was at school who'd always take things the wrong way. When he sees the Buddha in a nook between the second and third floor landings, he gives a low whistle and raises his eyebrow at me. He flashes his watch and, passing the hall mirror, grabs the stiff collar of his shirt with two thumbs to pull it upward in a rapid motion.

My own clothes feel wrong here, my hair like something from a hairdresser's window. Mark's showing off in front of these kind people who have offered us a bed seeking nothing in return, bores and embarrasses me. I want to wriggle out of myself, shed this sterile skin, and start all over again, like a newborn yanked into a foreign, dazzling world.

Dolls

Worry dolls (6), 2cm in height, made from wire and colourful cotton and yarn, in yellow oval hand-painted box made from reeds, handmade in Guatemala mid-1980s.
Accompanying paper slip reads: 'According to legend, Guatemalan children tell one worry to each doll when they go to bed at night and place the dolls under their pillow. In the morning the dolls have taken their worries away.'

Trauma is a strange thing. It can lie dormant and then resurface years or even decades later, the cells of it multiplying until it takes you over. Its return can be prompted by the most random of occurrences: the way the light flickers through a window, the smallest and most imperceptible of movements, the smell of must, and fear, or the faintest imprint of a long-forgotten tune. You'll find such things will goose at you, forcing regression to a long-suppressed horror. It was twenty years since we had left that house for the final time, but it and the serene complacence of the people in its thrall had made me a puny, fractured thing. The residue of what I had witnessed prodded me each night when I slept, leaving me jumpy and strung out. I didn't know this then, of course, merely that I had to come back, that something of me lingered in that house, somewhere in its darkest corners.

I was born into Longhope. Legally, the product of my two parents, but emotionally, at least in my early years, raised by a collective. This arrangement – an urban commune of sorts – eventually proved too unconventional for my mother, who took me and my father away when I was four. We returned a year later, Stella and I, during the summer in which she left my father for the first time. It is a period we do not talk about, the prohibited topic of my childhood. Yet it had its echoes in my mother's torpor, her wall-staring; in my own childish desire for asylum. My return was prompted not only by a desire to know more, but because of a need for structure and stability. The house was the only place that felt like home. Its walls felt solid.

I had given up all hope of ever living there again by the time Josh and Lou accepted me as their new flatmate. I'd had a Google Alert set up on the place for months without much luck and had begun looking at other flatshares when the room finally became available. The house was not only much changed, but it also seemed smaller. I could remember standing in the cavernous hall as a child on the day we ran away, my small, moonlike face turned upwards in wonder at the winding spiral of the continuous stairs. I stared up through the hole in the middle and marvelled at the ceiling's height.

Lou's furniture, bequeathed by her mother the year before when she had renounced all worldly goods and moved into a Buddhist centre up north, may have had something to do with it ('She lasted three months before running back to Quentin,' Lou sniffed, 'but by that time he'd bought new things.'). It certainly added to the air of bohemian poverty that she was no doubt cultivating. The carpets were tangerine, while the textured wallpaper in the hallways was a jarring salmon pink, scuffed and peeling in places, but the pieces themselves were stylish. It's funny, I had always assumed my parents' taste, with their spider plants and their arty clutter and their mismatched antiques, was somehow unique to them, because everyone else's homes appeared so different. Then I moved to North London, and got into the habit of peering wistfully through other people's windows at night as I trampled home, only to see the places, with their built-in bookcases and Victorian fireplaces, all resembled each other.

The flat wasn't especially clean. Old milk flaked off the shelves of the fridge like nail polish, there were cobwebs on the cracked cornicing, and the wallpaper in my room puckered with mildew. When it was quiet enough you could hear the fluttering of tiny moths, so many you might think them native to that part of North London. Lou blamed all the Turkish rug shops on the Highgate Road.

As a child I had padded around that same building and squashed them against the walls with my fingertips, leaving dark smudged traces of moth-guts all along the magnolia. It was a habit that I retained as an adult, much to Josh's disgust. Resuming the ritual had reminded me of a long-buried childhood nickname I'd had for the place. I had called Longhope the Moth House, to differentiate it from the Northumberland cottage we had left behind, but also to annoy my mother, who, in the same way one feels about a relative, was happy enough to complain herself about the house, with its dust and its damp, but was vehemently intolerant of anyone else's remarks – however mild – if they could be construed as negative. After that, whenever I mentioned it, a twist of discomfort would pass across her face that, unaware of her remorse, I perceived as embarrassment, and she would most often say nothing, or change the subject with false lightness.

When Stella and I returned to Longhope, in the summer of 1991, it had taken me a while to settle back in. The house and its transient, eccentric inhabitants had been a poor replacement for the comfort of living with a mother and a father, as other children did. I was too young to know that many of them were also on a desperate hunt for a stable surrogate family.

Children need routine, and in Northumberland, I had had that. Picking peas in the vegetable garden, and shelling them in the stone-walled kitchen afterwards with Stella. Running along the windy coastline as my father's calls to slow down drifted in the distance, the fronds of my hair flapping at my cheeks as I turned around and jumped into his arms, his beard scratchy on my cold skin as he tickled me. Cosy nights curled up with them both under a blanket, watching the flames flicker in the fireplace, and the smell of woodsmoke. My father reading to me in a soft voice – hard to believe now.

Watching from the top of the stairs as they swayed together to the scratch of a record. The way he made her laugh, her face delighted at the revelation that she could, as though his ability to make her happy were a magic trick.

'He really tried,' she said to me, once, and I believe her. The most vivid images of my dad are hosted in that period in the cottage, when I saw his clownish, loving side come out in silly games and stories, and he touched me all the time, giving me cuddles and Eskimo kisses, swinging me around the room by my arms or holding me upside down by my feet, or waltzing me around as I stood on the tops of his shoes. We'd take daddy–daughter trips to the supermarket, to give Stella some quiet time when she went for a 'lie down', and I would skip behind the trolley with joy as he tossed strange and wonderful things into it. Years and years of chickpeas and lentils later, I can still recall that feeling of being held up at the waist at the deli counter to take the little paper ticket knowing I could choose whatever I wanted.

Here he was a joker, a playmate, a friend, my idol. I watched him constantly, Stella said, my little face tilted towards him in awe as though his ebullience were the only guiding shimmer on a starless night. That's the thing about fathers. They sprinkle you with enough love early on that you'll know forever what you're missing.

Having known him this way made the Bryn I came to accept a preoccupied, distant man whom I rarely saw and whose interest in me seemed mostly academic, an even starker contrast as I got older. 'Now you know how I felt,' Stella would say, during our heart-to-hearts. Even years later, she often brought up the divorce, explaining her reasons as a way, I think, of justifying her decision to leave him. We would drink wine and reminisce, and I would play the part assigned to me: exempting her through empathy. 'I understand,' I would say. 'Of course I understand.'

Now, here I was, an adult, settling in once more, having actively sought it out. It took several weeks to unpack, and even then suitcases remained on the floor due to lack of wardrobe space. I had accumulated a lot of clothes, probably more than anyone I knew, and was sentimental about them, as I am with almost all material things. I'd always had trouble throwing things out; objects were, are, important to me, and I like to surround myself with them. It makes me feel safe. I was always an anxious child, even before that summer. I worried all the time. When I was a toddler I'm told I talked a lot, asking incessant questions of all the adults in the house ('Why is the sky blue?' 'What is time?' 'Why don't fish die when lightning hits the sea?') until my mother learnt to simply respond with 'I don't know' and taught them all to do the same. I had to know everything, but once I knew, I would only go and worry about it. This was how she protected me. Perhaps Josh is right and we are obsessed with our parents. They're the only people we struggle to see as fully human, to admit are flawed, and sometimes craven.

Yet another thing I found when I was unpacking – my talismans. My parents bought me worry dolls. You know those dolls, little ethnic things, the size of a thumbnail, and they all have different costumes and live in a little yellow box made of rushes, a tiny box, painted yellow, with strange symbols in primary colours. And I would write my worries down, on notepaper, my worries and my wishes, and then roll it up and put it in the box, and sleep with it under my pillow, to try and magic it all away.

And did it work? I can hear the hypothetical therapist's voice now. Not that I ever had one – apart from the university counsellor I went to see, once, after the freak-out at the party. She told me it had been a panic attack, then asked me lots of questions about my parents. There was something in her demeanour I disliked. Pity, I think. So I lied and said I had a normal family, but I think she knew I wasn't telling the truth. I didn't go back.

We're more of a self-help book kind of family. My mother has hundreds, ranging from organic cookery to Reiki healing to Feng Shui to past life regression. *Potatoes not Prozac*; *The Highly Sensitive Person*; *Five Minute Meditation*. There's a whole bestselling subgenre regarding

22

messages from angels that I won't even go into. No one approaches cod psychology with such verve as boomers. The fervour of a generation who think they discovered self-analysis. They seek the path to enlightenment and then use everything they have found out about the vagaries of the unconscious to market products back to themselves.

I know people who have spent five years in analysis at the behest of their parents, but not me. There was never any money and, in any case, we had books. There was a point in the second year of university where it seemed like everyone I met had some kind of mental health issue. The corridors practically echoed with self-aware choruses of 'my therapist says ...', 'According to my therapist ...'. They always said 'therapist' even to describe a weekly one-to-one session with a counsellor funded by the NHS – it sounded glamorous, I suppose. Less mental health crisis on a budget, more Woody Allen.

From late childhood onwards, I began to receive self-help book after self-help book, usually as presents from my mother, who, in hindsight, was probably concerned about the impact of events at Longhope upon my fragile psyche. I've accumulated quite a library. I never read them, but couldn't bear to throw them out. The dolls, however, were some comfort. I could have done with them now to soothe away my nightmares.

I used to be obsessed with things that went missing. I still am. Objects take on a strange significance, and when they become lost I made lists, and I pasted them up in the kitchen as though they were missing persons, and ticked them off as the things were found. Here's an example: I remember bouncing a ball in the kitchen downstairs at Longhope, in what became the basement flat, below the one I moved into decades later. It was a super bouncy ball, the sort you get from corner shops, and I can picture it vividly, it was half purple, half blue, and about the size of a small tangerine. We were about to leave. There were boxes everywhere, and I stood in the kitchen and I bounced this ball, and it bounced higher, and higher again, and then vanished. Literally vanished. My mother helped me search, in vain, for it. 'Oh well,' she said, lightly, after some time. 'Perhaps it's gone over to the other side,' and I wondered if that was someplace where all the lost socks went, too.

The same thing happened the other day in the kitchen when I was unpacking the shopping. I dropped a lime, bought for making margaritas, and it bounced away from me, and then: nothing, gone. The thing with the ball still bothers me. Shortly after I moved in with Josh and Lou I went out into the garden to look for it, though I didn't admit to myself that that was what I was doing. It was as overgrown as it had ever been, though a few more mattresses had been added to the collection. What could you expect, after eighteen years of heavy bodies on springs? Perhaps the ball was there somewhere, amidst the brambles, like the motorbike we had discovered buried, in some mimicking of a prehistoric grave, by its sentimental owner underneath the mound of the lilac tree. But as soon as I started searching, I realised that I didn't really care. I had lost so many things since.

I suppose to an extent we're all fanatical about losing things. It's not the ones we keep that stay in the mind – they blend mundanely into the background of our lives – but the things we lose along the way: the time the car was broken into, the antique ring left by the sink, the burglary all those years ago, the photograph from the wallet. So maybe I am not so different after all.

My parents always tried to lessen my anxiety through objects. When I was little I would pick at scabs until they bled, and it was somehow comforting to see the crimson trickle run down my leg from an insect bite, to feel the sting of alcohol from my mother's antiseptic. 'Don't do that darling.' It felt almost enjoyable, the pain. To break the habit they gave me worry beads, teal-turquoise ceramic, looking like a Catholic rosary, the idea being that I would fiddle with those instead of picking apart my own skin. I had dreamcatchers to catch the frequent nightmares; a block of rose quartz to bring me love; crystals and amethysts. It makes them sound like hippies, which let's face it, they were. But also I think they realised that I set a lot of store in things. I treasured their solidity and their defined margins, because, while I could reassure myself of my limits – 'I begin here, at the tips of my fingers, at the surface of my skin' – the fact remained that I had periods of feeling outside myself, unreal, as though I lacked the materiality of the rest of the world. I was very young when I first experienced this vague, dreamlike feeling of being in third person. It was terrifying. I no longer belonged to myself.

I outgrew these things eventually. But sometimes, when I am walking down some steep stairs, or a train flashes past, or I am standing on the balcony of a tall building, I will put my hand in my pocket in search of some solid thing to hold. In these moments it strikes me how fragile we are, how feet can trip up, can stumble, and that heads can hit concrete and bones can be crushed, and that skin and ribs and guts can come apart like soft bread torn between the hands.

Cheque

*Cheque for £600 (paper), 3.5" x 7" (8.9 cm x 17.8 cm). NatWest,
made out to one Harmony Brown by University of London
student welfare office. Some water damage.*

I hadn't known either Josh or Lucia before I moved
into the house, though I had found out their names
several months before they knew mine. Just in case
you thought my background wasn't eccentric enough
already, then there you have it, Harmony, a classic,
hippie-parents name. Still, it could have been worse:
Crystal or Moonbeam or something like that, and at
least the explanation for their choice was level-headed
enough. None of that guff about planetary alignments;
I was named for a friend of theirs who died tragically
young. An asthma attack, they said.

One morning, the February before the May that
I moved in, I was walking past number 26 Longhope
Crescent as had become my habit, and saw that someone
had left the door ajar. Slipping into the musty hallway, I
breathed the air of that place for the first time in almost
two decades. I did not want to risk the chance of being
caught so I only lingered long enough to notice that
someone had carpeted over the lovely black and white
floor tiles with some brown monstrosity. That and the
post, lying on the side table. Having their names made
things easier. Pre-internet, I would have had to scour the

back pages of the *Evening Standard*. It could have taken years to get back in.

I am not surprised that my new flatmates thought me friendless. Despite being a student, which I still was, then, at least officially, I hadn't really collected many close friends. I spent a lot of time in the British Museum, not just because it was relevant to my course but because it was one of the few places that made me feel calm. The neatly organised and catalogued objects were soothing when contrasted with the slapdash chaos of my own life, and I used to wander between artefacts, imagining the people to whom they had once belonged, what they would think if they could see their treasured keepsakes on display. Once, shortly before I dropped out for good, I stumbled across an exhibition about death rites. I was especially struck by the tribeswomen of Papua New Guinea. When a loved one or relative dies, they enter a period of mourning where they cover themselves all over, including their faces, with thick clay. The clay stays on for several months, cracking and stinging in the sunlight, giving them physical pain instead of the grief that they are unable to express themselves. That is how I felt. I felt wrapped up in clay.

I was not entirely alone. I had had superficial friendships with several girls at university, but when I wasn't out drinking with them I generally ran solo and preferred things that way. We certainly didn't take baths together or plait each other's hair, things popular culture would have you believe such female friendships involved. Instead, we took coke in the toilets of richer people's houses and smoked fags out of kitchen windows and danced, and said crass things like 'honestly, my vagina was in such a state I thought he'd run home crying.' We tried on terrible clothes in charity shops and, one memorable time, a low-rate wedding dress boutique. We laughed at most things and discussed nothing of importance, and it was wonderful most of the time, but none of us wanted to live together, not after the last flat we'd all been in, which had ended in a disastrous eviction following a series of noise complaints. If we did we might never come down.

And as for men, well. Earlier that year (my third year, it was supposed to be, though by the time I moved into the house I had stopped going in) I had slept with two or three undergraduates, having fiercely avoided doing so throughout the rest of my time there. I preferred to pick my men up randomly, which was not without its own set of problems. They were all fairly nice middle-class boys, what you'd expect. They divided into two camps: when they graduated, they either wanted to write for *Vice* or to work for the Foreign Office, both ambitions of such crushingly dull predictability that I struggled to find the energy to even engage in conversation with them. Not that much talking was required, and not only because of their tendency to sexually objectify me (I'm not complaining – I did the same to them), but also because of the kind of dates they took you on, which were, respectively: electro nights and lectures at the LSE.

I'd never been virginal; I didn't understand the decision to wait. Every man I slept with offered up a different quality, a different part of themselves, for me to sample. No two were ever remotely the same, and I relished this opportunity for discovery, especially in terms of what they could do to my body. Then again, I could be surprisingly prudish. 'How many people have you slept with?' I asked my mother once, when we were drunk. We had had a lot of wine, and for some reason she was sitting on the floor in the living room. It was at times like these, when we drank and talked candidly of the past with exuberant, piss-taking scorn, that I felt closest to her. Perhaps other daughters of single mothers feel something similar. There's a fierce power to your relationship that sometimes manifests in a charge so negative it can threaten to overwhelm you, but then, at times like this, you feel a defiant, hilarious camaraderie in having both somehow survived.

She considered the question, and I watched, giggling on the sofa, as she counted on her hands for what seemed like an age.

'Thirty-three,' she slurred, finally.

'Hold on a minute,' I said. 'You lost your virginity when you were sixteen, and you met Dad when you were eighteen. You've been with two people since you got divorced. That means you slept with thirty-one people in the space of three years?'

'Are you terribly shocked? An average of ten people a year is hardly the last days of Rome. And it was pre-AIDS, darling.'

I stared at her. Little did I know then about what had gone on in the house, about how their political principles when it came to ownership had extended to people, too – what a shame that they failed to follow the same rules. How disappointing it must have been for my parents, the realisation that the desire to possess could override a utopian ideal and worse, could hurt the very people it was designed to liberate so profoundly that that hurt became ravenously destructive.

When I joked with people that I was born into an urban commune, I could see in their faces what they wanted to ask, but my mother was uncharacteristically reticent about that period of her life. All I knew is that

I seemed to have an awful lot of unofficial aunts and uncles. When I probed more, she'd get that look, a pained grimace laced with stormlike warning, and I'd know it was better to pipe down for the sake of a more peaceful home life.

I will admit I found her disclosure unexpectedly startling. It's not that I thought she was a slag. I was used to these kinds of revelations ('When I first met your dad, he was speedballing.'). I once met a girl who boasted proudly that she had the most liberal parents in North London. 'So your dad's done smack too?' I said, innocently. I think I was just relieved to have found someone whose parents did not inhabit the static, semi-detached worlds I had grown up both fearing and secretly desiring. The look she gave me. Wrong kind of liberal, as always.

In fact, I was faintly impressed by my mother's sleeping around, which was undoubtedly the reaction she was going for. She must have endured an awful lot of boring conversation, unless people were more interesting in the seventies, which I doubt. Parents would have you believe this, but it was patently not the case.

My own sex life, in comparison, was deathly dull. By the time the student protests came around, in November of that year, I had all but had enough. The previous week a boy – for that's what they all were, *boys* – had quoted Nietzsche at me, after sex. He followed this up by informing me that 'love does not exist, it is merely a question of chemicals', typical university stuff. I hadn't been expecting a lecture, nor did I especially like the assumption inherent in his words: that he was pre-empting some kind of tedious and cumbersome hormonal attachment on my part from which he would have to extricate himself.

'What about your parents?' I said.

'I don't think they've ever loved each other, either,' he said, taking a self-conscious toke on his rolly.

The next morning, we had gone down to Camden to get the morning after pill, together. 'We can go halves,' he said, and being skint as per usual, I consented. As I handed over the £25, the cashier asked me if I had a Boots Advantage Card. 'Slut points,' my charming companion commented. I think he wanted me to be upset, to embark on a feminist rant. Instead I just popped the tiny pill onto my tongue, stuck it out, then dry swallowed. 'Thanks for the memories,' I said, and headed off towards the Lock. 'I need a burrito.' Modern narratives would have this obligatory morning after trip to the chemists as representing something profound and meaningful about youth and loveless sex, but in fact it's just an errand, an insignificant interval in your day that makes you feel a bit dizzy afterwards. You take the pill, it dissolves the miniscule cluster of cells, life (yours at least) goes on. It may sound flippant, but there it is.

Though it was clear, after that interlude, that I had absolutely nothing in common with this self-professed Übermensch, we still marched alongside each other down to Millbank, yelling 'No ifs, no buts, no education cuts', him a parody in a khaki donkey jacket. He held my hand as some kids in black balaclavas smashed their way in to Conservative Party HQ. There were raised plummy voices as around the back a group of befuddled civil servants tried to negotiate rationally with the righteous anger of the young, left-wing and newly politicised. The words 'capitalist hegemony' were mentioned. A red-faced middle-aged man in a trench coat, overweight and balding, tried to articulate to a group of eager manarchists how this small skeleton team of admin support staff weren't the real enemies here. 'My dad was a miner,' he said. True Yorkshire. 'If you only knew what that were like,' his voice cracked. 'You kids, you don't know you're born.' He was so angry I thought he might cry. 'Tory scum!' yelled a guy in a bandana. We kissed. It was all quite fevered and romantic until some fool threw a fire extinguisher from the roof and we all had to go home. Just what we needed – the pointless endangering of young lives coupled with the flagrant disrespect of the war dead as a millionaire rock star's son swung from a cenotaph. For kids raised in an era in which every human relationship is mediated by images, they were impressively shit at PR.

I remember Bryn speaking once about growing up in the aftermath of the conflict, of how the older generation crushed their offspring with the weight of their anticipated gratitude. 'You were expected to feel grateful to them, all the time. It was this constant, stifling expectation,' he said, with heavy sarcasm. 'They had salvaged civilisation, they had *saved us*, and anything you did that was remotely counter-cultural and rebellious, even the act of having long hair or flamboyant clothes, was deemed a desecration of their sacrifice.'

'But wasn't freedom what they had fought for?' I said. This was how we talked, on the rare occasions we saw each other, as though we were sitting around a seminar table. At times his interest in me, his only child, seemed purely intellectual, but then he would astonish me with a comment so emotionally perceptive that I felt a surge of love for him, and guilt at having misjudged his capacity for empathy. Then he would start talking about Marx's dialectics, and the moment would pass.

'They were traumatised, that generation, I think. They wouldn't talk to their children, as I do to you, now. Not about anything significant, anyway. I felt like a cardboard cut-out at home.'

The words stayed with me. I had felt a similar flatness that university term, a time when I responded to everything with the woodenness of a bad actor. I was an automaton in a ratty fur coat and tight jeans, just going through the motions, laughing at boys' jokes as I took drags of their cigarettes, lying naked on their grubby sheets not knowing how I could even begin to love them. There was a lot of politics going on, but passionate though I felt, even taking part in protests felt like an act being carried out by someone else. No wonder it all came to a head that night at the party. Every day, it felt like another part of me was snapping off.

That winter we spent hours kettled by the police into submission, once on Westminster Bridge with the freezing, churning Thames below our only means of escape. This disappointing boy and I huddled together out of no bigger a desire than to keep ourselves warm. I felt an acute sense of outrage at being kept there. Never before had my freedom of movement been so brutally curtailed. It was fury-inducing at first, but by the time dusk fell a palpable feeling of submission emerged. By that time, everyone just wanted to be at home in a blanket. Perhaps that is why the students took their political protests indoors, into the warmth of one another's company. Ensconced in their ivory quads they were safe from the flying glass of angrily lobbed bottles, impervious to the temptations of deliberately placed police vans. There, these brocialists and manarchists, these pale aesthetes with even paler politics did not have to pretend they had anything in common with the kids livid at the loss of their EMA, to whom smashing up a bus stop felt like creating something.

This boy I was seeing had appointed himself one of the ringleaders of a small group of students who were occupying the admin corridor at the university in protest at the rise in student fees, and was behaving exactly as you'd expect someone with a privileged upbringing and a copy of *Das Kapital* poking out of the back of his skinny jeans to behave. At the time I thought the so-called 'solidarity' this group claimed to feel with low-income students was laughable – their presence in the admin corridor meant I couldn't pick up my hardship fund cheque, for starters, and they were so frightened of repercussions that they did all their graffiti work in chalk.

A couple of weeks into the occupation, I was on the way back from yet another failed mission to get my hands on some cash when I decided to see for myself what these armchair anarchists had achieved in their struggle against our neoliberal overlords. They had succeeded in creating a working community of sorts, though absolutely every decision had to be passed by complete consensus, which made their nightly meeting mind-numbingly long. They even had a kitchen. 'Your mum doesn't work here, so clean up after yourself,' a sign read, and under 'mum' some smartarse had added 'dad/guardian/carer'. I didn't know who these students thought they represented, but it wasn't me or really, anyone else I knew. How perfectly and exhaustingly right on they were in every way. They proudly paraded their virtuous courage, but any fool could see how terrified they were of tripping up by expressing the wrong opinion.

As for our dear Leader – he was becoming more and more obnoxious by the day. The whole situation reached its unbearable nadir when they held an evening poetry slam and, during the course of a maudlin poem that

34

invoked a lot of heavily vaginal sexual imagery, it slowly dawned on me that the girl in the black turtleneck on the stage was reciting an emotional missive about the boy I had been sleeping with. She was bitterly imagining us in bed together, via the metaphor of an avocado. 'She is / a stone / wrapped tightly in your bearded flesh,' I think it went. I made my excuses and left for the pub, alone.

I stopped going in, after that. I suppose I felt disillusioned with the whole performance, and there was the issue of my hardship fund, too. It was nearly the Christmas break by the time I got my cheque, only for it to slip out of the pocket of my coat somewhere on Upper Street. The coat itself fell apart, mid-escalator, only a few weeks later. It was too late in the term to go and have a replacement cheque made out, and after the holidays, over which I decided that university wasn't really for me, I just didn't bother. The nightmares were already drawing me back to the house, which, despite its unremarkable appearance, burned like a balefire in my memory. The nuances of structuralism (or, in my own opinion, a lack thereof) were of little interest in comparison. I had a job in a pub as a waitress and had inherited a small amount of money from a distant aunt of my father's, a stage actress who had died the year before in an Equity nursing home with a proper cocktail bar and a grand piano; a real live peacock in the grounds kind of place. So I had enough to get by, and to put a deposit on the room in the house, once it came up. I hadn't really thought much beyond that.

My initial introduction to Lou after moving into the flat at Longhope was entirely aural: the second night I spent in the flat was spent listening to her orgasm through the wall. Unlike other flatmates I had had, however, Lou's gasps and screams were not ostentatious attempts to treat sex as a theatrical performance; there was no real concept of audience. She had a lack of awareness of those around her, and their needs, that was entirely innocent and this, coupled with an admirably untroubled love of sex, always drew people to her. The roster of partners, both male and female, that passed through her room betrayed a refusal to accept any kind of stigma when it came to her own pleasure, but at the same time lacked the self-consciousness of the self-styled polyamorists I had avoided at university.

'Morning darling,' she said, yawning as she heaped coffee into a rather dirty looking cafetière. 'I haven't had even a moment of sleep, so do excuse the unkempt appearance.'

She looked like a fashion plate. Her black bob was hardly ruffled, and she wore the kind of Victorian nightgown that would have made anyone else resemble a crazed Bertha Mason, but somehow its voluminous nature only lent the sharpness of her figure more definition. Despite the nonchalance of her gestures, Lou's body had a fragility to it that bordered on shocking, betraying as it did a fraught relationship with food (I had known enough private school girls by this time to discern this), and a young adulthood privileged in its access to cocaine. On that morning and every other morning I have seen her since, she ate nothing. At other times she picked daintily at her food, like a bird.

Our first conversations were tentative. I was aware that she was attempting, very subtly, to get the measure of me, and I was determined that she would not. Despite the fact of my being a waitress, I suspected Lou thought I was rich, like her, though I realise now, like all wealthy people, she was probably just too polite to ask and knew exactly where to place me. University had stamped any trace of an accent out, and we never discussed money, except vaguely once, when she told me she'd been at Bedales. I pretended to know what she was on about and then looked it up in secret later. I wasn't actually sure what Lou did for a living – something loosely thespian, or to do with the art world. She never talked about it and never seemed to be at work, except when she was guzzling sparkling wine at friends' openings, straddling the social scenes of Mayfair and Shoreditch like the 'society slut' she proudly proclaimed herself to be. Francis Bacon once described his early years in London as having been spent 'between the gutter and the Ritz', and Lou wished to cultivate a similar impression. She was drawn to the putrid glamour of the down-at-heel as she was anything alluringly transgressive, but, like a good little rich girl she would always, eventually, be led back to the comfortable salons of her childhood, even if she was smart enough to proclaim them odious (when we did finally visit the Ritz, for cocktails, she declared the decor as resembling 'the inside of a tart's handbag').

One topic we did discuss, however, was that of our parents. In contrast to my own wry forbearance, her guileless zealotry for their bohemianism was almost embarrassing. 'Daddy dropped out of Westminster in the sixties after being hospitalised for taking too much acid on Parliament Hill,' she said, one evening early on, as we made our way through most of two bottles of red wine. 'His father was furious, though it was a serious breakdown you know. After that they weren't on great terms so he moved in with his friend Freddy who lived in a gypsy caravan and they formed a folk ensemble. They spent the next few years travelling around England. Quite romantic really.'

'And what about her? Your mother I mean?' I had learned that asking Lucia lots of questions about herself meant that my own family background, namely the bizarre catastrophe that was Bryn and Stella's marriage, was left relatively unmined. Lou took a drag on her super slim menthol.

'Oh, she used to model for British *Vogue*, so never did much of anything. And then she met Daddy, who by that point had sent Grandfather to his early grave and inherited the Hampstead house, and soon after they had disappointing little me who absolutely ruined all their fun.'

Others would have found Lou's knowing, cartoonish self-deprecation irritating, but I couldn't help but warm to her, seeing it as I did as her way of acknowledging the subtle ordeals of privilege; her sadness and her skinniness, the faded scars along her arms, the directionless nature of her ambition. Her rent got paid like clockwork every month, though certainly not by Lou. I couldn't understand why she had decided upon a shabby flat in an unfashion-able part of North London. It certainly wasn't from neces-sity. All the friends she ran around in her little 2CV seemed to be writing screenplays or books of autobiographical essays or running pop-feminist cultural criticism blogs and art collectives ('I'm a waitress,' I said, when I was asked what it was I did by one of her drag queen hangers on. 'A waitress and what?' asked the drag queen, yelling above the disco beat. 'You can't just be a waitress. Everyone's "—and something".' 'Just a waitress,' I said.). They were all like that. I remember a conversation with another one of her friends particularly vividly.

'I'm working on a new idea for a blog at the moment,' she told me, late one night as we sat on the carpet next to Lou's record player, smoking a spliff. 'I think it'll be huge.'

'What's it involve?' I said.

'Well, it's like, a fashion blog. Basically I hang around outside Archway jobcentre and take photographs of the people after they come out from signing on. It's called "dole queue fashion". I think it's, like, a really good way of showing that well-dressed people sign on too, you know. Like, everyone is signing on now because of this fucking government, even cool people.'

I made eye contact with Josh.

'And have people been ... receptive?'

'Not really. Like, I got chased once, and I have to stand across the street or the staff come out and yell at me. Also some of the people look so sad. But I think it could be really cool, provided I get enough black people on it.'

I focused hard on her face as she was speaking, but from the corner of my eye I could see that Josh was holding one of Lou's satin cushions up to his face and that his shoulders were shaking.

I spent most of the time when I wasn't working at Longhope. I was barely sleeping, and my absconding from university had removed me from the outer peripheries of my old social circle.

Lou and her friends went out six nights a week, loved MDMA, and thought of themselves as London's new bright young things. Left-leaning but politically complacent, they looked down on the start-up nerds on the Old Street roundabout and the advertising boys with their thought pods and their brightly-coloured American

Apparel hoodies, but they weren't so different in their tastes and values. They lived in a London whiter than I could ever envisage, never mixing, rarely leaving the comfort of their suites and cars and parties. It was as though they inhabited a series of closed-off rooms, all adjoined so that those that walked within them never had to feel the cold of the outside air, never had to make conversation at a bus stop or see the peach-coloured vomit that dotted the pavement of the Cally Road in splatters every Saturday dawn (ketchup). Their money was old, as were their friends, made in childhood. As cordial as they would be to you when mixing you a drink or rolling you a joint they were, ultimately, unreachable.

Josh, in contrast, worked in the social housing department at the council and rolled out of bed each morning at eight-thirty, a habit he learned during his first job with Morgan Stanley. 'I was one of those blokes on the news walking out of the office with a cardboard box,' he told me, with a grimace, when we met. Lou used to joke that he was single-handedly responsible for the financial crash, in the kind of voice that showed she was fond of him but she didn't entirely approve. He had grown up in a normal, working class family in Manchester, with normal parents, meaning that his mum had never given head to Keith Richards and his dad had never injected himself with a combination of heroin and cocaine for a laugh. He was five years older than we were, and from what I could tell regarded the pair of us with a mixture of superiority, bafflement and lust. He thought our conversations pretentious and idiotic, our fixation with the past strange, and our clothes wildly eccentric, but he also looked at our tits while we stood smoking in our slips late at night at the window. Josh wore jeans and T-shirts, read music biographies and went to the pub with his friends. He had a normal, 'boy' haircut and he did not read fiction or enter cocktail bars, and because of this Lou had ruled him out as a sexual prospect entirely; he would never join the parade of lovers entering and exiting her room at all times of the day or night. Not that she would have had much chance had she wanted it. Lou was beautiful, but could also be astonishingly shallow. According to Josh's mate Jamie from work, who had tried unsuccessfully to sleep with her, she was 'all mouth and no knickers'. 'She's like a frozen pie, bruv,' he told Josh as he sat in the kitchen one night. 'You get the packaging off and you feel you've been mugged off, you get me? Then you notice the small print says "serving suggestion" and that nice tasty meal you were expecting is just a frozen slab. The actual product's bland as fuck.'

'I was drunk', reported Lou, 'and then suddenly I was sober, and calling time on his slobbering tongue.'

Josh was also out almost every night, though unlike Lou (who could reliably be found tearing up a dancefloor in Dalston while wearing a headpiece made from found objects) he was most likely circling some secretaries in an All Bar One while doing the white man's overbite, gel in his hair. When he wasn't out, there was usually a girl in his room, and she usually had highlights, the sort Lou would describe as a 'belt-through-the-loops' kind of girl. You'd hear these women giggling sometimes through the wall in high-pitched, little girl voices, the way they'd been taught, the way men like it. He'd often sneak them out in the early hours, before either of us was up, and would then sit at the table drinking tea and waiting for us to wake up so we could conduct the post-mortem. How was it? we'd say. 'All right. I bought her some chips from Chicken Cottage and one thing led to another. Terrible

41

chat, though' – they always had terrible chat – 'She asked me what tog my duvet was.' At first, I credited myself with seeing through this affected carelessness, but then I realised that he genuinely didn't give a toss.

As a result of my flatmates' nocturnal habits, and my equally nocturnal job in the pub, I didn't see all that much of them. Having made it to Longhope, I was unsure what I was supposed to do next. I hadn't thought beyond getting there, and once I was installed, the calm I had hoped would wash over me failed to materialise. My nights were as disrupted as before, but I felt more awake than ever. My skin tingled, and every nerve within me seemed to be on high alert, flinching at the slightest noise.

I still hadn't met the downstairs neighbour, even after a month in the house, and I was curious about her. Once, when I had gone down to the cellar to try and scope out some extra furniture (no such luck, though I did come across an eerie Victorian pram before I retreated rapidly up the stairs), I caught a glimpse of a tatty dressing gown disappearing into her flat, the door slamming hard. I hadn't heard the early morning howling again, though I did sometimes hear her voice through the floor, or two voices, hers and another, shouting. Hers was deep and gravelly, almost like a man's, scratched raw from years of fags and arguments. Even less often I saw her cat (or traces of its shit in any case). Being apparently incapable of using bin bags, she left traces of herself in the garden: cat food, fag ends, loo roll, rotting takeaway meals, little plastic drug baggies and empty cans of Fosters, and, once, a used sanitary towel. Part of me pitied her – she clearly had problems – but I also hated her a little for making me face how squalid people can be. She barely seemed to venture outside and yet there were fetid signs of her sad existence everywhere.

'I'm starting to think she's a ghost,' I said to Josh, one evening in the kitchen. We were always in the kitchen.

'Yeah, a ghost who snorted coke off this table,' he said. He was fiddling with a discarded rizla, rolling it into a tiny ball between his fingers.

'Sorry, what?'

'She used to come up here, before Lou moved in. My old flatmate Trish used to have her round. They'd rack up lines together.'

'Really? What's she like?'

'Weird,' said Josh. 'What do you want me to say? She's odd. She lives in a flat with no furniture. I saw it once when I first moved in and knocked on the door to borrow a hammer.'

'She never seems to go out,' I said.

'I think she's agoraphobic,' said Josh. It made sense. Sometimes, when I entered the hall through the front door I got the sense that someone had just been there but, on hearing my key in the lock, had made a hasty exit. There wasn't much evidence to support this feeling apart from the fact that, when you enter a room that has just been vacated, that recently departed person leaves a trace. That entire house was full of traces.

'She went to Woodstock once, you know,' said Josh.

'Everyone that age says they went to Woodstock,' I said.

Summer 1984

After the march we return to the house to drink, spent but elated. Mark was hit by a copper and nearly got nicked. A bruise on his cheek now blooms purple. We sit in the candlelit living room, huddled around gas heaters that click metallically at unpredictable intervals. There are lots of us, about twenty, making it hard to tell who lives here and who is a hanger-on. They are all friendly, but I can sense their unease with our poverty. The men of the house talk proudly about signing on and Thatcher, wearing their politics like a pantomime costume, its flimsiness obvious from their vowels.

The women talk amongst themselves, but I sit with Mark, who is listening quietly to a man called Bryn speaking passionately of socialism and the workers' struggle, dropping in words like dialectic and materialism, words he turns to me and explains as though I have never read a book before. His young wife watches from the corner of the room, darting her glance sideways as she conducts her own conversation, with an expression that could be weariness or could be fondness. She is hard to read, but it's obvious that she has heard this speech before, many times. Her obvious boredom makes me bristle.

'Why's he dressed like a poofter?' asked Mark, when we arrived. Yet despite this pompous tone and his odd clothes I am drawn to Bryn. He seems happy. His conversation may be earnest in a way I am not used to – back home, it's not good to take yourself too seriously – but his eyes are laughing when he looks at me as he passes me a joint, the first of my life. It makes me feel calm and dreamy, and I lean back against the arm of the sofa, cross-legged on the carpet, and look upwards at the plaster ceiling rose, which is moulded into an extravagant arrangement of floral swirls, reminding me of the peaks and points of stiff egg whites as they are beaten into meringue.

I stare at it for a long time, until the flowers become faces, the shapes resembling open-mouthed devils in a ring, performing a ritual dance around the globe of cheap paper lantern, their arms raised about their horned heads. The voices and the music drift in and out. I am somewhere else for a long time, only reviving at the feeling of a soft hand placed on the bare skin above my knee.

'Everyone has gone to bed,' Bryn says. 'Time to call it a night, I think.' He helps me up, and I am struck by the bulk of him, the breadth of his chest and shoulders contrasted against my half-starved frame. Although I am now standing, he keeps hold of my slender wrist, his thumb and middle finger forming a bracelet around it. I am surprised to find that the room is empty apart from the two of us, though an imprint of the night remains from the hiss and drone of a record that has reached its conclusion.

'You're so thin,' he says, almost with reverence.

'Thank you for letting us stay.' My voice is hoarse from the smoke. 'I love your house.'

We stand and listen to the hum and fuzz from the speakers for a moment, not looking at each other, and then he slowly removes his hand, reaches across, and tucks a strand of my hair behind my ear.

'It's ludicrous how beautiful you are,' he says.

45

Fruit

12 x loquat ('Eriobotrya japonica') fruit in plastic supermarket bag, petrified. Harvested 2011. Not for consumption.

It was a hot early summer, the year I dropped out. I spent much of it lying on my bed, dozing off the late shifts, the large sash windows all wide open, the gauzy curtains barely rustling in the stagnant air. The sky outside required no filter, you couldn't see without squinting. At the height of the heatwave a news crew had successfully fried an egg on the pavement. In the garden, a man with a ponytail burned rubbish in a can and the smell of melted plastic found its way into the upholstery and walls. People paddled in the fountains and lay in parks half-dressed, kissing. Old people died. Teenagers became restless; political dissent bubbled wirelessly through the stagnant air on networks not hidden from but little understood by the authorities. An incentive to rebel delivered in emoticons, building, but yet to explode. It was too hot.

Outside, in the front garden, the tree was bearing small, strange fruit. About the size of an apricot, and orangey yellow, we did not know their provenance. But others did, and they came with carrier bags. Some would knock on the door and ask to harvest, others didn't. I recall particularly a little boy, plump and olive-skinned, standing shyly on the doorstep. At the end of the path was a stationary black cab. 'Can we pick your fruit?' asked his father, the cabby. 'We were driving past. We haven't seen them since we moved here. They taste of home. He is so excited.' Smiling, the child handed me some and showed me how to peel them. 'Sheseq,' he said. Loquats. 'You must eat them right away,' his father said. 'They perish in a matter of hours.' They tasted sickly sweet, sticky. I imagined the boy and his dad returning to their kitchen, devouring them, telling stories about the old country. I liked them.

Less so, the woman I found up the tree as I left the house one balmy evening in early June. She was right up in the highest branches, armed with plastic bags and watched fretfully by a younger relative, a son, perhaps, from the pavement below. 'That's our tree,' I said, standing there in my cocktail dress. I had just dip-dyed my blonde hair pink and had a cigarette in one hand. There was a bottle of wine tucked into my armpit. He looked embarrassed. From behind the leaves, in a foreign tongue, the woman let out a stream of what I assumed from her tone was abuse.

'I'm sorry,' he said, in heavily accented English. 'She says that it is her tree.'

'I live here,' I said. 'It's my tree. I don't mind, but I wish you had asked. I could have been naked up there.' I gestured at my bedroom window, which, to her, was eye-level.

The woman shouted some more, her words unfurling rapidly like a party streamer.

'It's fine,' I said. 'Take them.'

'She used to live here,' he said. 'Her father planted this tree. She says it is her tree.'

'When?'

'Fifty years ago.'

It was possible, I concluded. This house had histories that predate that of my parents.

47

Afterwards, I wished I had not been so harsh towards the woman, but I have to admit that my thoughts did not linger on the subject for long. I went to a house party in a tatty ex-council in Whitechapel and drank warm rosé, danced to all the songs we loved as teenagers. The nineties: a nostalgic night of remembrance for people who were barely adults. Sitting next to a girl in a high ponytail in an upstairs bedroom, I dabbed MDMA into my gums to the tinny sounds of a laptop, and then moved so much and for so long that the pink pigment in my hair mingled with the sweat pouring down my face and coated me in a fluorescent sheen. Outside, I kissed a boy on the patio and when I pulled away it was all around his mouth in a clown-like smirk. Time to go, but it was three night buses home and I had misplaced my oyster card. Inside the holder I had tucked a note from my father, giving details of his new address and telephone number. The phone was as modern as he got, on the communications front.

It was nearly dawn when I stumbled up the path, barefoot and swearing, my heels dangling from a finger as I rummaged one-handedly for my keys. As I finally located them at the bottom of my handbag, I heard a crash and realised, with the slow reaction speed of an extremely inebriated person, that our downstairs neighbour was amongst the recycling bins and struggling to regain her footing.

'I'm your new neighbour,' I said, helping her up as she swore.

'I know who you are.' Voice thick with special brew, a suggestion of Irish, via Archway.

Inside, the hall light was broken again. Her words were barely a croak, coming somewhere to my left. 'I know what you're all thinking, up there. Judging me,' she said. Slurred.

'Why would we be judging you?' I said, judging her. In the gloom I could make out a face puffy from alcoholism, framed by greying hair straggled and too long for her age. I couldn't see her teeth but they were probably crooked and yellow. I swayed on my feet as she began to cry softly.

'Hey,' I said, reaching out to catch her sleeve. And then just like that, I was holding her as she wept into my shoulder. Despite her fleshy countenance, she was all bone. 'We're not judging you.'

She broke away and pushed open her front door as I stood, wobbly and confused, in the dark hall. She was about to shut it completely when I saw her face appear in the black gap. It shone bright and hollow, like a skull.

'You look just like your mother,' she said, and for a moment, I found I could not breathe. She slammed the door.

Photographs

Job lot miscellaneous photographs, subjects unknown (majority feature a man, c.35 years, Caucasian, shoulder-length dark hair, beard, and a woman, also Caucasian, c.20 years, waist-length dark hair, though several unposed group shots also included featuring persons unknown), colour (Kodak instamatic film), black and white (Ilford 35mm HP5 plus 400, taken using Nikon EM SLR). Taken circa late 1970s-early 1980s.

I suppose she was right; I do look like my mother. In my favourite picture of Stella, she is in her mid-twenties and standing on the street. She's wearing high-waisted drain-pipe jeans, probably black, although it's hard to tell in greyscale. Her hair is long and unstyled, thick. Black and white striped waistcoat, leather jacket, boots, cigarette. A slight smile that shows on only half her face. Huge eyes rimmed with black eyeliner. She looks beautiful in this photograph; all the best parts of me and none of the worst. While I am blonde and washed-out, less vivid, she is dark, unreadable. In the background, you are just able to glimpse the house.

'Your mother was a trophy wife,' my father said once. A strange thing for a self-confessed male feminist to say, and about a woman who, when she was up, was so much more than the most beautiful woman in the room. She was the only one who you wanted to talk to: charming, and quick to laugh, with a self-taught intelligence. At these times, she was barely recognisable as the red-eyed, dirty-haired wild woman at home who periodically gobbled up my mother. She would wear her sadness so lightly that the only hint of it was manifested in a deep and encouraging sympathy. I've seen her do it. Some stranger will tell her all his sorrows and her hand will grasp his arm as her eyes widen and fill with tears at whatever misfortune has befallen him. I don't mean to imply that this is by design: it's authentic. It's just that at the same time she's already plaiting the strands together to create the story. She's addicted to stories, my mother, and she loves to tell them. When she does, she captivates. It's one of the things my father fell in love with. 'She was so young,' he said, of the schoolgirl he had taken from her parents. 'But she was full of all these tales.'

In the photograph, he's standing next to her, offsetting her smile with a brooding expression. Despite it being the mid-eighties, he is still wearing flares; corduroy, from the look of it. You cannot tell from the picture but I know that they were lime green; my mother told me, laughing, how embarrassed she was. Everyone else had moved onto punk by then, and there he is, his hair far gone past the point of touching his collar as a delayed rebellion against his schoolmasters, and a collarless shirt accessorised with a ridiculously long hand-knitted Doctor Who scarf, knitted for him by Stella. I used to love that scarf, scratchy and moth-eaten though it was. When I wound its knitted stripes around me, it would almost conceal my entire body, and I would roam about the house with my arms out in front of me, a stripy scarf mummy.

I was five when Stella decided that the conventional family life that she had tried to build with Bryn on leaving the commune was intolerable, and she and I went back to

Longhope less than a year after having left. I remember standing alone in the checkered hallway surrounded by boxes, as she sought out her old friends somewhere in the depths of the house. She had had enough of living the hippy countryside dream, she told me later. 'You can't imagine the boredom, darling,' she said. 'There we were, way up in this isolated cottage on this mountainside, miles from anywhere. I had to get out before one of us did a murder–suicide.'

The night my mother left him, she told me that she made him the most beautiful salad. She had been supposed to prepare a meal for both of them, but she was alive with a calm hungerless anger and so only laid out one plate. Then she set about carefully arranging the ingredients; the grilled courgettes in concentric circles, dotted with perfectly symmetrical slices of tomato and perfect little new potatoes. Asparagus positioned to form a star, and the centrepiece: a flower formed of slices of boiled egg. 'Your dinner is ready,' she had said to him, and she had walked out of the room and out of the door, putting me and our stuff into the old yellow Datsun and driving four hundred miles back down to London, blasting Elvis Costello and the Attractions all the way and smoking roll-ups out of the window. In a final act of defiance against years of imposed vegetarianism, we stopped at Wimpy for a burger.

I once asked her what the catalyst had been, and as was typical of her she said that she didn't really know, only that the fact of the perfect salad seemed to her an affront. Her guilty desire to furnish my father with this perfectly ordered, balanced meal was so reminiscent of the life that she had tried to escape that she felt she had no choice but to flee immediately. 'Everything I didn't want was on that plate in front of me,' she said. 'So I gave it to him, like a good wife, and then I scarpered.'

This was the first of many road trips we took together; Stella was never able to stay settled for long. Throughout my childhood, usually during a manic upsweep, she would come across someplace and become convinced that this was it, this was where real life would begin for both of us, and she would truly believe it, even though there was often a man waiting conveniently in the wings.

'We'll grow vegetables!' she would declare, as we stood on the edge of an overgrown patch of land that, having discerned a wonky 'for sale' sign in the rear-view mirror, she had pulled over to examine. 'We shall open a farm shop!'

Another time: 'I will establish a studio that restores antique furniture, and we shall become rich because wealthy people with taste will come to buy it from miles around.'

And another: 'It may look decrepit to you, but soon this will be transformed into a highly desirable relaxation and yoga retreat.'

She was always full of these schemes: a health food shop, an art gallery, a community theatre. My childhood is littered with discarded grand plans, and though the failure of them would always hit her hard, their inception was part of what made her fun. As I grew older, I began to recognise the symptoms of her restlessness purely from noticing a certain look in her eye, and though it would frighten me (usually I would have just settled at school, or made friends, established a routine), her enthusiasm was catching. That's the thing about Stella – she is capricious, unstable and deeply unreliable, but she also has a charm that you see rarely in life. If you were a stranger lucky enough to meet her, she would make you feel privileged by the very fact that she was drawing you into the story of her life. There was little concession made to the truth, granted; it was always the telling of it that mattered. If you let her wrap you up in all her twists and turns, it can feel almost like love.

Though I can barely remember the journey back to London, I do recall finally arriving and staring up at the imposing staircase in our new (old) home. The ceiling seemed to stretch for miles above my head. Suspended from it was a grubby chandelier that hinted, jarringly, at one of the place's many past lives as a home for wealthy Victorians. The doors and windows were thrown open, as they so often were, and the breeze caused it to swing back and forth in ways that were not entirely unthreatening. Such a theatrical centrepiece didn't exactly fit amongst the Indian batik wall hangings, the strong cooking smells and the spider plants whose dust-covered leaves my mother would wash on Sundays with soapy water. The place felt enormous, too big even for the eleven adults, two teenagers and four cats living there at the time.

At the rear of the hallway there was a large kitchen that smelled perpetually of curry. This was where the adults would congregate and cook while the teenagers, both dropouts from the local comprehensive and living at the top of the house, would blast out jungle music from the attic. Fleur, an exercise in heroin chic and the girlfriend of Rufus, who headed the DJ collective and was the only guy I'd seen in real life with high top fade hair. He didn't seem to mind the fact that she lived with her parents – not just her parents, but also her mum's new boyfriend and her dad's new girlfriend. Then again, they both spent most of the time stoned. As a five-year-old I was unaware of the complex sexual dynamics in the house, or even who belonged to whom, just as I couldn't really understand what my daddy had done that was so terrible we had had to go away and leave him in the countryside. My memories of that time are mottled, and it's difficult to know which parts I can actually recall and which are the consequence of years' worth of family legends, fictions that have built up like limescale, no longer brittle enough to be scraped away.

It was a sweltering summer in 1991, not dissimilar to the one I would spend at Longhope twenty years later. I spent most of the time in the garden, either alone or with one of the many other children who passed through for varying periods of time dependent on how long one, or sometimes both, of their parents were sleeping with one of the inhabitants. Together, we would rough and tumble in the wildflowers, carefully avoiding the sharp points of rusted metal protruding underneath, as the sound of reggae played through one of the many windows thrown open to let in precious gusts of cool air to the surrounding houses. It was a happy time. Though I remember seeing my mother – who had taken to her room – very little, and my father not at all, I was always surrounded by people and lavished with attention by the other adults. The strangeness of the situation became clear only later.

The house was a hippy experiment. The ghost of the sixties lived on for that generation, and communal living was as much a political act, a utopian ideal, as it was an affordable form of housing. That part of North London had paid host to the squatters' movement of the seventies, and many of the inhabitants had lived there since then, though by this point the council had got canny to the potential of its Victorian housing stock and was renting such houses out via housing associations for a few pounds a week. Children were just a matter-of-fact part of the community, the natural consequence of all that free love, and we were largely left to our own devices. Mum spent a lot of her time upstairs in the big bedroom, crying and smoking while lying on the double mattress on the floor, listening to Joni Mitchell's *Blue* and occasionally throwing a picture frame against the wall.

Most of our boxes and suitcases remained unpacked, but I have a vivid memory of the excitement I felt when one evening, after several glasses of red wine, Stella one-handedly opened a trunk to reveal a dressing-up box of treats that I had never seen before. 'I put these all away when I met your dad,' she told me. 'He didn't like them.' Lying within were layers and layers of brightly coloured silk and chiffon, taffeta and velvet. Cocktail dresses of all styles and moods, bought by eager parents for their teenage sweetheart in preparation for her attendance at suburban parties and dances, receptions and the theatre, events at which she would chat politely with the sons of doctors and lawyers, her laugh a murmur as she brushed dust from the shoulders of their fathers' borrowed suits. How disappointed they were when she ran off, instead, with a much older waster who had been speeding for six weeks. How bitterly they regretted allowing their teenage daughter to go on that march.

That evening, we tried the dresses on and laughed and twirled to the music of the record player on the floor. It felt wonderful, as though she was giving me access to a secret world of girlhood that I barely understood, a girlhood which she had cast away like an unwanted coat and was now regretting. I believe now that she was having some kind of breakdown, the first of many 'difficult periods' that would come to define my adolescence. For days after this joyful ritual I would come upstairs, muddy from the garden, and find my mother sitting on the mattress on which we both slept, staring at the wall in full cocktail regalia. Sometimes, when she felt better she took me to one of the big paddling pools in the city's parks. When I look back on that summer now, I see mainly bright squares of blue, and little white feet refracted, as though not my own.

The area has changed beyond all recognition now. In the mid-eighties, despite the fact that it was rapidly gaining a reputation as an enclave for the North London intelligentsia, Longhope's part of town was still generally regarded as a run-down shithole, somewhere you'd come to buy a gun. The rents were cheap, the houses crumbling, and the locals mainly of Irish descent. I remember little of the high street aside from a Post Office, an Indian restaurant and a junk shop, dirty brickwork rendered even darker by the fact of being in the shade of the incongruous Archway tower, a building that everyone local hated without exception. In the tower was the dole office, where at least half of my new adult housemates would go to sign on, some still clad in the splattered painter's overalls they had been wearing on the job (you could always lie and tell them you were an artist taking a break from your latest abstract masterpiece).

The change was slow, but inevitable. Even in 2011, the year I came back, the area remained stubbornly grotty, though the houses were already worth millions. The five chicken shops were defiantly holding on in the face of rising rents and the buildings, especially around the main road, were covered in a thick layer of hardened exhaust fumes, bricks the colour of soot and ghost signs long faded.

'FANCY WORK
OVERALLS
BLOUSES
CORSETS
GLOVES
HOSIERY
LACES
RIBBONS
HABERDASHERY
FLANNELS
FLANNELETTES
CALICOES
UNDERCLOTHING
MAIDS' DRESSES
CAPS & APRONS'

said one such sign, which you could just make out. Another: 'CATERING FOR BEANFEASTS'. But by far my favourite was the yellow, smiling sun on the side of a house at the top of Hargrave Park, now almost vanished but in my childhood brighter, not long painted. 'ATOMIC POWER/NO THANK YOU' it read, and I would often ask whichever adult had been granted custody of me for the afternoon to take a detour home so that we could go and see it. I found out years later that it had been painted in the middle of the night sometime in 1976 by a squatter in the grip of a mushroom-induced vision.

By 2011, the council had long sold off its dilapidated Victorian albatrosses and almost all were either privately owned town houses or had been turned into flats, like our house, but the area still clung to its soul. No longer did the pubs do a whip around for the IRA at closing time, but you'd still hear Irish voices in the street and in the shops. These days, I hear the place is unrecognisable. The pubs, all of which have long 'gone gastro', are full of children. There's an artisan bakery and a pretentious gift shop. The French have moved in, with their patisseries and their nurseries, and many of the houses are now houses again, homes to Parisian BoBos on the run from Hollande's taxes. Such is London's property cycle.

But the year I returned, that corner of North London was the only place where I wanted to be. There I was, in 2011, pink-haired and pissed off, trying to rediscover the strange, lost, summer I was five, that I suspected marked the point where it had all gone wrong and my parents buried their secrets. Five is a strange age for making memories. Some recollections are lurid in their vigour, others slippery. I suppose, in my adolescent way, by going back I was trying to claim some part of myself as my own, and not theirs. They had put so much of themselves in me that I wasn't sure what would be left after I tore up their legacy, because how do you rebel when your so-called bohemian parents have already taken all the drugs and slept with all the people? When they've excused themselves from the mainstream, turned their backs on an orderly existence in favour of self-rule? I suppose you become a doctor or an accountant and, worst of all in their eyes, are happy living that kind of life.

It could have been me, had I allowed the momentary lure of stability to stick. Maybe I even wanted it to be. But what would have been the point? To rebel against my parents, as they had theirs? They would have doggedly continued loving me, their only child, regardless. They would have loved me in the baffled, bemused way of parents whose children who have taken everything they hold sacred and told them to shove it up their arses, not in the midst of an easy to handle teenage tantrum, but in a series of quiet, purposeful, adult manoeuvres too subtle to identify in isolation, barely noticeable until one day, you're someone they no longer understand, in a suit.

Besides. In teaching me to question everything, they had conspired to make it difficult for me to function effectively in any real system. I was always getting reprimanded.

'You look like your mother.' The downstairs neighbour's parting words remembered as I stood in the kitchen mixing myself a vodka Berocca the following afternoon. So she had been here all this time. The last mad hippy standing. And she had known my mother. I had not anticipated this, not in this transient city of rising property prices and revenge evictions. Everyone I knew moved about once every year, yet here my seventies throwback downstairs neighbour was, a museum piece. A generational relic. I wanted to know what she knew, but her dawn screaming, the suggestion of abuse, disturbed me.

I had slept until four, having sat up long after our encounter, smoking, my teeth grinding against one another. Now, mid-comedown and maudlin, I wondered about Josh's comment that we were girls fixated upon the past. 'Why glamorise a generation', he had said to me, once, 'when their commitment to their principles only lasted as long as a twenty-five-year-old's lease on one of their buy-to-let properties?'

'I don't know,' I had said. If only Bryn and Stella could be so easily dismissed. I thought back to Lucia's words in the kitchen. 'Because they did it all first,' I said. 'And because they did it without caring.'

Summer 1984

Mark says it's time to go, but I do not want to leave this place. It has cast a spell on me and I can't go home.

Last night, Bryn walked up to me as I swayed to an old soul record, handing me a beaker of cheap red wine. 'Stay,' he said, looking at me. 'We all want you to.'

I glanced at Stella dancing next to me, her cool gaze unreadable beneath her dark fringe. But she did not contradict him, and after he had walked away to get another drink she placed her hand in mine and twirled me under her arm in an imitation of a 1960s dance couple at a contest. 'Follow my lead,' she said.

In the few days that I have been here, the possibility of another life has intruded with sharp-elbowed insistence. There's nothing for me at home. My measly job at the shop, my knackered mam, stewing panacalty for hours next to the stove to try and soothe Dad's pain and fury when he returns from the picket; Pete, his rough hands rummaging underneath my skirt as I stare at the patterned wallpaper of my room, peach and pale blue, counting the petals on its sprays of faded forget-me-nots in time with his grunts. He doesn't know how to love me. My moans are a false balm to his ego. He's a good man, kind; a catch, even, but when we are together it's like he needs a dictionary and I, a tranquiliser. He's never made me come.

I have noted the way Bryn looks at me. I know that look well. Famished. It scans the half-moons of my breasts and backside, greedy, but it is also shot, like silk, with warmth and friendship, and this is something new. I know he wants to sleep with me, and Mark knows it too. My brother watches me possessively, as though he's loyal to Pete and not me, the little girl who would skip after him down the chares, pleading with him to let me play.

We spend hours talking, sitting up into the small hours. Bryn's wife, too, who seems to have a fondness for me I don't deserve. 'It's so great to have a woman closer to my own age here,' she says, and she puts her hand in mine. 'We are not so different, are we? You and I? I was young and innocent too when I came here.'

I think that I am not that innocent but I say nothing. Instead we talk about painting and poetry, surrealism and Simone de Beauvoir. When I reply to her questions she seems struck by the breadth of my knowledge, but quickly hides it. 'I read a lot,' I say; 'it's my way of being somewhere else.'

There is another life for me here. What fun it is to laugh and talk and drink and feel that, finally, I am understood. This is a world of music and ideas and freedom, and a whole city at my feet, unrolling before me like a magic carpet, rebuking my threadbare childhood at home as it beckons. This, I tell myself, this is the place.

Slip

*Slip, vintage (1950s), nude silk-trimmed with white lace
(Valenciennes), size 38, label reads: 'Fabriqué en France'.
Frayed hem on right-hand side. Faint grass stains on the back.
Accompanying receipt for £3.50 from Marie Curie charity shop,
27 Junction Road N19, 22nd May 2011.*

London in the summertime. I've always loved it, maybe
because it was there that we ran away to, or maybe because
it's the only time when the city truly feels like itself. People
come out of their houses to slacken their straps and lie in
the parks, or sprawl out of the pub onto the pavement
in after-work hordes, collars damp, ties loosened, pencil
skirts straining, cool liquid rinsing the sweat on their
upper lips. Londoners will even, sometimes, sit relaxed on
the steps of their houses, drinking beers filtered through
slices of lime in the warmth of the evening sun. London
in summer is the sound of reggae and soul floating from
cars and shops and bedroom windows, and saxophones
too. No one ever seems to play the saxophone except in
summer, when, as the heat of the day dissipates into the
early evening, some neighbourhood musician must feel an
urgent need to dust it off, walk over to the open window
and make it sing. In the sunshine, all the houses appear
whiter, and everything that was, in winter, a source of
dissatisfaction or disgust is filled with a sense of vivid
promise. Even the fumes of the traffic seem romantic

somehow, the buses wobbly and marbled when admired through the waves of heat rising from the tarmac, the horns and sirens more muted and distant. It feels safer, too, with the nights only drawing in when you want them to, as you lie hazily on the grass, giggling, watching the sky turn puce.

When you are young, life plays itself out in a succession of summers. School comes to a close and the days stretch before you, filled with countryside wanderings, fruit-picking, sticks and stones thrown across streams and ditches during unspoken battles with the kids from the other side of the cul-de-sac. Then, later, sex, drama, weed. Guitar music, sixteen-inch-long spliffs because you don't know any better, virginity loss, and four-mile walks home through the fields because the buses haven't started yet. Before we grow old, we live a life of summers.

I always found it strange and slightly laughable how British people still harp on about the summer of 1976 – the hottest summer to end all hot summers. That it held so much cultural weight was surely more of a symptom of our horrendous climate than a reflection on the unique magic of that three-month stretch. But as a summer, there's no denying that it is fixed immovably in the minds of those who were young then, a witness to the freedom they experienced in casting off hundreds of years' worth of ingrained desire for shelter and warmth and becoming, briefly, an outdoor society. Breakfast on a patio in Solihull may not be dinner by starlight beneath a cypress tree in the Tuscan hills, and a quick fumble down the bottom of the football pitch may not be a romp through the lavender fields of Southern France, but for a brief period of time at least, our parents and grandparents embraced the feeling of being European. Fewer clothes, fewer hang-ups; Cinzano; olives. Sticky afternoon sex, limbs coated in the coconut sweetness of Hawaiian Tropic.

My mother's memories were less romantic. Having been urged by a friend to visit the local lido despite the plagues of ladybirds congregating there, she vomited insects on the lawn.

Wife-swapping was still going on in the mid-seventies, my mother told me. Those poor suburban squares who missed the actual summer of love, who felt the lack of it so profoundly that they thought a bowl of keys would help kick off their own sexual revolution in the bedrooms of their Essex new builds. The husbands blamed *Cosmopolitan*, Stella said. Divorce inevitably followed, though not for her own parents, who never swung, instead opting to sit, suffocating in the front lounge throughout the heatwave, a still life in brown and mustard polyester as the grass yellowed outside and the neighbours sunbathed, oiled and topless. When, in the early eighties and not even out of her teens, she met my father and he led her by the dainty hand into a life of sin and squalor, she had been glad to get away from suburbia and come to London, where the houses were older and the people younger and more alive, their bohemianism more instinctive. After the static electric shocks of her mother's daisy-patterned curtains, her suburban semi in its shades of nausea, what she sought was authenticity. Even now, she has a hatred of synthetics – materials, smells. She will leave a room if there's even a hint of air freshener.

But we were elsewhere, deep into another summer. Not hers, but mine, a time in my mid-twenties when, as a dropout, my only real responsibility was to turn up at the pub when I was needed, and even when I was needed I was replaceable. The absence of air conditioning meant that, when I was there at all, I spent a not insignificant amount of time standing in the walk-in freezer, or smoking in the cool little courtyard, dodging the drying pools of blood from the huge joints of meat that were unloaded weekly from the van. In mid-June, there was talk of a hosepipe ban, and there had been no rain to wash the blood away, so its metallic, rusty smell endured. The loquats in the garden had all been picked, or else were puffing and withering amongst the wildflowers, soon to be dust in the mouth of cats. I was working very late shifts, and, though I had banged on the door a few times, finding out about how the woman downstairs had known my mother became less of a priority than it had once felt. Simply being there, in that house, was enough.

Also: I had a boyfriend of sorts, a rekindled university fling who had strolled into the pub on a boiling after-noon that month after a ramble on the Heath. He was an academic. Eastern European, Jewish, older. The genre of well-educated, liberal, North London-based person who had taken to frequenting the pub since it had been done up and the manager had advertised for nice, well-spoken, polite staff fluent in English – hence my new job. Rumour had it that the pub had been bought by the manager Mattie's mother for the sum of one million pounds and, as is the way with rich people, she and her son had turned it into the exact place that their kind would frequent. Never mind the regulars and the loss of their local. What the poshos wanted was somewhere dog friendly that has guinea fowl and bowls of quails' eggs on the menu, and suppers just like nanny used to make. The kind of place that reminds them of the little tavern on the fringes of the country estates they grew up on, but not so far from

Hampstead. Good luck getting a bag of scampi fries, in other words.

I suspect they chose to employ me, with my hint of a London accent, to give some local flavour. A month after opening we were still getting the cockneys coming in and asking what the hell had happened to the slotties, and where was the picture of the old Queen that used to be behind the bar. Mattie's prices had put a lot of them off (the staff couldn't afford to eat there either) but there were a few stragglers tenaciously holding on, refusing to leave, stubbornly doing lines in the toilet like they had every Friday and Saturday nights for years. Sometimes, when I wasn't on the bar or being made to accompany my boss to Sainsbury's to buy ingredients we had run out of (Mattie had smoked too much weed at Durham and now had a terror of crowded spaces), I would join them and they would say that I was not like the others. It sounds stupid, but crowding into that Farrow & Ball-painted cubicle with Kev the painter–decorator while we chopped up coke on the reclaimed Victorian tiles is the closest I'd ever really felt to belonging anywhere. 'Of course you're one of us, you were born in the Whitty,' he said, using the nickname for our local hospital, his wrinkled hand resting on the back of my neck as I bent over and switched nostrils.

It's true I was born there, unusually for my mother's natural birthing crowd. 'Have you signed her up for YTS yet?' said my father, on seeing me that first time, pink and new and most importantly, unlike the newborn daughter of the Orthodox Jewish woman in the bed next door, a much-wanted girl.

A barmaid. It was as good as anything else that was going. You can't be too choosy in the middle of a recession, though I think the academic was surprised when I turned around and poured him an Addlestones. 'Harmony,' he said, in that peremptory tone of voice he had. 'You work here now.'

'Yes,' I said. 'Just here. I'm not a waitress-and.'

If he had no idea what I was talking about, he didn't let on. He just smiled his dirty smile, and raised his glass to my tits.

God, he was beautiful. I had never thought that word about a man before, but there simply wasn't another for what he was. I could try to describe him, to mix and match the adjectives to try and make a picture of him in your mind, but it would be by the very nature of its mode of creation blurred and indistinct. It would be easier to mould his slender but muscular body out of plasticine. I knew its every tendon and crevice, the weight of it, the tautness of his stomach, how it tightened when he was trying to hold back. Just looking at his bare arms made me crazy. If I had to sum up the effect he had on me, I'd say he made me want to miss a flight.

The rare power he had, the way he seemed to peel back the rind of me so that what was left was slutty and compliant, had made him difficult to give up; it was also the reason why I had. It felt electrically cheap to be so willing, and now, seeing him in front of me meant I could no longer remember why I had ever thought to stop.

We stood looking at each other. It was a busy afternoon and the pub was filling up with sweaty families who were staggering off the Heath in search of organic refreshments, so there wasn't time to talk. But he said he would call me and had done so, and I met him in another bar, in town, late one night after my shift. He was polite and attentive, insistent that he pay, listening carefully to my thoughts about my abandoned course while he shifted his knee so that it sat between my legs, forcing them open.

'Take me somewhere,' I said, when we had barely finished our first set of drinks, and he smiled as though he had known all along what I would say, that our attempts to talk across a table and be interested in one another's thoughts on higher education were only play-acting, our way of saying, see, I don't want you that much, of delaying the moment when our need for each other's bodies became tacky and obvious.

Since then we spent the late afternoons at his place, carefully angled away from his curtainless window that looked out onto the next-door neighbour's garden, in which a child bounced on a large trampoline for hours at a time. We fucked to the rhythm of it and sometimes, he tied me to the bed. It wasn't and never had been love. In many ways it felt better and easier than that.

We fucked in parks, too; Finsbury Park particularly. Once, we were nearly caught. It was a particularly hot day, even by the standards of that year, and I had been out for lunch with Lucia, which meant drinking throughout the afternoon. I was wearing a silk dress. The colour was what you'd call 'nude', meaning that, if seen from a distance, it looked as though I was naked. It was more of a slip, really. The material was so thin that it stuck to the sweat on the backs of my legs, and as we walked through the park the academic slid his hand up between the fabric and my skin, separating them. The inside of my mouth still tasted like gin and cucumber, he said, but my head had begun to feel tight and sore, and after we kissed a little I fell into a long, deep sleep and he lay next to me, reading.

When I awoke it was getting dark, and I could only

vaguely see his shape over me as he blew cool air on my face. 'Harmony,' he said, and there was laughter in his whisper. 'You look just like a little girl when you sleep.'

'My mother told me that once,' I said, feeling fuzzy, and hungry, as I always do after a nap. It was still hot, and my skirt had ridden up as I slept, but when I tried to pull it down he placed his hand firmly on my wrist.

'Oh no you don't,' he said, grabbing my other wrist and placing them both above my head. He shifted his hands so that one pinned me down and the other was free, and used it to lift my skirt so that it was entirely around my waist. It occurred to me that the park was empty, but it was still not quite dark, and I could see the look in his eye; his pupils dilating, as he ran his thumb over my nipples, hard through the silk, then placed his hand inside my underwear. It didn't take me long to come. It was only afterwards that I noticed the headlights. Had he known someone was watching?

I walked all the way home that evening. The air felt heavy and balmy and there wasn't much of a breeze as I made my way through the streets of Hornsey and Holloway; a circuitous route, but I was in no hurry to get home. As I walked past the groups of men smoking outside the Turkish restaurants on Green Lanes, they all hissed, and I wondered not for the first time what exactly the sound signified – was it desire or condemnation? And is it wrong that I felt a little bit pleased? As I had many times before, I longed to call their bluff. To turn around and say, 'come on, then, big boy. Let's do this.' Watch them back away, embarrassed.

I was halfway home when my phone beeped. A text, from him. 'I want to rape you,' it said, and immediately it felt as though the spontaneous moment we had shared

71

had become sordid and base. I felt ashamed, as though the words themselves were acts of violence, and I had somehow helped form them, had aided and abetted. I deleted the message without replying.

It must have been a reminder, because for the rest of the way home I could not stop thinking about the woman in the downstairs flat. The sound of her strange, animal screams would not leave my mind. She is the reason that you should not use such words lightly, I thought, as though my mental admonitions could somehow reach him across the park and back in his poky little Stroud Green flat stuffed with books and bongs. I wasn't angry, but the message was further proof that he was unknowable. It wasn't just that he was circumspect, although I was sure that there were many things about his life that he kept hidden. It was the fact of his inconsistency. Every line was incongruous, as if, each time, I were meeting a different stranger.

'You're beautiful,' he said once, brushing the hair from my eyes like a leading man. Then, two days later, as I dressed: 'Your arse is getting fat.'

And, 'I hate London. The people here are so uncultured. I include you in that, little girl.'

Followed by: 'I can't imagine being anywhere else than here with you.'

He didn't seem to care when I slept with other people. He'd be eager to hear all about it, not from jealousy but because it turned him on. He'd ask questions, imploring me to leave no detail out. 'And then what would he do?' he would ask, his thumb circling my inner thigh. 'Did you like that?'

But later, in bed, he would push my face into the pillow and breathe into my ear that I belonged to him.

It was all just words. Words which, instead of blending over time to form some sense of a personality, simply sat there, cold and out of context. Each time it felt like a meeting with a different man. That afternoon, for instance, a disturbing desire to rape me, but two weeks later, a hotel room in West Hampstead, an Italian dinner and a declaration of love. None of it made sense, but then everything was disconcerting that summer. I was not completely in my right mind, you could say. Memories long inaccessible were beginning to rise to the surface like scum and were sitting there, waiting to be sifted through.

When I got back to the house and entered the hallway, I noticed the downstairs neighbour's door was ajar. The room's dark interior beckoned.

Spider

*European garden spider ('Araneus diadematus'), female, grey
with mottled white abdomen. 17 mm.*

Her flat had the same layout as I remembered. There was
the kitchen in which I'd lost my treasured bouncy ball,
the French windows, the overgrown garden. As Josh had
said, there was hardly any furniture, and from the direction of the back door there rose a fetid smell. There was
no fridge. Dylan sang from somewhere too indistinctly to
make out, a radio probably. I had heard her singing to
the radio before, through the ceiling, in her gruff, rasping
voice. Motown, Smokey Robinson. Several flies buzzing
in time with the strip lighting danced around the unshaded
ceiling light bulb, trapped. Though the sunshine outside
was still blinding, the interior of these rooms was dark,
mould-smelling.

'I knew you'd come eventually,' she said, and I saw her
standing in the corner, then. She was barefoot and wearing
a stained nightie with a greeting card teddy bear on it with
a heart-shaped nose. Her grey straggled hair reached past
her armpits. I couldn't tell for sure, but it looked as though
she had lost even more teeth since I had seen her face close
up, in the hallway. I felt a sudden, dismaying wave of pity,
and I think she sensed it, because she pointed at the door.
'Get the fuck out of my house.' Slurring, drunk as usual
and me, as she had said, judging her.

I looked at the empty pile of bottles next to the overflowing kitchen bin, and had a thought. 'We have booze,' I said. 'In the flat.'

She said nothing, but I knew her interest was piqued. 'Shall I go and get it?' I said. 'Come on, let's have a drink together.'

She bowed her head slightly in acquiescence, and I hurtled upstairs. Josh, naked but for basketball shorts, was in the kitchen smoking a joint. I made a beeline for the sideboard – a great, hulking piece of early twentieth-century furniture that he'd salvaged from the curb. All that was left was the 4am stuff: Cherry B, Crème de Peche, a dash of Cointreau. I grabbed it all. It would have to do.

'On it already?'

'No,' I said. 'It's for her.' At the word her, I nodded downstairs.

'I meant to ask you about that, actually,' said Josh. 'I swear I heard you both, a couple of weeks ago. Pissed in the hall.'

'Yeah, that was me,' I said. 'Christ, I was hammered. You'll never believe this, but she was going on about us being judgemental of her sad existence and I ended up ... hugging her.'

'You should be careful.' He tapped the joint against the side of a teacup, and watched the ash fall.

'What do you mean?'

'Letting people like that into your life. She'll take advantage. She's mental, you know. All she wants is a slight crack in the door and boom! She's in. There'll be no getting rid of her.'

'She seems lonely,' I said. 'You're too cynical.'

'You're naïve. You mark my words. You'll be filling

in her benefit forms and picking up her coke before you know it.'

'I thought your Albanians delivered to the door?' I said. 'See you later.'

'It's not great,' I said, as I entered, 'but it's better than nothing.'

She had moved to the centre of the floor and was sitting there cross-legged, smoking a fag, ashing into a Perspex bowl of cigarette butts that was almost overflowing.

'I'll get us some glasses, shall I?' I said, when she made no response. I started opening unit doors and rummaging around, eventually settling for a cracked teacup and a ramekin.

'Bottoms up,' I necked it, the artificial peaches turning sickly in my mouth. I shuffled over onto the floor and sat down next to her, shifting slightly when I realised that the laminate was sticky, sliding a cushion beneath myself. Silence. Dylan croaked on despite the awkwardness. The song was 'Just Like a Woman'.

'I used to like this one', I said, 'when I was a teenager. I liked how cruel he sounded. The disdain in his voice.' It was true. It had given me a thrill, this song, and not just because of its evocative talk of amphetamines and pearls, the mythology that it had been written about Edie Sedgwick, but because it felt like he truly hated this woman, this debutante, whoever she was.

'Your mother always said it was misogynistic,' said the neighbour, after we had listened to another verse. 'But then that's the type of woman she wanted to be. Parties. Cocktail cigarettes. Touched a nerve.'

It sounded like Stella. The aspiring middle-class party girl who never could quite wear a kaftan comfortably. My mother had secretly smoked Sobranies the entire time she had been married to my father. I found them once when I was very small and rummaging in her dressing table, opening her silver case with my clumsy fingers to reveal the candy-coloured stripes inside. The smell and, I hate to say it, taste of them is unmistakable. Perhaps you've chewed tobacco and so know to an extent what I am talking about, but unless you've actually eaten a cigarette in the belief that it's some kind of sherbet sweet, it's difficult to convey the level of nausea it elicits.

She looked at me, expecting a reaction, but what could I say? She may never have worn a bra, but my mother had not been built to be a hippy; it was plain for anyone to see.

'I prefer "Don't Think Twice, It's All Right", now,' I said, taking another swig of Crème de Peche. 'I gave her my heart but she wanted my soul ...' my reedy voice came out louder than I'd intended in the staleness of the room and I abruptly stopped singing. The neighbour looked at me as though I were the mad one.

'How is the old slag, anyway? Still shagging her way around the West Country with some toy boy, last I heard.'

I considered contradicting this. No one likes to hear their mother spoken of that way, but to be completely honest, it wasn't too far off the mark. I presumed she was talking about Ziggy, the latest slightly-useless-but-ultimately-benevolent stoner she had shacked up with in Cornwall, but then it could equally have been River, or Floyd, or even Xavier. It depended how far back you wanted to go.

I suppose I could have told her about life with Stella; the constant moving, the rows and the rages, the time in the orchard when she had made a half-articulated confession about what had gone on with them in that house. 'I'll never forgive myself,' she had said. 'Or your father.'

77

Then another time: 'There are things in life that are fine to be blasé about. But the hearts of other people are not one of them. I learned that the hard way, and it still haunts me today.'

But judging by the hatred I could detect in the cadences of this stranger's voice, I gathered the neighbour knew much more than I did about the whole, messy affair.

'Send her my love.'

'I can't. I don't know your name.'

'It's Coral. Tell her Coral sends her regards. The old bitch.'

The fury in her voice threw me. People never normally hated Stella. She was too charismatic, and too talented at making people feel good about themselves, for that. Even my father, despite the baffled wonderment she inspired in him, never said a bad word about her.

Coral reached for the bottle of Cointreau and lit a cigarette. 'I have to say, the day you moved in, I thought for a second it was her, gone blonde. I watched you through the net curtains, unloading your stuff out of the car. It was uncanny. Same face. Like she'd come back to wreck it all, all over again.'

'Wreck what?'

'Everything she touched. She was a careless woman, your mother. Careless with money, careless with objects. You couldn't lend her a dress or a record without her losing it, or breaking it. I remember I lent her my white cheesecloth summer dress once, for a garden party she sneaked off to in Chelsea, with some rich friend of hers. She jumped in an ornamental pond. "It was just so hot," she said, when she came home dripping, her skirt muddy and covered with weeds, all torn. Ruined. She was careless with people, too.'

'Wait ... did you live here? In this house?'

'Don't catch on quick, do you, you stupid cow? Granted, you were a child, so I doubt you'd remember much about me, but how else would I have known your cunt of a mother?'

'Don't talk about her like that.' Even I have limits. I topped up my drink.

'After what she did, I'll talk about her any way I want. I imagine I know her better than you do. I've lived with her long enough. The world wasn't formed the moment you walked into it, love.'

'I know that. Believe me, I'm well aware of that.'

'I've lived here since the early seventies, way before her time. Helped break into the place myself. I'm the only one left now, obviously, but I was one of the very first. Me and your father, and Rowan and Mikey, and some goggled-eyed groupie whose name I can't remember, who I think was Swedish. This was before your mam would have had blood in her knickers. I'd been kicked out of my squat in Chalk Farm, so we decided to start a "new model for communal living–".' She said 'communal living' with real venomous sarcasm '–and we broke into this place, which was all boarded up.'

'I knew it had been a squat,' I said, 'but I didn't realise how long for.'

'I'm the last man standing. They not tell you anything?' Coral said. 'I suppose your dad was always too busy skinning up and lamenting the death of the counter-culture, the pretentious arse. He was a poser, Bryn, but his heart was in the right place. At least he believed in what he was doing, unlike your ma. You know the first thing we did when we moved in was remove the bathroom doors? Bathroom doors were bourgeois, you see, and why should we feel any shame about nudity, and bodily functions? We weren't squeamish about sex, either. Gawd, when we first moved in here, no one was allowed to sleep in the same bed – I say bed but it were bleeding mattresses on palettes, nightmare for your back – two nights in a row. You weren't allowed to own things, let alone people.'

'I had a bed when we came here,' I said.

'It was the eighties by then. Everyone had calmed down. Still shagging each other like rabbits, of course, not that you'd have known. Do you remember anything about that time? I suppose you don't.'

'Parts,' I said. 'I remember how the house and garden looked, and some things that happened, but it's all very hazy. We weren't here for long. I know that it didn't end well.'

'Oh, you were here long enough,' said Coral, as she downed the last few drops of liqueur. 'Speaking of, it's about time you buggered off. I've got someone coming round, or "calling on me" as that posh tart who lives upstairs would say. Do you think you could get her to stop her and her mates braying in the hallway all hours of the day and night? Ridiculous accents. It's like having Margaret Thatcher in your living room, and eleven years was quite enough.'

I stood up and made my way to the door. 'Of course,' I said. 'But do you think you would mind if I visited again? I know there was no love lost between yourself and Stella, but I'm ever so keen to hear more about that time, and about my own childhood. You see, I'm not really sure I know much about it at all. She won't discuss it. It makes her cry.'

Coral let out a bitter laugh.

'And I don't really know any friends of my parents.

She's never mentioned you. My dad lives up in the mountains somewhere in Wales, we don't really talk, and it would just be so good to hear something about how it was, then. This house is so different now ... '

Tailing off, it occurred to me that I was drunk, and I stood, swaying slightly on her threshold, waiting for her response, but all she said was, 'Take care', and closed the door quietly, leaving me alone in the shadowed hall. I wanted a cigarette, but I had smoked them all, and the kitchen was empty. Josh had undoubtedly gone for a nap, and Lou hadn't been home for several days, so I gave up the search for tobacco and went to lie down on my bed.

The room was mercifully cool, the window having been open all afternoon and the early evening sun was in the process of disappearing behind the terraced houses opposite. As I scrunched up my pillow to a comfortable consistency, I could hear Coral's wind chimes gently nudging each other in the garden below. I thought about her strange, furniture-less flat, with its crystals hanging from every window frame but no couch, and I wondered who it was who would visit her and if they wished her well or if, any moment now, the screaming would start. The feathers and teeth of my dream-catcher were shifting slightly in the breeze, and as I watched the sky turn pink through the knotted cells, it occurred to me just how much the netting resembled a spider's web. I thought of all the spiders' webs I had ever seen since I was a child, listing them as you might see them in a curator's catalogue: 'Robin Hood's Bay, Gate Post, 1996 (?), medium-sized.'

As I did this, a recollection began to form itself in my mind. An afternoon of playing in the undergrowth outside, in the garden of that house, that summer, with Gabriel, the first ever boy to hold my hand. His mother, Vita, had been in my mother's consciousness-raising group, and had stayed with her here at the house during the Brixton riots, before I was born. They moved to Manchester not long after we left Longhope, his father sick of the sus laws, the constant stop and search; not wanting the same biweekly ordeal for his young son once he grew tall and muscular, the overnight leap from child to perceived threat.

I had seen Vita and Gabriel only once since then, one August when we were older but still easy around one another in that pre-pubescent way, and they had come to the country to visit us. The two of us had been walking through the main village street in the late morning, towels rolled neatly under our arms, on our way to swim, when we heard the high-pitched whooping of an ill-conceived monkey impression. Three children, several years younger than us, followed us all the way to the river, gibbering ceaselessly, and Gabs never said a word, even as they sat above us in the trees as we swam, mocking in their arm gestures as they scratched their armpits. I remember how high he held his head as he walked, and how I had said nothing because I did not have the words, even as we reached the safety of the kitchen and sipped our home-made lemonades, shaken but relishing the sharpness. This was the point at which he tried to raise the topic of what Stella called 'that awful summer'.

'Do you ever think about it?' he had asked me. 'Do you ever think about her?'

I don't remember what I said in reply. It was the last time I saw him. My mother stayed in touch with Vita and later told me that he had had a breakdown in his first year of university and had come back to his mother's house, to lie quietly in his room.

I have always struggled to think of him as grown.

Instead, Gabriel is cemented in the garden of that summer, grinning chubby-faced in the hours we spent lying in the wildflowers, eating them, crushing them between our fat little fingers, splitting their stems to reveal the lurid chlorophyll beneath, our hands linked, giggling while our mothers sat inside drinking herbal tea, and a fat-bodied garden spider spun a web across the entire width of the dark void left by the propped-open French windows. We sang, 'Daisy, daisy, give me your answer, do.'

Finally, when it was growing dark and we were called inside, for supper, we stood together looking at the web as it blocked our path, its engorged queen plump and hideous in the centre, and I cried at the sight of it, as Gabs gripped my hand tighter, because when you're five a spider is enough to make you that scared. Nearly two decades later, drunk, I lay there on my bed thinking of how the first boy to kiss me had also been the gentlest, because he had been afraid of the horrible creature but refused, despite my wailing entreaties, to wreck its home and cut it lose from its translucent thread; we would just have to stay outside and miss our cake and sleep under the stars. And as I wept for him in a half-sleep, I remembered something else, a flicker of a moment that had long been lost: a woman's face appearing behind the web as she stood there bony in a pair of cut-off denim shorts, red hair long enough to almost reach her waist, and plucked the spider from its web delicately between her two fingers, laughing.

Summer 1984

Mark is upstairs, packing. I can tell he's seething, though he was quiet when I told him I was staying here. 'I'm not coming with you,' I said, and he clenched his fists, his arms taut by his sides, and in that moment he looked like the little boy I once knew and worshipped, mute with frustration at the shit injustice of our lives. 'I don't need you to protect me,' I wanted to say, but he had already left the room.

I sat there for a long time, waiting for him to come down. The house was quiet, as it so often is in the daytime, as people sleep off the excesses of the night before with the languor of those who aren't needed anywhere in daylight hours. When I first came here I wondered how they made their cash, though it seemed rude to ask. Giros, odd jobs, family money, I imagine. How lovely and safe they must feel.

Mark comes in, holdall in hand. 'What do I tell Mam and Dad? That you're shacking up in a squat with a load of punks and hippies and weirdos? They need you. We all need you.'

'There's nothing for me up there,' I say. 'I'll get a job, send money home.'

'They probably don't believe in money,' he says, with bitterness. He hands me a tenner, but does not move any closer. I make a move to embrace him, but he shakes his head.

'It's your funeral,' he says.

I cry a bit after he's gone, from relief rather than regret. Then I begin to climb the stairs to what is now my new room. When I reach the third landing, Coral strolls out of the bathroom to face me, her beads jangling. She puts a hand on my arm. The amethysts on her bracelet are cold on my goose-pimpled skin.

'I'm glad you're here,' she says, 'but you need to be careful.'

'What do you mean?' I widen my eyes. Though I know, and she knows that I know. She's seen how he looks at me. How she looks at him looking at me.

'Don't get too mixed up with them. They may be a pretty pair, and they may be very taken with you, but their loyalty is always to one another. Do not forget that.'

China Lady

Royal Doulton porcelain shepherdess figurine holding lamb, pale blue frock. Made in England. 20.5 cm high. Modelled by R. J. Tabbenor. Production dates between 1987 and 1988. Significant damage (has been reassembled using superglue).

They say that arachnophobia is evolutionary; that some primal, atavistic fear of these eight-legged creatures is triggered when we see one crawl across the floor – 'it's the way they move', phobics so often say, as they shudder voluntarily, and for emphasis. My mother has a horror of them, but said it was because her own father did. Spiders, she said, were the only things that frightened him, and as he in turn frightened her the fear was passed down.

They don't scare me. As I woke in a beam of almost agonising sunshine, it struck me that they hadn't done since I had seen the young red-headed woman pick one up so easily. I wondered who she was and what she was doing in the house. There were always people drifting through but for some reason this memory left a disturbing trace, a sense of loss. It had been months since I had had a full night's sleep, so often would I wake from some fearsome dream, gasping. In the mornings my face would be wet, but I'd remember nothing of the phantasmagoric perils my brain had thrown at me during the night. Whenever I woke up like this, I was filled with such a profound sense of sadness that I knew instinctively that there was no use getting up today. I assumed, because of watching my mother, that everyone had a certain number of days like this, where they just can't bear to face the outside. It felt like a mixture of what Holly Golightly called the 'mean reds' – being afraid but you're not sure what you're afraid of – and the blues. I call them the purples.

Dreaming of Gabriel and the garden had not been like that. Instead, I felt bereft, with an urge to ask my mother to phone his, but although my fear of the spider in the dream had been tangible, the object of my fear had been so tenderly removed. In showing me both him and the garden as they had been, the dream felt like a gift. I had forgotten there had once been wildflowers out there among the cat shit and the mattresses. I wondered where all the flowers had gone.

I got up, and cutting through the living room on my way to the kitchen for a coffee, I saw that Lou was back. She'd been looking even skinnier over the last couple of weeks, and in this particular dress – a clinging, floor-length number in shiny yet translucent lamé, metallic raspberry pink with spaghetti straps, like something that belonged on the floor of Studio 54 – she looked even more so. It clung to her hip bones and the ribs beneath her bee-sting breasts in a way that made me feel simultaneously envious and pitying. She was so terribly thin. Her heavy fringe against the paleness of her skin as she stood, backlit by the bay window, made her look like a model with make-up smeared down her face.

A Godard film flickered on the television, the sound muted. I'm not sure which one it was – one I hadn't understood, which could be any of them. As I looked at her it struck me that I could see her bush through her dress, and I felt shocked, and then embarrassed by my shock, because if anyone was going to cultivate a full bush, in London in 2011, then it would be Lou.

'Where have you been?' I said.

'Oh,' she said, with a slight toss of her head. 'Here and there, and everywhere.' She was holding a cut-glass whisky tumbler that was almost empty. 'We ended up in Harry's latest squat, in Mayfair. You know Harry, my old friend from school, the artist. I don't know how long ago. What day is it?'

'Sunday,' I said. 'I've got to be at work in an hour.'

'Sunday ...' she said, in a vague way. 'But it couldn't be.' Her pupils were massive.

'I assure you it is. Your voice sounds very dry. Do you want me to get you some water?'

'Please. I'm dehydrated. My mouth feels like something crawled into it and died. My piss was this horrible colour, almost green, with a sort of film on it. Vile.'

'Are you ok?' I said, coming back in. 'You look ...odd.'

'I'm fine. I drove home. There was a bit of drama with Cosmo.'

A year ago I'd have questioned the plausibility of there being a human being in existence with the name of Cosmo, but now I knew better.

'We were in one of the rooms, fooling around. I was wrecked. Then we started fucking, I'm not sure how.' She looked me dead in the face. It was the first time I'd ever heard her talk about sex, which for someone whose bedroom door might as well have had turnstiles, I found strange. You knew she had it; everything about her, the way she dressed and spoke and moved, was geared towards you knowing that she had it. The sound of her orgasms pierced the stillness of most of our afternoons. But to talk about it? Never. At least, not with me.

Lou downed the dregs and looked away.

'So he flips me over, on the bed. And we're doing it that way, from behind, and he starts pulling my hair. Not in a sexy I-can't-control-myself way, either. In a painful way. I screamed.'

'What an arsehole.'

'Right? I wish I could say that I told him to get the hell off me, that I hit him. But I didn't. I just lay there, silently. Until he finished. And then I drove home.'

We were both quiet for a moment. Then Lou spoke again, louder this time.

'I'm just so fucking sick of these men, Harmony, with their "liberal principles". The way they treat us, like we're just holes. Before the sex, I was talking to Cosmo about a play I'd like to write. He didn't even pay me the courtesy of pretending to be interested. He just wanted to get me in that bedroom so he could ram me like the porn stars he beats off to. I can't do it anymore.' At this, Lou let out a little scream of frustration. The glass, which mere seconds ago had been in her trembling hand, hit the wall on the opposite side of the room. We both stared at it without speaking.

A door slammed open and then shut.

'What the fuck is going on?' Josh's voice was thick with the incoherence of sleep. He was wearing a pair of boxer shorts and a T-shirt, cut tight to his body, that he had obviously got at some work training day: 'Keeping Islington Active'. 'I was asleep. It's Sunday morning.'

'Do you think we're not aware of that?' Lou walked through into the kitchen and got herself another glass. The whisky was on the counter. She poured herself another three or four fingers.

'So you're not even going to apologise?' His accent got

stronger when he was angry. He was more awake now.

'Apologise? Grow up, Josh. Are you saying you've never smashed anything before? Of course you haven't. Because you don't get angry, do you? People like you just bury your pain until it festers into a tumour, and then you die in your fifties.'

'Oh, please. Posh people don't own the patent on anger, Lou. If anything, you've got far less to be angry about. Do you know what it's like where I'm from? You haven't got a fucking clue. What it took for me to get here. Work in a factory, marry a local girl, like my dad did, that's what was expected. And you're here, crying your eyes out, smashing your expensive crystal glassware all over our lounge. It's you who should grow up.'

'God, you're just so bloody honourable. Tell me, then. Have you ever smashed anything? I bet you haven't, have you?' Her voice was goading, mean.

She sat down in front of the television. A man in a hat was talking to a woman in sunglasses as they drove along in a convertible, the shot cropped close, like her hair. We all fell silent as though we could hear what was being said.

'I have, actually.'

'Oh yeah, when?' She pretended indifference, her eyes not moving from the screen.

'I was ten,' said Josh. 'There was this adventure weekend that we were going on at school. It included a day trip to the Cadbury factory. Did you know that Cadbury was the first company to build a tailor-made town for their workers? Obviously I didn't know that then, I just wanted to go for the chocolate. But my mum said I couldn't, we didn't have the money. Even though she'd just spent £150 on a steam carpet cleaner from JML.'

The absurdity of the steam carpet cleaner broke the tension, and we all laughed.

'What a cow,' said Lou. 'So then what happened?'

'Well, I was angry, obviously,' said Josh. 'Everyone else was going. After school, on the Friday, I watched them all get onto the bus with their rucksacks, all excited, and I was so pissed off at the unfairness of it all, that when I got home I went into the front room and picked up one of her china ladies and smashed its head on the mantelpiece.'

I could just see a lanky, ten-year-old Josh, freckled and shaven-headed and furious in his school jumper, standing in a pristine living room with its steamed carpets, smashing up a shepherdess. I felt a new affection for him that came from knowing where he fit, and guilt at my pity. He had grown up in what, as a child, I used to call an 'ornament house'. I first became aware of their existence when Stella began taking to her bed in the afternoon and I started going home with friends after school, noting how different their immaculate homes were to mine. When I think of them now they are always presided over with a sense of stifling gloom – the velveteen settees, the painted wildlife scenes, the women in lampshade dresses clutching parasols in the cabinet. No books. These silent houses were not places for children, so we played in the garden or the bedroom. Our house, where there was always music of some kind playing, may have been eccentric and chaotic but it felt like freedom in comparison. I'd run through the door into my mother's bony arms and bury my head in her shoulder and she'd say, 'How was it? Did you have a nice time?' and I would say, 'It was an ornament house.' She would clap her hands and laugh with delight at my snobbery. After Thatcher there was little to distinguish the lower and upper middle classes for that generation other than matters of taste. Josh's mother probably thought the china ladies elegant. To my own, they were aesthetic monstrosities.

Lou (who may have been thinking something similar, though when would she have ever been to a house like this?) stood up and walked over to him, placing a hand on his cheek.

'I'm sorry,' she said. For a moment I thought she would kiss him, and the imagining of it alarmed me.

He shook her off. 'It's fine,' he said. 'I'm sorry too. You know how I am, in the mornings.'

'I should go to bed,' said Lou, and walked out.

I remained where I had been standing, feeling like a failure. It struck me that I should have said something to Lucia, some comforting thing, but I hadn't had the chance and I knew that next time we saw each other the subject would be closed. Like many rich people I had met, she pretended openness but maintained an impenetrable inner core. So, while she would regale us with tales of her bohemian childhood, of trips to India and Marrakesh and teenage drug binges on friends' country estates, it was all told with an aloof distance, so you went away feeling as though you didn't really know her at all. Lou spent most of her time acting like a caricature, her poshness offset with a knowing campness. Now she had shown me a rare hint of the vulnerability residing in her roped-off heart, and I had forgone the opportunity of allowing her to confide in me and, in so doing, had failed in my feminine duty.

What had happened to Lou was a violation. An example of the almost-rape that so many of us had suffered, and talked about, at university. It brought it all back: the tender trip to the tube the next morning, the pain of rough sex that we hadn't desired and hadn't asked for, either, the sometimes-bloody crotch of your underwear. And the excuse-making, the twisted feeling of pride. The neat validation that came from being a girl who was wanted. It was just what boys needed, wasn't it? No one had ever told us otherwise. My mother had talked to me about sex, of course, from when I was at an early age. It would have been difficult not to, in light of the community she had joined in her tenderfoot youth and birthed me into. We had never talked about the seedier side of it. Sex was the free and beautiful expression of desire between two or more consenting adults. It was a spiritual experience, not an ordeal, she implied. My stop-start relationship with the academic, how after weeks of silence, one flick of his thumb on a keypad would see me open my legs for him: that would be beyond her understanding.

When she first came to the house in 1978 she had only just turned nineteen. On reaching London she decided she was no longer a suburban ingénue in a Biba dress and white, plastic high-heeled shoes but an artist with a desire to translate the mysteries of the world. It didn't suit her; despite her commitment to the counter-culture, her middle English ideals remained steadfast. On marrying my father, which she did less than a year after joining the commune, she demanded total fidelity, something he adhered to, he later told me during one of our more honest chats, because of his physical obsession with her. She would have it that his hippie ideals were embarrassingly outdated by the late seventies. The bathroom doors had long been reinstated. She hid her conventionality behind an eccentricity of dress and a furious and unpredictable temper, but it never really left her. She would dispute this, inhabiting as she does now a converted chapel in the West Country with a boyfriend fifteen years younger, a regular at the Glastonbury solstices, but she has always exhibited a blinkered omission when discussing the past, especially when it comes to anything negative that might reflect on her. 'Remember how you slapped me around the face, when I was fifteen?' I said to her once, and, drawing therapeutically on her talent for selective memory, she denied that she'd done anything of the sort.

Ask her about the seventies and she'd tell you she was living the bohemian dream. Perhaps in some ways she was, but, despite feeling a profound envy of my parents with their romantic idealism and of their luck in inhabiting a world of hedonistic certainties, I have always, secretly, been sceptical. It seems to me that no other generation has ever so successfully mythologised itself as that of the boomers, and, in my more cynical moments, I would question the validity of their reminiscences as sounding as though they were lifted wholesale from some collectively produced, crowd-sourced memoir. They pick and choose their pasts as I would carefully select pick and mix after school, with all the old favourites making an appearance – fried eggs, flying saucers, cola bottles. And she was no different. An acid trip here, a Stones concert there. I make it sound as though we were never close, but the opposite is true. The closeness I felt to her, as a child particularly, was almost oppressive in its fierceness. I can see her faults as clearly as she sees mine. I am, after all, an extension of her, living and breathing in the world, with philosophies as thin and arms and thighs and breasts as fleshy and cumbersome as hers were. That is part of the problem. When I thought about my mother jumping in that Chelsea pond during a sweltering garden party and how she turned up laughing on the doorstep, indifferent and flushed in Coral's mud-sodden borrowed dress, I knew I was supposed to have shared her old comrade's feelings of disapproval. Instead, I felt a fierce, unconditional love for the ebullience of her selfish youth. It was a kind of awe.

Harmonica

Hohner 'Great Little Harp' harmonica, 1960s. Made in Germany, 4" long. 10 holes, key C. In the original box with original instructions. Hand engraving on reverse reads: 'Bryn Brown'.
Songbook, 12 Bob Dylan hits for harmonica and guitar (arranged by Jerry Sears), published by Warner Bros Music, London, England, 1966. 26 pages 30 x 22 cm in size. Coffee cup stain on cover. Includes such classic hits as 'Don't Think Twice, It's All Right', 'It Ain't Me Babe', 'The Times They Are a-Changin''. Contact seller for more details. Check out my eBay shop for more Dylan memorabilia.

There was a Situationist working at the tube station, that July. I could tell this because of the boards. One morning, the 'Thought for the Day' was a Lenin quote: 'The way to crush the bourgeoisie is to grind them between the millstones of taxation and inflation.' The following week: 'Humanity will not be happy until the last bureaucrat is hung with the guts of the last capitalist.' It made me happy, that somewhere amidst the increasingly corporate-seeming Transport for London network, there remained a strident revolutionary idealist who was probably boring the tits off his colleagues with his visions of left-wing utopia. His politics may have been deeply unfashionable, but seeing his words nonetheless felt like the last gasp of the old, anarchic spirit of London making itself known like breath forming fleeting clouds on glass.

I do not take the tube regularly, and didn't even then. The pub where I worked was within walking distance, but it wasn't just that. The space felt sick and unnatural to me, and whenever I went down there it was as though I could feel the weight of the earth above us as we scuttled like rats between one station and another, in darkness. I preferred to get buses, as they made me less anxious. I would happily sit on one going from one side of the city to the other, even if it took hours, even if it was late at night, even if it was the 29, which was nicknamed the 'death bus' because of its reputation for criminal activity and violence, and where I once asked a man who was smoking a crack pipe 'do you mind?' and he responded by courteously opening the window.

Living in the north of the city, I could go weeks without seeing the river, and then all of a sudden I'd be on the top deck of a night bus, drunk usually, and we'd cross over and there it would be suddenly: London, all marble bathed in light. I'd feel this surge in my chest at the knowledge that this was my place, and their place: my parents'. The seat of our muddled, non-linear history; a nest of legends and recollections. As we passed through the streets, I would try and imagine what it was like, in the sixties, seventies, eighties, that summer. I saw the pavements strewn with rubbish and the boarded-up tube stations and the bombed-out houses, backdrops to men with long hair and clove-scented cigarettes, and girls you called 'love'. I saw the pub where you went when you wanted to take a contract out on someone, now a paean to 'British tapas' and salted caramel, where a man once played the spoons in the back bar and my mother cried with laughter because she had never seen such a thing before. As I rode the bus and zigzagged through ancient streets, I saw the place I

97

was born shift and ripple and transform, all the while looked over by a nuclear sun smiling faintly as everything was painted duck egg blue. Now, on the pavements, sandwich boards are popping up. The same marketing slogans – which give the illusion, much like the packaging on a smoothie bottle, of emerging unmediated from the lips of a single, quirky human being – repeated over and over. 'Unattended children will be given an espresso and a free kitten'; 'Soup of the day: the tears of our enemies'. Each statement calculated for maximum virality. But take heart, I think, take heart: there's still a Situationist waiting at the tube gates, a Rasta with a megaphone at Victoria. A soul still beating somewhere.

'Everything is so clean,' my mother said, when she came to see me shortly before I dropped out of university, 'it's as though it's all been sandblasted.' It is true. There's a man who has been taking pictures in the London Underground for nearly thirty years, and that's the first thing you notice when you look at his photographs: the dust and the dirt. His pictures are all skinheads and men with afros smoking, old ladies in trench coats clutching their handbag clasps tightly, people kissing and pissing and fighting and singing. Stella would say it was more alive then, but that could be nostalgia talking. Though buskers must play in clearly delineated semi-circles, you'll still catch 'Here Comes the Sun' drifting through Euston on a gloomy day. And though there are fewer teddy boys and gutter punks and girls with fluorescent orange Ziggy Stardust hair, you'll still spy an original every now and again, fishnets torn and bloody knees, rolly hanging limp from chapped lips. Back then, you had the characters, your tapdancing Lord Mustards and your Stanley Greens, the 'Protein Man' imploring you to buy less protein; meat;

fish; bird; egg. They may be long gone but they're always replaced. In 2010 it was the Jesus freaks and 'Angel Nigel' wrapped in an England flag, ranting in Holloway Morrisons. It'll be someone else now, no doubt, some street poet, or glittering drag queen.

This place can survive the sandblasting. There are still drunk kids roaring with laughter as they throw bits of chicken at each other, perching en masse on walls like crows, before charging down the high streets. The knackered commuters still sleep standing up and giggling freshers still sit on each other's laps, their arses grazing each other's crotches. Snatched, electric glimpses of life.

What legacy are we left by our parents? For me, it's the past. I see my parents' history rolled out in a shimmering trail behind them. They made me at Longhope. Some would say I was infatuated by the aching coolness of their youth, but they would be wrong. I've never found it cool. And I can spot the children of other hippie parents a mile off. When they're toddlers they have odd socks and a ratty bit of hair that grows longer at the nape of their necks, and when they're adults they find it impossible to settle at doing anything without the uncomfortable feeling that they're selling out. There's a vague sense of embarrassment that surrounds us. Our reference points are slightly off. We missed too much television. We know people who were born on boats. We care both too much and not at all.

I was not infatuated, but I felt a tenderness for them that propelled me back to the house, a place I thought I knew because it had been immortalised in photographs now lost. My mother in the bath with me, backlit by the gaps in a dusty wooden venetian blind; my father, smoking at the table with the other men, a bowl of half-eaten curry in front of him and no women in the room apart from a pair of ankles and a sheer, sweeping skirt visible from where I sit under the table; Gabs and me lying side by side in the wildflowers, smiling at one another (if I could have one, just one, it would be that one). The things we lost in the move, in all the moves, there were so many of them. All those photographs, left nonchalantly on the curb, or burned in the back garden.

I felt the tenderness well up in me as I walked through Longhope's rooms again, as an adult. It felt strange not telling Josh and Lucia about what had led me there, this attempt to reconstruct my history. Particularly Josh, to whom I became close as we sat up late into the evenings, smoking, or embarked upon long walks as Lucia slept through the oppressive heat of the day. That summer we spent many hours snaking our way through Islington, from top to bottom, east to west, past the giant mysterious white letters that spell out 'H O P E' at various locations across the borough, watching the scenery switch from multimillion pound houses to scruffy estates and back again. How the world can change in the turn of a corner, I thought, as we crossed a wasteland of a street near the prison, where black spiked railings protruded from the brick and concrete instead of trees, and then moments later entered the lush greenery of a dappled Georgian square.

The first time we walked together, on the pavement of a busy road, we almost collided when he tried to cut across from my left-hand side to my right. 'What are you doing?' I had asked, laughing, as we jolted one another. He flushed with embarrassment, explaining that he'd rather walk on the other side. 'It's so I'm the one that gets hit by a car, not you,' he said, and I wanted to burst into tears because the kindness in his gesture made me feel bereft at never having experienced anything like it before.

On these walks, we mapped dead teenagers, passing and noting their memorials: the flowers, the bicycles and football shirts, the faded, streaked portraits of their baby-faces, the choking goodbyes of friends and classmates spelled out in rounded letters: 'sleep tight, mate'. A heart on the dot of the 'i'. And each time we would stop for a second and Josh would inhale sharply, and swallow.

He told me about his family on these trips, about the wars on his estate, the petty and not so petty rivalries, his school, the girls, so pretty and clever, all mothers now. I liked talking to him. He had a way of listening intently to the things I said and retaining them, then bringing them up in conversation weeks later, agreeing, interjecting, 'It's like that time when you said ... ' before quoting myself back at me. Even throwaway flippant things he treated with enthusiasm and curiosity. It wasn't so much that it was unusual to feel listened to by a man, though when you are young that is in itself exceptional, but it was more the feeling of him seeing me as a person in the world with things to say, as valuable as – perhaps I dared to hope even more valuable than – any other. It was as though he were trying to tell me, 'your words matter to me as much as the things you could do with your body', though I know he thought about those things too; I would catch, for instance, his fleeting glance at my lips, my breasts, and hold that knowledge in my fist like an amulet, telling me I could be beautiful.

I was less honest with him. I was always taciturn where my family were concerned, partly from not knowing. Stella's talent for editing the past rendered any enquiries pretty futile. Anything that would show her in a bad light would be discarded on the cutting room floor. She'd come off best no matter what.

And my father? Along with his girlfriend Mokomo (not Japanese; not the name given to her at birth; a mere five years older than me) he was ensconced in the mountains, busy with his latest sustainable living project; a self-sufficient organic farm in the forest, centred around a yurt that he had built himself. There was no telephone and he rarely switched his mobile on, not that I'd have been able to hear him through the sounds of the ritualistic drumming. Plus he'd been emotionally off-grid for years before that. We didn't have a particularly close relationship and I rarely saw him.

The last time had been in the winter of my first year of university, when he'd spent a weekend at a Buddhist retreat in the city. He'd insisted we meet on Carnaby Street – there was a vegetarian curry restaurant that he had frequented in the sixties – for lunch. I had tried to explain that the street was not what it once was but he hadn't listened, and it was difficult for me to argue with a man I barely knew. To me, he had always carried the authority of a stranger, and that, mixed with the strong desire I had for him to show that he was interested in me, made it very difficult to contradict him. So he led me down the pedestrianised street only to stop outside one of Carnaby's many designer clothing shops looking baffled, and a little sad.

'It was right here,' he said, as house music blasted from the darkened, spotlit interior. He looked so out of place, in his Docs and his liberty print shirt, his beard and shoulder-length hair unkempt and greying.

'We should have gone to Drummond Street.' The hot air from the fan above the doorway was blasting in my face, making my hair move.

'I used to bring you here as a baby.'

In that moment I had wanted desperately to protect him. He looked so crestfallen. I reached out for his hand.

'Come on,' I said. 'Let's get the bus up there.'

They say you can't halt progress, but it was clear from my dad's face that what had happened to his old haunts was, in his opinion, the opposite. But for all his ranting about advanced capitalism it was something else that I saw on his face that day: a thwarted desire for shared experience. With me.

He'd be alarmed to see Soho now, as Crossrail excavations tear the belly out of London's sleazy epicentre, and the old, dingy institutions of a thousand dragged-up disco queens and misfits are boarded up, the lights having gone up for the final time. Madame Jojo's followed Vortex and the Marquee Club into oblivion. In the place of the dingy strip clubs and smutty bookshops, chains and street food restaurants have cropped up, and young professionals with too little disposable income for houses but enough for ceviche snake around the corners that were formerly manned by whores and hawkers. The Coach and Horses serves vegetarian, now, and the Nelly Dean has been gutted; its brick walls, if not its soul, exposed.

Even that summer of 2011 things were changing at an alarming pace. 'I know a place,' you'd say, to your assembled group of fellow drinkers, and you'd all snake through Soho's alleys, dodging the pint-and-rosé-after-work crowd spilling on to the pavements, only to find that it was gone or replaced by a joint specialising in polenta.

But there were bastions of old Italian Soho if you knew where to look, the sorts of places where a payment on the door was sometimes necessary, but often not, depending on whether or not they knew your face. My particular favourite was Julie's, an underground drinking establishment situated in the basement of a building just off Brewer Street. It had an unmarked door, but not as a marketing conceit – faux speakeasies had become common by then – but because it was simply part of someone's house. It marketed itself as a private members' club but it only cost a fiver to join and your membership card consisted of the barman's scrawled signature on a scrap of paper. You did have to sign in, but I suspected that it was more to do with keeping track of who was there than anything else. The place was run by gangsters.

I took Lou to Julie's one Wednesday in early July. We'd hardly seen her since she had come home from that party; she had stayed in her room, or else was out, though no one knew where because she was eschewing all social invitations. A week passed during which I didn't see her, and, having knocked on her door several times, I began to feel a bit concerned. By the following Saturday, I feared the worst.

'Have you seen Lou?' I said to Josh. 'I've knocked on her door. I'm worried.'

'I haven't, no.' Things were still frosty between them, and he didn't look up from the book he was reading.

'I'm scared she may have been taken ill.'

'What do you mean?'

'I haven't seen her for a week. What if she ... '

'What?'

'What if she's *in there*?'

'You mean ... ?'

'Dead. What if she's dead, Josh.' He looked at me.

'Don't laugh. I know someone that happened to, at university. She lived with an international student, a girl

104

who barely spoke any English and didn't really socialise. They hardly noticed when she stopped coming into the kitchen. Until it started to smell, and then they found her. She'd been dead for two weeks. Heart failure.'

He said nothing for a second, then put his book down. 'Oh for fuck's sake, Harmony.' He got up and barged through to the hallway. 'Lou.' He knocked. 'Lucia.' No answer. As he ploughed into her bedroom I stayed in the living room, too frightened to look.

'Fuck *off* Josh,' she mumbled, from under the covers. Her room was dark and smelled of must, the only light, red, emanating from a lamp she'd draped with a scarf. The floor was littered with clothes and shoes. 'I'm on a vicious comedown.'

We left her alone, but a week later I'd finally succeeded in getting her out of the house to Julie's. 'Ok, I'll come,' she said, 'but I don't want to see anyone.'

'I think I know a place.'

'How *darling*,' she said, seeing as we descended the stairs the red and white checked tablecloths and mismatched bar stools. She took in the clientele, a mixture of hardened Soho drinkers, crims, students, strippers and lost out-of-towners. 'You're right, this isn't my usual crowd.'

'This isn't anyone's usual crowd,' I said, 'but I like it. Everything is £3.50.'

'In that case the drinks are on you. I'm going to explore.'

There was a crowd at the bar, all shouting their orders over the din of Motown. By the time I'd got our gins Lou was nowhere to be seen. I pushed my way through the throng – the pubs had just emptied out so everyone had descended here – and eventually sought her out in the small concreted smoking area at the back. She was talking to two youngish men who were regarding her with the fascination of a child who has just seen its first punk on the tube.

'Well, darling, I believe you. If you say you didn't do it, then of course you didn't do it.'

'This might be his last night out,' said the dark-haired one.

'I'm hoping for Wandsworth because my mate's in there,' said his friend and, it emerged, his cousin. They were both Sicilian with strong cockney accents, dressed in perfectly ironed cotton shirts and jeans, teamed with smartish leather shoes. Next to them Lou, who was wearing a turban, looked faintly ridiculous.

'Well I think that calls for another round. How about it lads?' she said.

As they headed for the bar she leaned in towards me. 'Oh come on, Harmony, it's not as though he killed a man. Just a bit of blackmail, he told me.'

The drinks kept coming; the boys had a family connection, they said. In return we were expected to entertain them, which Lucia did with aplomb as I sat, mostly silent, becoming increasingly wasted.

'You shouldn't be drinking when you're in court tomorrow,' I said, to the younger one. 'You could really fuck it up for yourself.'

'Oh, Harmony, let him have a good time. He may never see freedom again,' said Lou, her eyes suggesting that she thought this impossibly glamorous. 'Isn't it delicious? I've always wanted to be a moll.'

As the night wore on and the Motown changed to soul, we crammed together in the tiny dancing area and thrashed about. The unventilated basement air was sticky and my hair clung to my face. By the time the lights went up and the opera came on, always a mainstay at Julie's when it got to three or four and the punters began to dwindle, and grown men felt suddenly that they could embrace and cry, I was ready to leave.

'I want to stay here forever,' said Lou, who had had a joint out the back and possibly more. 'Forever in this moment.' I grabbed her by the arm and nodded towards the boys. 'Time for us to go. It's been a pleasure. Thanks for the drinks. And good luck tomorrow.'

'Ciao belli,' she waved unsteadily as I manoeuvred her backwards up the stairs. 'Let's get food.'

We staggered down the street to a 24-hour diner and ordered eggs benedict. It was approaching five, and that slow, easy drunkenness that comes with a new place and a brightening sky had begun to take hold.

Lou carefully unwound her turban and placed it folded in her lap. Her arms looked so thin and pale, there in the slightly blue light of the darkened diner, as she tapped her fingernails on the lacquered tabletop. Her eyes stared out at me from darkened pools of smudged eyeliner.

'That was wonderful,' she said. 'And as a bonus, I now have the number of a really good defence barrister. Just in case I lose it for good one day.' She laughed.

I put my hand on her arm. 'Are you all right, Lou? I mean, really? I know we don't know each other that well, but I've been worried about you, after ...'

'Eggs.' The food was placed down in front of us. Lou pierced her yolks with her fork. 'They go solid if you don't, my mother always said. Not that she ever ate much.'

'Lou ...'

'The question is, Harmony, whether it's you who is all right.'

'I don't know what you mean. I'm fine.'

107

'I was rather scared of you when I first met you, you know. I've never met someone so composed. It's as though you're surrounded by this thick shell of confidence. It was quite intimidating, actually.'

'I don't know what you mean.'

'I just get the impression that nothing, ever, could break you. Look at me, I'm a mess. That arsehole. I feel sick that I got with him. I can't get out of bed in the morning, I drink too much. I'm so sad, Harmony. So unbelievably sad.'

'We're all sad.' I looked at her.

'It's not the same,' said Lou. 'You're so … still. Have you noticed that? Look at me.'

She pointed at her leg, which was jerking up and down under the table, the pale flesh rippling through the diamonds of her fishnets. 'I feel like I can never stop moving, because if I do. Well, you saw the other day. A corpse in the back bedroom.'

'Josh told you about us thinking you might have popped it?'

Lucia nodded.

'We all feel like that sometimes.'

'What does that *mean*? That doesn't mean anything, Harmony. Look at you. You're fine, you're sorted.'

'I'm a waitress.'

'But you're swaddled by love. I can tell by the way you are. You're at peace with yourself.'

I was surprised that someone could get me so wrong. She had mistaken detachment for composure.

'Tell me, was there ever a moment when you thought, even for a second, that your parents might not love you?'

'Never,' I said. 'At least, I think they do in a certain selfish way. But that's because I'm a perfect combination of the two of them. To stop loving me would be to cease loving themselves, and they couldn't do that because they're egotists. Plus, what's love without stability? Neither of them have been able to offer me that. And for all their words of praise neither have ever really consistently been there.'

'Fucking families,' said Lou. 'I wish I could smoke in here. Can I get a scotch and soda?'

'Let's go home,' I said. 'I want to be in my bed.'

'Why?' She was slurring. 'It can't be that great in there. You cry in the night. I can hear you through the wall.'

'That's unkind.'

'It's true. Tell me, mystery Harmony: why do you cry in the night?' There was a taunt in her voice and a twist in her cupid's bow.

'I have bad dreams,' I said, 'but I don't remember them.'

'Well, I'll stay with you tonight.'

She did stay with me that night, but not until we'd nailed a half bottle of gin in the kitchen. As the sun came up and the birds chirped in the fruit tree outside the window, we pulled the curtains closed, and she wrapped her limbs around me and, for a few precious hours before Coral started screaming, we lay in peaceful darkness.

Autumn 1984

There's a restfulness to living with other women that I never had with my mam, who was always too concerned with larger things, like having enough money to buy milk, to have time for sisterhood. I don't blame her, but to sit around a table with other women, shelling chickpeas as we chat idly about this or that, gives me a feeling of missing. My female friends at school were mostly bothered with working out how to get boys, curling their hair and throwing their heads back in exaggerated, shimmer-glossed giggles whenever they strutted past, the boys' shoulders taut so that their bodies were hardened rectangles, dense with purpose. We would kiss the backs of our hands in practice for the inevitable lunge, reading articles in magazines about which way to tilt your head and how to tuck your teeth beneath your lips. Who knew there were so many things that you could do wrong?

Here, though, the women seem almost self-sufficient from the men. They form their own group, sharing child-care and cooking duties, and trading in spiritual guidance – reading each other's tarot cards (witchcraft, mam would have tutted, shaking her head), sharing macrobiotic recipes, recommending this or that healer or acupuncturist. They laugh not as performance but at the wit and cleverness of their friends. It feels peaceful, this separateness, a welcome respite from the charged deference of the men, especially

Bryn, whose charisma only seems to increase when he's drunk or on something. He can talk for hours, each topic more fascinating than anything I learned at school. He feels the injustice of the world deeply, his heart breaking in a way that reminds me of Mark when, as a bairn, he realised that everybody dies. Distraught.

Suffering seems to physically hurt him, but that suffering is always of the many; he lacks patience with despair when it's in front of him. I'm not so mad about him that I don't see his faults.

It is true that I want him, but in many ways it is Stella who interests me more. There is a spikiness to her. Her affection is not straightforwardly given. She's young, not much older than me, but has a composure and sense of authority that makes me think of a much older woman. She rarely smiles. She's in on that secret of all mysterious, sad-looking women, which is that when she chooses to look happy it means more, and it feels like you did it.

She rarely touches, either, but it's when she links her arm through mine or carefully brushes my hair before bed that I am struck by the fact that the caresses given to me have nearly always been from men. From women, touch is strange terrain.

I have been here several weeks when the topic of Bryn's interest in me is raised. Stella is lying on the sofa, reading in a pose that makes me think of reclining nudes in paintings, her head thrown back onto the armrest, her arched torso bowlike as she holds the book so that it hovers above her face like a shield. I find the natural way she moves intimidating. My own body feels artless and cumbersome in the presence of hers.

I am sitting on the floor painting my toenails crimson when she starts to speak.

111

'He has always liked young women, you know, and you're an exceptionally pretty one.'

'But you're stunning.' The darkness of her hair contrasts with the paleness of her skin, while my face looks see-through, almost blue. I take in her round breasts curving under her blouse.

She makes a movement with her hand as if to say, irrelevant.

'We're married. And that means something. Not much, but something.'

'I won't try anything with him,' I find myself saying, as she looks at me, eyebrow raised.

'It's only a matter of time before he tries something with you. I'm not asking you not to respond when he does. It would be pointless. I'm not even asking you not to sleep with him. You probably will, and I couldn't stop it even if I wanted to. Bryn is a law unto himself, and that's one of the reasons I'm in love with him, so it would be wrong of me to reject this aspect of his character now.'

I say nothing, not used to such frankness.

'All I'm asking is that you remember we're married. That he is my husband. As long as this fact stays in the forefront of your mind, then we can go on being friends.'

I hear her message loud and clear: this trumps everything.

She jumps up from the sofa, startling me, and smiles. 'Come, let's go out. I'll find you a dress to wear.'

She puts me in a skimpy green silk slip that skims my narrow hips and slides down over my angular shoulders, nodding with approval as she stands behind me in the mirror. Outside, the sky brims with potential.

'Desiderata'

Framed hand calligraphy print (mid-1970s) of the inspirational prose poem 'Desiderata' written by Max Ehrmann in 1927 (see item for full text), wooden frame approx. 11.25" x 9". Masking taped at reverse. Glass cracked, smeared with fingerprints, slight cocaine residue.

Mid-July, and Lucia and I had been drinking for eleven days. Since that night at Julie's, we had spent most of our time suspended in an unthinking drunken void. Hours passed without very much happening at all. We were either lying flat on our backs in the living room listening to sixties girl groups and Joni Mitchell on Lou's record player or, on the rare occasions I had to work, having lock-ins at the pub. Lou had made a habit of turning up towards the end of my shift and charming all the locals into plying her with free drinks and the odd line until I knocked off, by which time she'd be thoroughly trashed and philosophical. Then the two of us would stagger back to ours and listen to more records, before tumbling into bed, if we made it that far.

It was the afternoons I enjoyed the most, when we threw all the windows open and the music up loud, and shouted along in between the puffs that burned the backs of our throats. Sometimes, if we hadn't passed out by the time Josh came home from work, he would join us for a spliff or two, remarking on our admirable stamina while at the same time maintaining an air of paternal concern for our well-being. By day eleven, however, he had begun to look more disapproving, perhaps because he wandered in just as Lou was halfway through a rendition of 'Why'd Ya Do It?' by Marianne Faithfull, having made the big bay window her own personal stage. She was standing there in her slip holding a crystal wine glass belting out the words while I sat on the floor clapping. 'Why'd ya do it, she said, when you know it makes me sore / 'Cause she had cobwebs up her fanny and I believe in giving to the poor / Why'd ya do it, she said, why'd you spit on my snatch? / Are we out of love now, is this just a bad patch?'

'Blimey,' said Josh, 'that's not one for karaoke down the Crown.'

Lou flopped down on the couch and lit up. 'She came for dinner once, you know. With my parents. I can just about remember her.'

'You inhabit a different world,' I said, and went into the kitchen to top up my Chambord and lemonade. We had run out of gin, vodka and whisky a couple of days in and were scraping the back of the cabinet.

'What are we doing tonight?' she called through. 'I think we should go out.'

The track ended. I came back into the living room and started flipping through the records, searching for something but not sure what. Lucia sauntered past in search of her cigarettes and clinked her glass against mine.

'To us.'

'When are you both going to stop? This is getting insane.'

We turned to look at Josh, who for once was not rolling up. He sat down on the arm of a chair.

'We're having a good time,' I said.

114

'Really? Are you really having a good time? It feels like you're hiding.'

'Hiding,' said Lou. 'You're so dramatic. We're just taking a little break, aren't we darling?'

'We are,' I said. 'A little break from life. Like Coral does.'

Coincidentally, Coral had embarked on what appeared to be an almighty drinking session at around the same time as we had. We hadn't seen her, but we'd heard. The muffled, faraway strains of 'Gimme Shelter' though the floor, with its high-pitched lead, the 'oooh, oooohs' floating up through the garden in the early hours. The sounds of breaking glass and the clanking of bottles before dawn as she staggered out to the recycling; the strained, gravelly tone of her protestations coupled by the deep, harsh yells of a man. Crashing, and then banging on the door. We had almost called the police several times, but our own dreamy excesses had made us lackadaisical. She'd be ok. She always was.

'Our alcoholic, agoraphobic, benefit-scrounging downstairs neighbour is hardly a role model,' said Josh.

'I never took you for someone who believed what they read in the papers,' I said, tipsy and righteous. 'You know, we were on benefits. Do you and whatever shitty right-wing newspaper you read think that we're scroungers too?'

'Oh for Christ sake Harmony, have some nuance,' said Josh. 'Are you seriously telling me that Coral and whatever dodgy bloke she's got on the go aren't a serious waste of public funds? I'm not saying we should blame those on benefits for every ill in society. I'm not saying that anyone who's poor is a lazy shirker who can't be bothered to get off their arse and work. I'm not peering over our garden fence getting myself all riled up about how them next door aren't declaring their drug dealing earnings to the DSS. But for a moment, can we just be honest here? I hate the Tories as much as the next *Guardian*-reading Islington liberal but I also grew up on an estate in Manchester ...'

'Thought you owned your house?' said Lou. There was a hint of mockery in her voice.

'We did. Do. But Lou, Right to Buy doesn't mean your house suddenly takes off like a rocket and lands in middle class suburbia. I lived there all my life and I'm being honest here when I say that if you really believe that there aren't any lazy bastards out there who live out their lives on the rock and roll then you're living in a fantasy world.'

'But it's overstated,' I said. 'It's overstated on purpose to create an even greater divide.'

'Yeah! It's blaming the poor and vulnerable for social inequality when what we have is a defective and oppressive system.' Lucia looked quite pleased with herself, as though her comment was sufficiently insightful for her to be able to withdraw from the conversation.

'That may be. But can you really look inside yourselves and tell me that you don't feel something like disgust for that woman downstairs and her complete inability to look after herself. She can't even dispose of her own cat's turds properly.'

'You said she'd had a hard life. You said that to me when I had just moved in.'

'I don't doubt that she has. But let's face it. She lives a sad, pathetic, booze-induced existence. There's nothing there to aspire to.'

'I thought you had more empathy than that.'

'Come on, Harmony. You're misunderstanding what I'm saying. I'm not saying that the state shouldn't step in when it comes to Coral, I'm just asking you to consider the notion that some of the Conservatives' welfare rhetoric – hideous and brutal though it is – might have a grain of truth in it. The trouble comes when they pretend that grain's a whole loaf.'

'Please can we stop talking about those awful people?' said Lou, who came back in from the kitchen clutching a brown-coloured drink. 'I just don't have the energy for it.'

'Yeah, I'm too pissed for this,' I said. 'And I feel like I'm back at university. So what are we going to do with ourselves?'

Lou walked over and switched the record player off. 'I know a party.'

'A party? Where?'

'Swiss Cottage'

'Behind the Iron Curtain? It's a trek. And I hate West London. Everyone's so ...'

'Wanky? It won't be like that. It's worth it, trust me.'

'Is it someone you went to school with?' Josh crinkled his nose. 'Because if so I'll give it a miss, ta.'

The last time Lou had taken us to a party in West London it had been some banker she knew through school friends. It always astounded me how close these public school kids' networks were, the girls from Francis Holland and St Paul's and the boys from Westminster and University College. Everyone knew someone's sister Tilly through someone's boyfriend Hugh, the back pages of *Tatler* printed in shades of blonde and khaki on their brains like some *Debrett's* for the children of magistrates and businessmen. 'He's nouveau riche,' Lou had said, as we disembarked from the black cab on a leafy street bathed in the luxury of white street lamps, offset by the watchful red bleeps of burglar alarms. 'It's a veritable case of "pimp my house".'

It was. A relatively normal-looking suburban detached, of the kind you get in cities all over the country, yet strangely altered, as though they had whacked a turret on one side and tried to elevate it from family home to something altogether grander. The whole building seemed crooked, but I couldn't quite put my finger on what it was. It had, I remember, a circular kitchen of the sort where you expected a newly jellied flan to be sitting on the central work surface in anticipation, and a billiards room, the felt of the table a vivid magenta, the posed family photographs silent spectators to the hedge funders, still so young looking in their suits, who were racking up lines on the lacquered wood like overgrown pageboys gone rogue. The real *pièce de résistance*, however, was the back garden, a workaday English lawn waxed smooth and vivid green, as though dyed. One day, probably in the middle eighties, the inhabitants had walked into their newly bought home, gazed through the screen doors at their conventional family garden and thought, 'Versailles'. The centrepiece was a three-layered fountain surrounded by box hedges and guarded by topiary glades of cherubs. To the right, the pool extension, which was at that point host to a number of topless Frans and Lucindas. In my electric blue cocktail dress, which had layers of nylon and lace and gossamer and looked like something early Madonna would have rejected for being too outré, I had looked (and felt) completely out of place. Josh had left early muttering under his breath that he couldn't stand another second of these cunts, but I had stayed, defiant in the face of questions about where I had been schooled. Other than that I remembered very little of the actual party; the sour metallic taste of cocaine in the back of my throat that made me feel as though I was going to be sick

118

in a flower bed at any moment; a boy in a dinner jacket, tripping over a box hedge and declaring himself 'literally shitfaced'; the sickly taste of semi-ironic punch. Everyone had talked incessantly about themselves, but then isn't that what conversation is? One person waiting for their chance to speak, and vice versa, on and on. It was just that these people didn't bother to pretend otherwise.

'It won't be like that,' said Lou. She shuddered with the camp practised drama of a true snob. 'It's a girl I know from ... I'm not sure how I know her actually, but it'll be sensational. Promise.' And so we agreed.

This party venue was unlike any house I had seen in London, but then I never came out that way, nor ventured into Surrey. It reminded me of a photograph I had once seen of Alfred Hitchcock's country house, jarring in its lack of resemblance to the gabled, gothic palaces of his films. This too was mock Tudor and brown brick, humble-looking, yet enormous on the inside, once we made our way through the people who were spilling or hanging out of every orifice, laughing without, thankfully, their heads thrown back. Lou was right, it was a different crowd, art students mainly, state school pupils now at ex-polys. Because of the house it had a feeling of an illicit teenage party thrown because the parents were away.

'They're property guardians,' said Lou, of the people who lived there. 'There are at least eleven of them. They live here for free to stop it being squatted. It's due to be demolished, that's why they paint directly onto the walls.'

Everyone seemed to be property guardians in those days. That year the rents had been rising on a month-by-month basis and, for those who resented shelling out for identikit buy-to-lets painted white with laminate flooring and aspiring balconies made of glass, it provided a realistic alternative. All over the city, homes stood empty.

The unoccupied mansions on Bishop's Avenue – the road that ran from the top of the Heath to Finchley that was also known as Billionaire's Row – were crumbling and overgrown behind their wrought iron gates, their moss-covered fountains dried up, their swimming pools empty and melancholy. Poor young people would willingly become cut-rate guard dogs to live in such a place. The guardians paid very little rent in exchange for their physical presence, so it suited many of those of our generation whose squatting ambitions had been thwarted by legislation.

'I feel ambivalent about it,' a girl I knew who 'guarded' an abandoned school in Peckham told me. 'On the one hand ... practically no rent. But on the other, I know that the owners are sitting on a goldmine here. And what are we to them? Meat. Meat that stops slightly smellier meat coming in and depleting the value of their asset.'

'And then they'll divide it into flats and sell it on, and then where will we be? In the same situation – onto the next place, helping rich landlords protect their property interests with no hope of that stability ourselves.'

The Hitchcock house's interior was an odd combination of faded grandeur – chandeliers and ceiling roses, peachy damask wallpaper – and the sad echoes of family life. The kitchen was panelled in dark wood cut in narrow strips and had not been updated since the seventies. You could almost see a bowl-cut child in a crew neck striped T-shirt sitting there at the breakfast island, eating a newly fashionable yoghurt, as a housekeeper in a pussy-bow blouse tidied in the background. Everything about the place spoke of a certain style of childhood, so clearly was it divided into those spaces which were for the adults and those which were not, and I wondered where that boy was now, whether he ever drove past on late summer evenings, slowing at the curb to remember the kickabouts on the lawn as his mother sat watching with her gin and tonic, her large floppy sun hat, her paperback novel, her barbiturates. They had all moved out long ago. 'Shall we take this?' I imagined the grown-up son saying, perhaps to his brother or sister as they cleared the house. But neither had wanted the framed 'Desiderata' that remained defiantly suspended from a hook above the kettle.

We had intended to eat the mushrooms on a pizza as a way of mollifying their floury, dirty taste, but the neighbourhood was such a wasteland that we had not passed a single shop on the way from the tube. Like many rich parts of West London, there seemed to be so little a sense of community that you wondered whether people didn't just ossify in their houses as they waited for the Ocado van. As Josh cracked open a lager, we boiled some water, and, after nursing our pilfered mugs for ten minutes or so in the crowded kitchen, had them in tea.

Shortly afterwards the edges of my thoughts began to blur and wiggle, making it, I decided, a good time to explore the house. I left Lou in the kitchen staring at her fingers while Josh chatted to a girl with a buzz cut, and pushed my way through the new arrivals armed with clinking plastic bags. On the ground floor there was a half-empty ballroom with the lights dimmed, a DJ ready at the decks for when the guests descended, gurning, from various bedrooms, demanding electro. I stumbled in and wandered to the back of the high-ceilinged room, where patio doors opened onto a large back garden that was in surprisingly good shape. Perhaps it was a condition of their guardianship that they mow the lawn. At this point I was starting to get some mild visuals – nothing disturbing, just an increased sense of clarity, as though everything within my line of sight was being passed through a pin-sharp filter. I stood swaying slightly on the periphery of a conversation. Someone was talking about the cuts to education maintenance allowance and the project they were working on based on it, and they asked me something but I smiled vaguely in response. I had come to the realisation that I could see every leaf on every tree and it was magical. Their edges shimmered silver in the moonlight and just the fact of them seemed at that moment indescribably beautiful and hilarious. I began to laugh.

I don't know how long I stood out there staring at the trees but eventually I returned inside. The house was filling up past capacity, the party's activities no longer mainly restricted to the outdoor areas. People were shouting in order to make themselves heard over the music. The staircases were packed, meaning that to reach the other floors you had to squeeze past people pressed against the banisters as their drinks sloshed. I kissed a blond boy on the second landing as we waited in the queue for the toilet, until his tongue became a worm that was trying to suffocate me and I pushed him away in horror.

The main bathroom had been papered, for some unknowable reason, in tin foil and was bathed in a blue fluorescent light. Next to the sink, which was full to the brim and contained a ladle, was a handwritten note saying 'gin and tonic'. I helped myself to a cup as the reflections of the light in the walls began to move. Three people sat in the pink corner bath talking as a guy with an afro skinned up. 'It's ok,' he was saying. 'Pretty derivative and anguished. Sub-par Bacon.'

'Bacon,' I said, stupid, and began to giggle.

Into the next room, and I found Josh, cross-legged on the floor and talking about Poirot. 'I never got why my parents loved it so much,' he was saying, 'it goes on for fucking hours. Oh my God, Harmony, you're tripping out.'

'Did you see the leaves?' I said. 'The leaves were amazing. It's like I'm inside and outside myself at the same time.'

'Let's get you some water.'

My memory of events is hazy after that, but Josh told me later that we went for some fresh air and that I lay on my back for an hour telling him we had the same body. Lou was nowhere to be seen, as was often the case, but I knew she hadn't left because every now and again I'd see someone trying on her hat. I'd lost all sense of time by that point. The sky was still dark but the birds, confused by a house all lit up, were singing. The music pounding through the screen doors had changed from electronic to old school hip-hop; the packed ballroom heaved and swelled. I floated through the crowds moving to the beat, the strobe accentuating the feeling that I was wading through treacle as the floral carpet, muddied from a hundred and fifty pairs of trainers, swirled and churned like lava beneath my shoes. It wasn't unpleasant, but I was beginning to feel a profound dislocation from my body. I was somehow standing upright and yet also horizontal, lying down kicking like an infant in a cot, all in time with the music. I finally spotted Lou vogueing in the corner and went over to her and danced with them for a bit. Who knows how long? Time had ceased to be linear, it was an amorphous accumulation of every moment ever lived. I was fucked.

'Did you see the moonbow?' said Lou. 'I'm a moonbow, too.' As she laughed her grimace turned into a horror-show mask and I took a step backwards, grounding myself.

It was just as I was imagining the technicalities of a moonbow that it happened. I caught a glimpse of red hair somewhere near the centre of the room, a scrap of white lace, and there she was. I stood staring before pushing my way over to her as she danced, her skinny arms flailing wildly from what appeared to be a diaphanous vintage wedding dress that had been hacked at with scissors. A druggy, pre-Raphaelite beauty. Her eyes, rimmed with dark eyeliner, hovered disconnectedly above the other dancers, dreamlike. In contrast to her arms her legs were moving almost languidly. I looked down at the swirling mass of carpet and saw that she wasn't wearing shoes. Her small, delicate feet almost shone set against the dark of the floor.

'So milky white.' I wanted to touch them, then felt complete repulsion. They were like doll's feet. Waxy. Bloodless. I looked away.

She focused on me, finally. It was as though the music had been cut.

'It's you.' I realised then that I was crying, that my cheeks were red and wet. 'It's you.'

I touched my face, then hers, grasping through the air. The ends of her hair, which went down to her waist, were damp. I ran my fingers through them, fascinated. In hindsight, I'm surprised she didn't push me off her. Instead she looked bemused.

'But where have you been?' I said. I was gripping her hard against me, crying into her shoulder. 'It's been such a long time. Where did you go?'

Wings

Child's fairy wings, 55 x 42 cm, white, wire and mesh fabric with silver glitter, bought Hamley's late 1980s. Made in China. Small hole.

The year I was five was dedicated mainly to experiments in human flight. I had a pair of white gauze fairy wings and, though I had not yet succeeded, I was convinced that the answer to flying lay merely in a certain tensing of the limbs, the unique propulsion of the torso at the moment you jumped. The arm of the sofa was my launch pad. I would teeter on the edge of it, poised, bending my knees, before leaping forward in breaststroke motion in an attempt to swim through the air. These attempts continued throughout the summer we came to the moth house, as my mother lay upstairs, listless on the mattress, her vitality dissipated by the heat and the self-inflicted tragedy of separation. Her love of frivolity was all played out.

Mine, however, remained intact. When I wasn't trying to solve the mystery of human flight, the only thing I viewed with any real seriousness, I spent my days adventuring, discovering new lands in the wild meadows of the garden, or sliding down the steep mountainside of the banisters. I'd make funny faces out of the vegetables piled up on the kitchen table, plunge my small chubby hands into the sacks of lentils in the pantry. Sometimes I would go up to the attic and sit as Fleur and Rufus mixed new tracks, or dance for them as they laughed. Despite my mother's baffling distance, I was never short of friends in that house, though their faces and names have long gone astray.

It's strange, what falls between the cracks of life, those things that slip, silken down the drain only to reappear as you stand, off your face and bawling, in front of a stranger at a party. A girl with red hair in cut off shorts, laughing, with milky white feet. How could I forget her? And who was she?

It hadn't been her, of course. She would be old now. But the party guest resembled the young woman enough that in my mushroom-addled brain neurons snapped and crackled, and a long-abandoned memory came to light. There had been a young woman in the house, and that young woman had been my friend, maybe even had loved me. The thought gave me comfort, not just because it led me to reassess that unsettling summer in which my solitary childhood stood in sharp relief, but because my sudden memory of her meant that there could be an answer nestling amongst my wayward thoughts. Events were as recalcitrant as ever, but at least now I felt that an ordering, a cataloguing impulse had started to kick in. Though I was far from a stage where I could place these scenes neatly in an album on a shelf and continue on with the business of living, at least my mind was starting to obey.

For as Josh shepherded me out of the party, as I sobbed and babbled in the manner of a deranged hysteric from a Victorian novel, arms flailing like Kate Bush, it was remembering my attempts to fly that finally broke through the stubborn mental barriers I had created.

I had been in the living room, as usual, on the sofa. It must have only been a few days after we arrived at the house, because some of our boxes were still in the hall, which was visible through the large, doorless arch adjoining the two rooms. Bright sun streamed through the windows, though the glass was so murky the light was imbued with a slightly polluted quality, and beams of dust shot through the air at jaunty angles, bisecting the space and providing me with visible targets from where I stood, poised, ready for my first proper flight.

This time, I decided, I would do it. I had made several unsuccessful attempts, failures, I suspected, because the muscles in my arms had not been sufficiently taut. The key was to stretch both arms and legs at the same time, as you jumped, belly-first, in the direction of the soft rug. Though I hadn't quite mastered the jump, I felt confident this would be the time. It was merely a question of will. My parents had told me I could do anything I wanted to do and be anything I wanted to be, provided that I wanted it hard enough. Why should flying be any different?

It took a few moments to dawn on me that they had betrayed me, because I was unconscious. I had overshot my target, banging my head on the side of a bookcase as I fell, belly-first, towards the floor. My left foot glanced a sturdy trunk that was being used as a coffee table, and several mugs and saucers had fallen to the floor and smashed. The almighty crash must have reached the furthest reaches of the house, because when I came to and my vision cleared, there she was, right up close, all anxious big eyes, telling me not to move. 'Oh, Harmony,' she said, her accent strange. 'My little darling, my sweetheart.' And then she drew me to her breast and rocked me from side to side as I cried over the bump on my head, and for my mother, far away yet just upstairs, and for my bedroom at home at the cottage, snug and safe and peppered in the gold stars she had made with stencils cut from cereal boxes.

This twenty-year-old memory, a vivid recollection of the young woman and how she had embraced me in the living room after I had fallen returned to me as clear as water as I woke up from my eventual, shroom-addled sleep. The trip lasted about six hours and, after Josh took me home, I finally crashed in the mid-afternoon, unconscious for almost an entire day. In retrospect it was obvious that I had confused some poor, harmless girl at the party with someone I once knew, a previous resident of the commune whom I had long forgotten. The laughing woman near the spider's web.

'You gave me a hell of a fright,' said Josh, when I surfaced in search of a coffee. 'You were like a wild thing. I could barely keep you still. Thank God there was hardly anyone on the bus, they would have thought I was abducting you the way you kept screaming.'

'I can't really remember that bit. I was quite drunk as well. I remember being in the garden, and then seeing the girl, and then barely anything.'

'It was a pretty bad trip,' Josh said. 'You were touching her face. I think she was amused at first but then she started looking freaked out. You were talking about the trees outside, and you kept pointing towards her feet – this was on the dancefloor – and then, for like, no reason at all, you just started hollering. As though you had seen the most horrific thing it was possible to see. You were screaming and screaming, and hyperventilating. It seemed like a panic attack.'

'I've had those before.' I looked away from his face.

'Me too, when I smoke too much weed, but this was full on. I thought I was going to have to take you to

A&E to have you sedated. You would barely hold still. You kept yelling about blood. Then the next minute you looked completely blissed out and kept talking about how much you wanted to fly. It'll be a miracle if you don't get flashbacks.'

'I'm fine, really. Thank you for looking after me.'

'It's cool. That party was shit, anyway. I was bored. I'm just glad you're ok. Come here.'

He drew me towards him in a hug. His chest felt solid. I rested my cheek against it for a moment and then raised my eyes to look up at him. His hand was in my hair.

'I worry about you, you know.' His voice was quiet. I could barely hear it over the hiss of the kettle.

'I don't see why,' I said into his jumper. 'I'm not on the dole, I'm making rent, I'm healthy. It's all good.'

'You just seem so sad sometimes. Why is that?'

I didn't know how to respond. Moments such as this, when I felt that he really saw me, only added to my affection for him. I wanted nothing more in the world to be the sort of girl he needed, but sadness rarely tallies with attraction. At least, not for decent men.

'Aren't we all? I don't know. I just have days like that I guess. Days where I know I'm not going to be able to get out of bed, and so I just … don't. The mistake is trying to push through it, to get up anyway, to go to work. That's how you end up weeping in the toilets or hyperventilating in a store cupboard or screaming at a stranger in the supermarket. So I just stay under the duvet.'

'So you're depressed? Or anxious? Have you seen a doctor? Tried medication?'

'I wouldn't say I was depressed, really.' I walked over to the window and looked out at the snarl of Coral's garden. 'It was suggested that I try Prozac, or beta blockers.

Everyone seems to be on those now, but I don't think that's right for me. It seems a bit. I don't know.'

'What?'

'I suppose I feel that I'd be dulling what is ultimately a justifiable sadness, you know? It's common to feel sad. It's a logical reaction to the way the world is. Why would I try and mute it? It's not as though it's affecting my life in any big way.'

'You dropped out of uni, Harmony.'

In many ways, I thought, university had been the saddest place of all. Almost everybody was depressed. A battered copy of *The Bell Jar* sat in every chunky knit-wearing female student's pristine leather satchel. And then you had the poetry. Later, after graduation, one of these girls would put her head in a plastic bag and fill it with helium in a bathroom in Berlin, thereby giving the others permission to shrug off their own undergraduate sadness. Things hadn't been so bad.

'Yeah, well. University's not for everyone. I'm ok, you know. I have bad dreams and sometimes I feel a bit low, but who doesn't? Anyway, I need to get ready for work.'

'I didn't mean to piss you off. You just seem lost to me. And you're so weirdly reticent. You've hardly told me anything about where you grew up or how or what it involved.'

What to tell him? My mother's peripatetic inability to settle meant an upheaval every few months. For years we zigzagged up and down the country as she followed a series of boyfriends with hair and politics of varying levels of ridiculousness. Curiously, her avowed feminism never prevented her from believing that men, ultimately, held all the answers. These boyfriends were rarely unpleasant, eccentric yet predictable in their attire (hemp hareem pants, skullcaps dotted with little mirrors, collarless shirts) and usually stoned. I didn't show much interest in them beyond realising that their flippant entry into our lives would signal an inevitable move and the usual shedding of things. With every man she met, whether at a drumming workshop or an organic farm collective, it was a case of serendipity, but to me, it spelled disruption – a new school and a new, scratchy uniform bought with vouchers from the council. Not to mention the things left behind – not just the Japanese lampshades and potted plants, the jam jars of beans and spices filled from the health food shop, the flotsam and jetsam of our improvised household, but my things, too. We would only ever take as much as would fit in the bus, the car, or whatever the latest man drove, and even these got lost as soon as summer came around and they embarked on their inevitable summer trips to Tuscany, Massachusetts or Morocco and I was dropped off at my grandmother's house for safekeeping. I liked it there – it was tidy, and cosy, and normal. She would tut and fret over me and make me cocoa when I woke crying out in the small hours from night terrors, then read to me until I finally went back to sleep. Hers was a life of Radio 4, cheese and crackers, rose pruning and McVitie's Gold bars. I loved being with her, but as soon as I got settled I was whisked away again.

In this, I think, partly lay my reasoning for returning to the London house. Its thick stone walls offered stability, a meaningful link to the belonging and history so many people find in the tangibility of things, that my parents never could.

Instead I said, 'There's not so much to say, honestly Josh. I'm just not a very interesting person.'

He rolled his eyes, reaching a hand out and using it to

cup the back of my head. I turned my face up towards his, but he let go with a grin.

'Now bugger off to work and promise me you won't do any more hallucinogens for a while.'

I laughed as far up to my eyes as I could manage, and went to put on some shorts, determined to find out the identity of the young woman who had held me so tenderly. I was going to go downstairs, into the room where a much smaller me had once naively attempted to defy physics and take flight, and I was going to speak to Coral.

Winter 1984

I am sitting shivering by the gas fire in my coat when he comes. The potential screw has been hanging in the atmosphere for weeks, building to the point where I think I will go mad if I don't have him. He has made me an expert archivist. When he's with me, I file every look and remark away for later when I am alone in my room. He has given me no guarantee and it is this possibility without a promise that has made me desperate. I would have gone to bed with him weeks ago, but he is older and also, married, so he decides when.

It's a Tuesday in mid-December. Stella and Coral have gone to get ivy and holly on the Heath, to decorate the house. Mikey is who knows where, the others working or at school. My face is so close to the warmth of the heater that I imagine it has turned red-raw. The ends of my fingers are itchy with chilblains and they struggle to turn the pages of the hardback I have borrowed from the library – a Czech novel about an adulterous surgeon that Stella recommended.

He says my name and I look up from it. Cold, grey light creeps in from the window leaving the room's corners in shadow, and he is slightly backlit standing there, in a stiff denim shirt. He's unshaven so that in the half-light I have to squint to catch his smile.

I feel as though I am standing on a platform and a

perverse urge is telling me to jump in front of the oncoming train.

He says my name, just once, and holds out his hand. I stand and walk over to him, taking it. He pulls me towards him, so that our lips almost collide, but he doesn't kiss me. 'Come upstairs.' A murmur into my mouth.

We pass the door of the room in which he sleeps with his wife and continue up to the top of the house. As he climbs the stairs I watch the muscles in his broad back, the curl of his dark hair brushing his collar. I find myself wishing that I had had a drink.

He strolls into the centre of my big room and stands a few feet from the foot of the bed. It's lighter in here than it is downstairs. I spent two days last week whitewashing the old psychedelic wallpaper, obscuring its oranges and browns. It still smells of fresh paint.

He turns to face me, grins. And then without knowing how, I am in front of him and I can hear my breath as he bends down and kisses me not on the neck but on my collarbone, with one hand pulling down the collar of my dress and jumper to present the skin to him, the other in my hair. I make a sound like I'm in pain and feel momentarily embarrassed. He takes my greatcoat by the lapels and pulls it off.

When I lay on my bed imagining what it would be like it was not like this. I saw us leaping on each other demented. Bryn is infuriatingly slow, deliberate. Holding my coat, he walks over to a chair and folds it over the back. I am shivering. There is no heating in this room and my dress, over which I wear a jumper pocked with holes, is only thin cotton. He walks back towards me and puts his hands on my wrists, raising my arms in the air. As he does this he finally lets my mouth meet his and I make another noise as he chews on my lip, trying to bring my arms down to put around him, but he lifts them up again and then his hands are at the ribbed edging of my jumper, coaxing it over my head, taking the time to smooth the static of my mussed-up hair once he has pulled it off. Again, he walks away and puts the removed garment on the chair.

I lower my arms, which are pink and stiff with goose pimples, and make to undo the dress buttons at my neckline, which hovers just above my breasts. He shakes his head no, returning his face to my collarbone, his other hand kneading my buttocks. My legs wobble but I continue standing there as he starts to undo the row of buttons on the front of my dress, which reach from just above the bow of my bra to the hem that skims my ankles. He approaches each button one by one, and even when the dress, now undone to the waist and exposing my nipples stiff against the lace that holds my breasts, is loose enough for him to pull it over my head, he kneels so that he continues to undo them with the same seriousness as before.

By now I am desperate, and the sound of my breathing seems to fill the still, white room. He is approaching the bottom third of the dress, pushing each side of the fabric away to reveal my body in the centre. At the tops of my thighs he pauses for a moment, then before I have time to react places his hand between my legs as though he is checking something. For a brief moment he moves his thumb there in a circle, grazing the cotton, as I buckle.

I say, please.

He takes his hand away, and, once all the buttons are undone, takes my arm through each sleeve and goes to place the dress on the chair. I stand there in my underwear.

'Turn around,' he says. He unclasps my bra. Again, I

wait, with my back still to him. Then I feel his fingers hook under the elastic at the top of my underwear as he pulls it down so it is scrunched below my buttocks, exposing them. He leaves it there for a moment, then bends to pull the knickers to my ankles. I step out of them.

He manoeuvres me over towards the bed and pushes me downwards, his body heavy on top of mine, kissing me. He traces his fingers over the thin skin on my ribs as he shuffles down my torso past the convex curve of my navel. He places his hands on the bones of my hips, and I know then what he is about to do, though it is not something Pete, or any of the other boys at home, ever did.

And then, it is happening. I can feel his breath on me, then, his mouth. And as I lie there, my body twisting as I try to be quiet, I envisage Stella standing in the room, still at the foot of the bed. She is watching, her calm eyes taking me in as her husband moves above me.

I open my eyes to meet hers. And this is when I come.

Wedding Coat

Cream stranded mink fur coat, size medium, fully lined in satin. Two pockets, high collar, metal fastenings. Sleeve length (underarm to cuff): 16"; length (shoulder to hem): 32". Hand-stitched label on interior reads: 'Estella Young'. Date unknown, though we estimate pre-WWII.

Pocket contains remnants of confetti, crumpled receipt for 1 x bottle of Moët & Chandon champagne (£12) from The King's Head, 115 Upper Street, Islington N1, 22nd April 1984.

'I knew you'd be back,' said Coral, who was unexpectedly practising some yoga poses in the middle of the floor, 'so I bought some cans.' She walked across the room to the refrigerator and got two. The dressing gown she usually wore – a grotesque, fluffy monstrosity covered in pink hearts and surely intended for no girl older than a teenager – had gone. Instead she wore a pair of pyjama-like batik trousers that hinted at her bohemian past, paired with a stained grey marl T-shirt, which didn't. She handed me the can with a gap-toothed grimace.

'How did you know?'

'You want to know about your parents. Why else would you be back here? Though I don't know why you're asking me. They're the ones with the answers.'

'I told you,' I sat down and opened my can. We both listened to the hiss. 'Stella won't spill, and I'm not sure I quite trust either of them to tell me the truth about anything.'

'Well you're not wrong there, lass,' said Coral. 'Your ma was always secretive, even when she first came to live with us. Barely out of school, she was.'

'What was it like when you came here?'

Coral took a breath. Though her face was as static as it usually was – she rarely smiled – she looked a little pleased that I had come around again in the hope of mining her past. Though she would never admit it, I imagined she was very lonely down here in the dingy must of the ground floor, and liked having a visitor. She shuffled over to the window and pulled aside the heavy faded curtains and their net counterparts to let in some much-needed light. It reminded me briefly of how, when I was a teenager and my mother happened to be in one of her more functional spells, she would come over all maternal and march peremptorily into whichever bedroom I had at the time and throw open all the curtains, saying, 'Let's shed some light on the situation, shall we?'

'When I broke in through that front door this street was half squats and half normal working families,' said Coral, pressing her finger against the cold of the pane.

'Now, see that house there?' Like the one we stood in, it was grey stone and white stucco, a natural counterpoint, the only difference being that it was double-fronted.

I nodded.

'Old couple sold it last year for £2.5 million.'

She gave a low whistle in the absence of mine.

'These houses were crumbling, lass. No one wanted anything to do with them. So we occupied. By the late seventies, squatting had become a movement, though the counter-culture was mostly dead. The seventies felt like one long hangover.'

'I thought people said that the sixties only really happened to most people in the seventies?'

'You could say that, but it masks an inconvenient truth, which is that most people abandoned the dream of alternative living pretty soon after it got started. Now, idealists like your dad would argue that it was because it got co-opted by the mainstream. I always liked that about him. Thinks the best of everyone. He's innocent, Bryn. But really, the commitment was never there.'

I wondered momentarily if Coral had once had a thing for – or even with – my father. Certainly her vehemence towards Stella seemed to excuse him completely of any wrongdoing, although to me it was patently clear that the entire commune project had been his idea from the beginning.

'But your commitment was there.'

'It was, yeah. It's why we petrified. You remember this house from your early childhood, what, twenty years after I first came here? It had hardly changed, I can tell you. The clothes a bit, and the music definitely, but everything else was mostly the same. Once a hippy, always a hippy, I suppose. The newspapers used to call us herbivores.'

'What happened to everyone else?'

'Dinner parties. There were lots of dinner parties at that time. Vegetable gardening. People bought up and renovated, rediscovered monogamy and nuclear families. The setup your ma always wanted really. Picked their causes from the broadsheets. Moved to the country. You know, like your parents.'

Coral made a suggestive face and I thought I might as well say it.

'So this free love stuff you were talking about last time – were they involved in that?'

She laughed a dry, dirty laugh, and winked.

'Your mother was always a priss. Even before they got married. I was there, you know.'

'At the wedding?'

'Yeah. Your gran and grandpa were there too. She looked like she'd sucked on a lemon. Your ma wouldn't even wear a dress. Had on this silk jumpsuit and a huge, white fur coat.'

'I remember the pictures.' My mother had looked as happy as I have ever seen her, her eyes framed by deep, beautiful laughter lines as she stared up at my father on the steps of the registry office. I used to love that coat. Her 'wedding coat', she called it. Sometimes, when I was little and she went out at night, leaving me with a boyfriend or a babysitter, I put it on and got back into bed, pulling the long, soft tufts of fur against my nose and face, until I fell asleep.

'The thing about your ma was ...' Coral stopped to light a cigarette, then exhaled roughly. 'She always dressed the part but it never quite rang true. She looked incredible but her heart was never in it. I think she always felt a slight regret at the life she chose when she ran off with your father.'

He'd been wearing a suede waistcoat and paisley scarf. I remembered her telling me that. She'd come down with some school friends, they'd bunked off sixth form for the day, and there he was. Leaning on a statue with a joint. Bearded, older (he was thirty-four), off his tits on drugs, and wearing a waistcoat.

'He seemed like he knew things,' Stella had said once. 'I wanted him to teach me everything, to show me a different way of living and being.'

'You never answered my question about the free love,' I said.

Coral kissed her teeth. 'We were all into it, before Stella came. Your mother wasn't. She insisted on monogamy. Your da' found that somewhat difficult, but he agreed. They used to argue like nothing I've seen before, and then they used to screw like nothing I've heard before. Your mother was a screamer, in both senses of the word.'

'So they didn't see other people after they got married?'

'Well, that's a long story, love.' She looked taken aback, for a moment, at the sudden term of endearment.

'I want to know. I want to know why it all went wrong and why we had to leave for good. Why I can't remember anything about why. What did Stella do that was so bad?'

I thought of that last day, at the end of the summer. Being rushed into the back of the car with only a few things. She had driven almost to the bottom of the hill before she had pulled over and let out a long howl.

'I'm not surprised you blocked it out, to be honest. It was awful for all of us.' Coral took a swig of her can.

'She never talks about it, you know. I've asked her over and over what went on but she says it's better that I can't really remember. I think she feels responsible ...'

'As she should.'

'I need to know, Coral.'

'It's difficult to talk about.'

'Please.'

'I'm not sure it'd be good for you, either. To you I probably seem like this messed-up, bitter old crone. But I know you. Cared for you. I've known you since you were wee. And you're doing all right. In many ways that is a miracle. I have a responsibility.' Coral walked across the room to the window and looked out again. I was struck by how light it was out there compared to the gloom inside, where it was dark and almost cold despite the thirty-degree temperatures we'd been having. Silence, then:

'Will you do something for me, Harmony?'

'What is it?'

'I want you to go and visit someone in hospital. As

141

you've probably guessed, I don't much like to go outside. But there's someone I promised I'd check up on, and I'd like you to go and see him and tell me how he's doing. Will you do that for me? And in return, I'll tell you everything from the beginning. Though we may need something stronger to drink next time.'

'Who is it?'

'His name's Mick. Mikey. He used to live here, too, until he lost the plot. If nothing else, it'll be a lesson for you in why you should never experiment with hallucinogens.'

'It's a bit late for that,' I said, and explained what had happened at the party, and about my sudden memory of the red-headed girl. 'It was really weird,' I was in the process of saying, but I stopped when I realised that Coral's face had gone hard, the plaster of her features set.

'Are you ok?'

'I'm fine. But it's time you went.'

She scrawled down the address of the local psychiatric hospital and told me to ring them to arrange a visit. At the door I paused.

'Do you miss it? How it was before I mean?'

'I miss the people. Well, some, not others.'

I turned to leave but she spoke again. 'I wouldn't worry about what happened with the mushrooms. Weird trip at the best of times, without what you went through.'

She gave me a look bordering on compassion.

'Besides, we've all seen faces of the dead in those of the living.'

Bathing Suit

Child's swimming costume (label reads: '4–5 years'). White nylon with red heart pattern. Frilled skirt attached.

Mid-morning, and already the air had taken on a lethargic thickness; it was like moving through soup. One of those days where all you could really do was lie naked in a dark room, twisted under sheets that have been run under the tap, moaning. Instead, we sought each other's company, and the three of us were sprawled across the living room, forcing mugs of hot tea down our dry throats; Lucia stretching and twisting on her back against the carpet like a restless cat.

'Let's do something,' she said, with sudden vigour. 'We can't just sit around all day.'

'I'm up for that,' said Josh, 'but it needs to be this side of the Cally Road. Don't want to bump into anyone.' He had called in sick that morning, after a night of heavy drinking. He looked tired. A couple of days' worth of thick stubble coated his jawline, and there were bags under his bloodshot eyes. He was holding one of the many novelty mugs that various transient flatmates had left behind when they departed. This one was a particularly bad example; a naked Greek-looking eighties Adonis with rippled muscles, cheaply photographed, whose penis became erect when hot water was poured in. Josh hated it and usually pushed it to the back of the cupboard, where we would retrieve it and move it to the front. He hadn't noticed.

Lou, whose mug bore the legend 'I pretend to work, and they pretend to pay me', sat up.

'The bathing ponds, on the Heath?'

'Yes,' said Josh, standing up. 'I'll get me trunks.'

'Have you been, Harmony?'

I nodded. I hadn't, but I disliked feeling like the non-Londoner amongst them. I felt such a fierce sense of home in this small triangle of city, but my territorial familiarity sometimes failed to stand up to in-depth scrutiny. I think I wanted to feel as though I belonged there more than I really did.

I threw a bikini on and a sundress over it and tied my hair in a messy bun above my head. It was too hot to make much of an effort, and I knew that once the dress came off there would be nowhere to hide. I stared into the mirror, holding a pinch of stomach fat between my thumb and forefinger. The skin around my collarbone was pink and mottled from the heat. I felt the unexpected hope that Josh would like my body when he saw it.

This was not an insecurity that I had usually felt with men. The academic, whose persistent late-night messages I had begun to ignore, could take it or leave it. It made no odds. There's a liberating element to a relationship that consists of sex and nothing more, I've always found. The only validation you need is that of your body being used as it's designed to be.

'Ready?' said Lou, when I walked into the living room. She was wearing a black and white striped short jumpsuit, a wide-brimmed white straw hat, espadrilles and a pair of tortoiseshell sunglasses. As Josh eyed her from the corner, I looked down at my faded floral button-through dress and mentally declared myself a frump. Lou adjusted her hat to reveal a smooth, white expanse of armpit, and I felt every prickle of my stubby short hairs.

The chill in the stairwell was welcome relief after the torpor of the flat. As we paused outside Coral's door while Lou flicked through the post – 'I'm waiting on a cheque' – I felt a guilty prod about the errand she had set me, and which I had yet to fulfil. It occurred to me that her weak, alcoholic heart could die of heat in there.

We bought cider in bottles from the corner shop and walked over Parliament Hill to the Hampstead side of the heath, too hot and panting and desperate for a drink to pause at the top to watch the glittering skyscrapers going up amidst a haze of smog and cranes. It was only upon arrival we realised we had neglected to bring a bottle opener. Josh struggled to open his using a lighter but eventually managed, before placing his hand over my drink. His skin felt rough against my knuckles. 'It's a question of leverage,' he said, as he sliced the side of his finger open and winced.

It was a weekday, and the school holidays had not yet started, so the yellowed grass was empty of the usual picnickers. We spread out a blanket and sat down, Josh sucking his finger. I looked up at the expanse of bright blue through the unruffled leaves and held the cool of the bottle against my forehead. I felt sticky and unfeminine, coated in a thin film of sweat that I could feel in the follicles on my scalp, matting my hair which would soon inevitably curl, though not attractively. I felt the acute, embarrassed pain of being a girl, these minute flaws we amplify when in the presence of someone whose body we crave. I wanted him, I realised, not only for his tall good looks, indisputable though they were, but for his kindness. I'll admit it was not a quality to which I had ever paid much attention in a man. All of a sudden it had become compulsory.

'Toke?'

I took the joint from him and noted the amber inner circles of his irises. In the preceding days I had become acutely aware of the proximity of our bodies in that house. Just knowing he was there, in his room, less than five metres away from mine – bar one sturdy Victorian wall – made concentrating impossible. When we sat talking in the kitchen I found myself absorbed, unable to move my eyes from his face. One night I had a dream – a welcome respite from the endless nightmares – in which he quietly wound the crook of his little finger around mine, no more than that, and I woke up longing to launch myself upon him. Instead, in an attempt to hide my feelings, I became more circumspect, sarcastic even. I wished him luck when he went out with other women, I made loaded references to my exes. I even brought a man back, one evening, and laughed loudly at all his jokes in the hope that he would hear.

But there he was, in my thoughts, to the extent that it had become almost irritating, like the two lines of a song you just can't shake. In order to combat this, I was stand-offish, sometimes even rude. Another symptom was that I often became incapable of speech around him. This was a side effect I was unfamiliar with until we held a party, and I ended up nose to chest with him in the packed kitchen, and due to some terrifying combination of alcohol, THC, cocaine and pheromones, was unable to utter a single word. Instead I stood and laughed, laughed right in his face, because it just seemed ridiculous – to want someone that much. I remember my grandfather

146

telling me once that seeing my grandmother for the first time felt like being hit by a tsunami. This didn't feel like that. It felt like floating on the stillest and deadest of seas. This suspended body felt unrecognisable as my own. It would not obey. There was something wrong with it.

Lucia yawned. It was too hot to talk, so we sat for a while, dreaming. After some time had passed, she stood up; the stretching of her slender arms and the tautness of her muscles drew your eye to her raised chest. All of Lou's gestures were like this; not mannered, exactly, but somehow theatrical. The movements of her body demanded that you look at her, while remaining at the same time entirely natural seeming. She was completely at ease, whether you looked at her or not.

In contrast, I cultivated a studied indifference, especially in the presence of men I desired (and even ones I didn't). I would manufacture nonchalance, ignoring them entirely if I could get away with it. But every movement, every utterance, every slight mannerism was performative, devised entirely for whichever man was present, as though I existed only through their eyes.

'Aren't we dull? I'm going for a dip.' Lou shimmied out of her jumpsuit to reveal a plain black swimming costume beneath, cut slightly low on the thigh in a fifties style. As she stretched her pale body she was all angles, her black hair an oil slick on a slab of snow. She saw me staring at it and giggled.

'I nearly forgot,' she said, rummaging in her bag until she triumphantly produced a white, frilly swimming cap. She put it on. On anyone else, it would have looked absurd, but Lou's aristocratic air lent her vintage mania and rejection of modern technology a precise authenticity. She was surprisingly tenacious when it came to avoiding the trappings of digital life – no social media, and for photographs, she used disposable cameras which lay gathering dust in her room for weeks until she took them in ten at a time to be developed and our overexposed faces with their blurred features were fashionably revealed. The only way of getting hold of her was via the rotary telephone she had plugged into our landline, or hoping that this would be the week she happened to look at her email. The rotary telephone had been particularly problematic because most companies have electronic menus necessitating the use of a touch-tone phone. Lou got around this by ceasing to check her bank balance.

'Coming?'

'Too high,' I said. 'Later.' Josh nodded and she ran off, looking like a photograph of someone's stylish great aunt.

'She's something else,' he said.

'You like her.'

'I do, but not like that. Well, maybe a bit like that, but not really.'

I raised my eyebrows.

'She's fragile. You have an urge to protect her, I bet.'

'Lou's always been one to look after herself. We've lived together for two years now, remember. She has her dramas and her crises but ultimately she pulls through.'

I thought about her face the day she'd come back from that party, and felt annoyed at his dismissiveness, but more so at the notion that he might be right. Lou did have a tendency to embroider and amplify other people's behaviour towards her. The thoughtless actions of a friend or acquaintance – an offhand remark, an absence of tact, or an innocent mistake – would be deemed an all-out assault on her very personhood, as she would sit there telling you about it in a spiked voice, chain-smoking and tossing her hair and calling them a cunt. The next, she'd be doing lines with them on the coffee table.

It could be, I thought, that I had been overanxious about her welfare. It was my role, as I saw it, to maintain calm amidst the whims of the more volatile.

'I suppose.'

'Why? Are you jealous?' he grinned at me. I held his gaze, then crossed my eyes.

'You think a lot of yourself.'

'Someone has to.' He handed me another cider. There was a pause in the conversation as we drank. I suspect we were both thinking about the girls he brought home; there had been four or five already that month. You'd see them in the kitchen, in the mornings, sitting at the table as he jovially made them breakfast but no promises. He had a knack for treating women with sympathetic distance. This, he believed, was for their own good when in reality it was entirely for his; 'here I am sensitively offering you a total absence of any guarantee, because I'm such a nice guy.'

The week before, I had come out of my room to see him shepherding a girl hastily through the front door of the flat. A beautiful girl, who looked very unhappy, as though she had already caught a glimpse of herself several weeks in the future, checking the screen of her phone for the thousandth time. After she left he turned and dismissed her almost immediately. She was dull, he said, and poor at sex. But all the same I feel an intensely physical envy for that nameless girl and where her lovely hands, her perfect mouth had been. I felt sick about it. At least the physical aspects of it were tolerable. Most tormenting was not the thought of his lips grazing her ear while he moved inside her, but the unknown words he might have whispered while he did it, words conferring a private intimacy that would only ever be known to the two of them. It was agony.

'Why is it that you hardly ever take anyone home?' he said, with affected innocence.

'To the flat, you mean?'

'Yes. I assume you do, you know ... shag people.'

'I do. But I tend to go to theirs, or else a hotel.' I stopped short of saying 'the park', or indeed, 'the occasional stairwell'.

'Mysterious,' he said. 'Why? Are you shy? You don't seem shy, but it is slightly odd.'

'You have more control that way. You're the one leaving in the morning.'

'Girls usually prefer it the other way, the first time at least. Aren't you scared when you go back to theirs that they might ... ?'

'What? Rape me and cut me up into tiny little pieces? Not really. None of them have got the backbone.' I was joking, but only slightly. The last person I had slept with had been a few days previously, a guy from university who had looked me up to ask me out and, being a Blairite, had suggested a David Miliband lecture at the LSE as the ideal setting for a date. I had gone, because he had a pretty face and was intelligent enough to be tolerable company. He asked me, I suspect, for almost identical reasons. A dropout waitress with mild substance abuse issues would provide him no challenge in the status stakes, so he'd not have to engage in the usual graduate career one-upmanship – one of the main reasons I avoided most of my former classmates. After the lecture I think he hoped that we'd repair to a wine bar where I'd stare up at him, all moon-faced, as he talked about New Labour. Instead, we got shitfaced in the Princess Louise on tequila shots and had some of the most lacklustre, reluctant sex I had ever experienced. It was so patently obvious that our hearts were not in it that when his mouth began to dawdle its way down towards my clitoris I simply grabbed him by the back of the T-shirt, pulled him upwards so that we were face to face, and said the thing every woman says when she can't face the drabness of incompetent foreplay, which is: 'I want you inside me.' I could face a few phlegmatic pokes of his dick but indifferent cunnilingus was another matter altogether. So utterly sexless was our encounter that when, the next morning, he accepted a mug from me with the words, 'you do make a very good cup of tea', I felt almost flattered at the compliment.

Josh was still looking at me when Lou came back from the pond – 'It's filthy in there, all slimy. Cold though' – and flopped down on her towel with a sigh, her eyes closed. Soon she was breathing rhythmically. I worried she might burn and thought abstractedly that perhaps I should wake her, but didn't. It was the hottest part of the day.

'Swim?' said Josh, taking off his T-shirt. I looked at his bare arms, strong from the gym and freckled from weeks of summer, and felt such a desperate desire to sleep with him that I thought my knees might buckle when I stood up. I looked at his slim hips and wondered if they would dig into the flesh of my thighs as he moved above me. If they would leave a mark.

Despite my earlier loss of confidence and the acute feeling that he was watching me carefully, I nodded and pulled my dress over my head. My bikini, which had come free with a magazine and was cheap and flimsy in comparison to Lou's designer suit, nevertheless had the desired effect. His eyes flickered downwards twice in quick succession.

'Let's do it,' I said, and walked briskly towards the wooden gate beyond which the sounds of splashing and laughter drifted towards us.

'C'mon, let's jump off the jetty,' said Josh. I thought of my flimsy bikini top and how I would probably lose it, then decided I didn't care. He grabbed my hand and we took a short run up, then launched ourselves into the muddy coloured water, which filled my eyes and mouth and ears. Grit beneath my tongue.

'It ain't Biarritz, but it'll do,' said Josh, in mock cockney, as he swam in circles. I brushed my wet hair away from my face, and watched his strong shoulders as they moved above the water. My foot grazed the bottom and I felt sludge between my toes, so I kicked them up towards the sky and lay, floating on my back in a Christ-like pose, for several moments.

It was a little while later, when I twisted my body back to a vertical and began treading water, that I noticed that Josh had moved closer and was staring at me intently. I laughed, and the noise sounded sharp and abrupt even against the oddly muted background noise of boisterous teenagers bombing from the jetty.

Josh spoke quietly. 'Come here.'

I swam towards him. We were about a foot apart when he placed a hand on my face. He looked at me through long eyelashes. I started to count the freckles on his nose as a way of steadying myself, preparing to lean in to kiss him. I was still high. He was brushing drops of water away from my cheeks with his large thumb, which then moved down to graze my lip. I came closer, so that I could almost feel the heat of his breath. He raised his other hand, placed it on my head, and dunked me.

My mouth, which had been open in preparation for Josh's tongue, was filled with brown pond water as I sank, and for some reason it didn't occur to me to close it. Nor did I really feel like going back up there, perhaps because of the embarrassment I felt from having fallen for his trick. But I was running out of air and would have to resurface soon, so to save face I swam several metres underwater until I was near the ladder, then climbed out.

I sat, legs over the side of the jetty, catching my breath. His face was a blurred pale circle across the water as I inelegantly spat out fluid. It was as I coughed that deep cough that seemed to come from the very depth of my lungs that I saw a flash of red and a memory assaulted me. A little girl with long brown hair, probably aged around four, was being chased along the side of the pond by her father, who was grasping a towel, but it wasn't the little girl that reminded me of myself: it was the swimming costume she was wearing. Bright scarlet, with a little frilly skirt attached, and covered in small white hearts all over. I had had the same one, I realised, the summer my mother and I ran away. She had bought it for me soon after we arrived, as it became apparent that this summer was to be a scorcher. We bought it in Camden town, and I picked it out myself. It is funny how an object that was once such a part of your life, so treasured and admired, becomes forgotten and insignificant. I had loved that bathing suit. I had worn it in all the padding pools to which she had taken me. I had worn it the time I nearly died.

This, I had not forgotten. The sensation of almost drowning is not something that slips the mind, though it was not something I spoke about often, mainly for reasons of shame. Because the secret thing about the nearly drowning was that I hadn't wanted to be saved. After the initial struggle, the gasping for air as my lungs filled with water, the fear in the knowledge I would die, I felt an incredible sense of calm. To horrified onlookers, I was a dying five-year-old face down in a paddling pool in Hackney, but to me, it was like taking a Valium pill. I was floating, beatific, and the last thing I wanted was to be dragged back to life, as I was, brutally and abruptly, and not – this was new – by my mother, but by the same red-headed woman who kept intruding in my thoughts, and whose presence I had hallucinated at the party.

She had held me, crying on wet concrete, as we both lay prone and shivering by the side of the water.

'You're all right, pet. You're ok. I'm here. There, there. I love you.'

She had been there that summer, I had gathered that much. My blurred recollections of her – playing ring a-ring o'roses, making daisy chains, teaching me to roll pastry between my palms – evoked a familiar fondness, and I was sure that she had meant something to me at a time when, in light of our running away from our lovely, safe family home, any five-year-old would have felt confused and off kilter.

Coral had suggested that this woman was now dead, and that Stella was somehow responsible. A strong instinct, the same kind that jumped to my mother's defence whenever I thought anyone spoke ill of her, urged me that it was probably better not to know. As Coral had said, I was doing all right. But as I sat there, dripping wet and hyperventilating, I vowed that I would not allow Coral's reticence to prevent me from finding out the truth about my parents. For too long Stella had fobbed me off with opaque, offhand remarks – 'oh it was all so long ago' – and – when my questioning became too pointed – veiled threats that my probing would provoke yet another relapse.

I was so absorbed that I had forgotten completely about Josh, who was now floating beneath me, at toe level, wearing a hangdog look.

'I'm sorry,' he said. 'It was just a joke.'

'It's fine. I'm just tired all of a sudden. I want to lie down.'

'Let's get you home then,' he said, climbing out and putting his arm around me with a gentle authority that was almost like a brother's. I knew then that we would.

Spring 1986

I'd know those signs anywhere. I've seen it time and time again. Back home, you're an old maid by the time you're twenty. They used to say Mam had a gift for telling, but by her age, I imagine she'd seen so many girls succumb that it was second nature.

'I was going to tell you,' Stella says, after she has run to the back door to be sick. She is half-bent, swallowing the cold fresh air. The smell of my boiled egg was what set her off.

Now we are lying on her and Bryn's bed, a patchwork quilt crumpled underneath us. Looking at her from this angle, with her smock pulled taut over her belly, I wonder how I didn't see it sooner. She is pale from the sickness but also vividly, radiantly beautiful, her face brimming with the warmth of her secret. She smells of soap and rose geranium, the bile a sour undernote to the sweetness tugging at my nostrils.

'Are you happy?' she says, and I smile and kiss her forehead, moving the damp hair away with my hand.

'How could I not be?' I say. 'A whole new little person. What could be better?'

And I am happy, of course I am. They are my friends, I want the world for them. The things that he and I do to each other in bed doesn't change that. What they are to each other doesn't change that. Husband and wife, yes, and in a few months, there'll be a child too. To the outside they are a unit, a family. But we're all of us a family. We are bigger than the sum of our parts, than personal agendas and petty jealousies. Just look at Stella and the way she has given me her friendship and generosity, allowed me to go into her bed and share her husband without ever saying a word. I know she knows.

She lets it happen because we all love each other.

Last time I visited Mam said I'd gone all happy-clappy. But she said it smiling. She knows that I'm better down here. 'You're in love,' she said, nodding at my fleshier figure. 'It looks good on you.'

I will love this baby because of who it came from. It may not have my genes but I will love it and care for it as though it were mine too, and I hope the bairn will come to love me, and look to me when it is lost or frightened.

'Have you told Bryn?' I ask.

'I'm telling him tonight,' she says. 'Do you think he will be pleased?'

'Of course he will,' I say, stroking her hand. 'Of course he will.'

Later, I cook a veggie curry for everyone, to celebrate. Stella and Bryn have been upstairs for a long time, and when they come down from the room they are flushed and shiny-eyed.

'Look at her! My clever wife!' he laughs, after they have announced it to the room and Mikey has opened a bottle of cava, the cork popping so hard it hits the ceiling. Everyone is hugging her, and she stands, smiling in the golden glow of the lamplight, her hand resting on her stomach. She looks like a queen, bright and fecund with promise, laughing as her husband dances around her.

Coral walks over and puts an arm around my shoulders.

157

'Such happy news,' I say. I cannot read her face, and she doesn't reply, and so we stand there, side by side in silence with our backs to the kitchen counter, my fingers tightly gripping the handle of the wooden spoon as we watch them bask in the joy of a new life.

Boule

Weighted boule in green plastic. Manufacturer unknown.
80 mm diameter.

Morning, and as the dust flitted through the stream of dawn light, in my half-sleep I felt his fingers flutter beneath the seams of my muddied bikini bottoms. I had not changed after returning to the flat – instead we had drunk and smoked more, until we had both collapsed as a tangle into his bed, too wasted for sex but craving that boozy closeness. Now, he was tiptoeing towards it, as I squirmed and let out a heavy series of breaths to let him know that I had woken and was decidedly into the idea. Then: nothing. I must have fallen asleep again, and when I woke for the second time he had gone.

I took a cool, lengthy shower in an attempt to break the inertia of the morning after, and succeeded to an extent, my hair a freezing sheet against my skin, which bristled with alertness. I had plans. I threw on a floral sundress and stepped outside into the arid fug, making my way down Longhope Crescent and through the streets of terraced houses, stopping to admire the acid green parakeets that congregated noisily in our local trees. Then up the steep hill, past my much-loved atomic sun, to the hospital. I passed groups of pale, nervy smokers on the steps, and entered a clinical-smelling reception area, noting the juxtaposition of the bright framed pictures and the ominous automatic locking systems. Their buzz resembled a tinny drill. Visiting hours had just begun.

'I'm here to see Michael Dunt,' I said. 'I phoned last week?'

'Take a seat,' said the Nigerian nurse, whose name badge read 'Progress'. I sat, the backs of my thighs sticking to the teal-coloured plastic of the seats, and hummed a tune under my breath. A fan standing on the reception desk oscillated noisily, but the people in the room were silent. A middle-aged white woman with the demeanour of a concerned mother avoided my gaze; a young Afro-Caribbean man who, with his smooth, dimpled cheeks and long eyelashes could have been a grown-up Gabs, tapped his fingers rapidly against the stiff fabric of his jeans. The automatic doors whirred and opened every time a smoker shifted slightly just outside. Somewhere in the distance I heard a guttural sob.

'Come through please,' said another nurse, sent to fetch me, and, taking me through several secure doors, led me to a closed ward, then, to the left of the nurses' station, into a common room in which people sat, murmuring, in groups of twos and threes.

'Michael,' she said. 'You have a visitor.'

A huge, brick shithouse of a man with grey, waist-length dreads, whose eyes had been fixed on the flat screen television, turned around to greet me.

'Bleeding hell. For a moment there I thought you were Stella.'

'Hi Michael,' I said, walking over to shake his hand. 'I'm Harmony, Stella's daughter. Like I explained on the phone.'

'I'll be having none of that gubbins.' He frowned at my hand and pulled me into a bear hug. 'And it's Mikey D, or

160

Dunty, or sometimes Cunty, if the nurses ain't listening. Or just Mikey.'

'Cool. I'm sorry I don't really remember you.'

'Why would you? You were tiny last time I saw you.'

'Coral sends her best.'

'How is my favourite sour-faced alchy? Haven't seen her for time.'

'She seems all right. I moved back in – upstairs. She's been telling me about the commune.'

'Yeah? I thought that might be why you're here. Take a walk?' He gestured to the door, which I eyed a tad nervously.

'Are we er … allowed?'

'Why? Were you expecting straitjackets and padded cells? 'Course we're allowed, let me just fetch an orderly.'

He walked away, then returned several moments later with an affable-looking nurse, who introduced himself as Martin and buzzed us outside.

'It's not Victorian times. They do let me out,' said Mikey D. 'He's just got to be up my arse the whole time in case I go mental.'

'It's for your own safety,' grinned Martin. 'And believe me, Mikey boy, up your hairy arse is the last place I'd want to be.'

Mikey D lit up a fag and swaggered over to the adjoining public park.

'Plus, it's been a while since I fed the ducks,' said Mikey D. 'Good to get a look at the ugly cunts every now and again.'

We meandered towards the pond, with Martin lurking at a polite distance.

'How's your dad?'

'All right, last time I heard. He's up in Wales, in the mountains.'

'Ah, the great Welsh exodus. How predictable of him, the bloody hippy.'

I laughed. 'He's got a yurt in the back garden if you fancy going up to visit him.'

'Yeah maybe,' he said, in a way that made it clear he didn't. 'So back at Delirium Towers, are we?'

'Sorry, what?'

'Just my private name for it. Christ, the things that went on there. It's a miracle you're not in an asylum yourself. That nasty business with the girl. So much for peace, love and understanding. Real hippie enclave, though, Quorn Crescent. Haha. The whole thing used to be squatted, you know, not just number 26.'

'Yeah, I know,' I said. 'What nasty business?'

Mikey looked at me with a raised eyebrow.

'Have you asked Coral?'

'She said she'd tell me, if I visited you.'

'Best leave it to her then. My brain's all frazzled, innit. I'm all mixed up.'

I sighed. 'How long did you live there?'

'Let's see,' said Mikey. 'I moved out in about 1990, not long before I first got sectioned. It was like a time capsule, that place. A fucking TARDIS, hurtling through the decades, nothing changing. Your dad still banging the old hippy drum well after the fact. Nearly twenty years I was there, I think. Yeah, I got sectioned in 1991. Though obviously there'd been times before then when I'd felt pretty fucking peaky. Too many bad trips, man. Too much time spent off my tits. Too much tragedy witnessed. Too many people I loved, gone.'

His sadness made me glib, and I said, 'Well, they say that if you remember the sixties then you weren't there.'

162

'Oh, I remember it, fuzzy though it may be. How could I forget meeting your old man?'

'I didn't realise you'd known him that long.'

Mikey sat down on a bench by the water and toyed with the beads at his wrist.

'1966,' he said. 'UFO club, Tottenham Court Road. We were just schoolboys then. We must have been, what? Sixteen? Neither of us had stayed past O-levels; we'd been too busy separately acquainting ourselves with the finest mind-altering substances that the West End had to offer. Then we came together at this magical place and the rest is history.'

'What was UFO club?' I said, pronouncing it 'yoo-fo', as he did.

'It was a hippy paradise, darling. Words do not do it justice. It was in an old Irish dance hall, got adopted by some hippies. Pink Floyd used to hang out there, it was radical. Poetry, music, art. The whole place stank of patchouli, these wide-eyed kids lying around, off their heads most of them, watching the light like falling snow. There was a room in the back you could go if you took too much, but mostly it was pretty friendly, like. This mop-haired geezer, can't remember his name now, used to live out on some nudist colony near Watford, had this thing he called the trip machine, and would do these light shows using bodily fluids – piss, spunk, you know. The lot. Mixed with food colouring. They looked so beautiful, Harmony. We used to lie there for hours watching the blobs of light move, then crawl over to the macrobiotic food counter for a snack. Not that I could ever abide that shit. Give me some good fried chicken any day.'

I eyed his bulbous gut then looked away quickly.

'Apparently the light shows had first been designed

for patients at mental hospitals. Ironic eh? Considering getting off my box and looking at that stuff is what got me here in the end. Amazing your dad made it really, considering the amount he was putting away. Anyway, so that's how we became trip buddies, lying in this club listening to whole albums until 6am, wearing bloody face paint and kaftans, looking like total ponces, listening to some fuckwit mime artist accompany a poetry reading. Embarrassing, really, but God, we had a blast. They were all there, all the beautiful people. Townshend, Hendrix, McCartney. Yoko doing some film where she got everyone to bare their arses. And don't even get me started on the pussy – no offence intended, girl.'

'Bryn met all those people?'

'You didn't really "meet" in the traditional sense,' said Mikey. 'You just … absorbed. Me and your dad, we were sort of in our own world, doing all this wild stuff. One time, we went to this event at Ally Pally called the 14-hour Technicolour Dream …'

'I think I've heard of that.'

'Yeah, it was pretty intense. '67 I think it was. The start of the Summer of Love. There was this big helter-skelter right in the middle, and all this mad stuff going on, as well as the music. Folk music and tarot cards, and circus performers. Some cat in a headdress that was on fire. We were off our nuts, because there was this guy there who always gave away his first 400 trips for free. There were thousands of people there, and some of them had climbed up the scaffolding near the big organ and were swinging by their arms. It was the middle of summer. I can just remember lying out on the grass thinking I could feel every single blade of it. It was all so clear to me. The sun coming up, miles and miles of rooftops, the people. And your dad was there living it all with me. What a summer it was.'

'What was he like?' My father, this man I barely knew.

'He was a vision in paisley,' said Mikey, chucking his fag butt at a duck and missing. 'Hair like George Harrison on the cover of Sgt Pepper – that was the soundtrack to the summer, by the way. And that quiet confidence that people would often mistake for arrogance. You have it a bit, actually, though you look more like Stella. And he was always going off on one about something. Clever bloke, your dad. Foucault, or R. D. Laing, or Eastern philosophy, usually after a shit ton of Nepalese temple ball. And he always had at least a few girls on the go, sometimes older women, even though he was just a teenager then.'

I tried to imagine Bryn as Mikey described him, strutting down Carnaby Street, a joint flopping between his lips.

'So when did you move into Longhope?'

'Oh, that wasn't for a good few years yet. Summer of '67 we embarked on various experiments in communal living, as was then the fashion. Usually chosen according to the number of willing girls in residence. We were near Dalston for a bit, in this house full of cats. The place was a dump. Then we moved to Islington Park Street for a couple of weeks, but your dad had a bust up about anarchism with one of the regulars so after that we were somewhere near the Ladbroke Grove. There were so many empty houses at the time, not like now. But we were constantly getting moved on by the busies. Your dad had gone out. I went to the pub. When they left we just nailed the windows up again.'

'And I suppose this was all during the free love period ...'

Mikey laughed. 'Oh yeah. In a lot of the places couples

were banned. They'd put all the mattresses in one room, and you couldn't close your door or anything. You had to share everything. We had a chest of pooled clothes and you just picked out what you wore that day…'

It was ironic, considering the last time I had seen Bryn he'd been living a thing-filled existence that saw him almost buried beneath piles of clutter.

'Can you imagine me in a dress, walking down Holloway Road like a moving target? Shared our bodies, too. Proper, ideologically-driven fucking. I think that's where your dad got all his ideas. You couldn't sleep with the same person for more than one night. It was fun for a while, until I got the clap off some girl in one of the Notting Hill places. Think she was a member of something called Tribe of the Sacred Mushroom, if you can fucking believe it. You'd come home from the shops or something and there'd just be some couple banging in the living room, as everyone else was sat around watching, out of their minds. Or else drumming. There was a lot of drumming. And chanting.'

'It all just seems like such a cliché,' I said.

'It *was* a cliché, girl. That's the thing, and the media jumped on it. But that wasn't really the sixties, you know. For us it was everything they said it was. Not for most people. The sixties happened to a couple of hundred people in London, and passed everyone else in the country by. While we were all experimenting with drugs and sex and general debauchery they were all sitting in their poky, dark living rooms watching *The Good Old Days* and mourning Churchill, ironing their doilies and popping in their diaphragms for a half-hour of socially-mandated how's-your-father. No wonder so many of their kids used to come down to the squats in town on the weekends. Weekend ravers, we used to call them.'

'So then you came up this way, after that?' Interesting as I was finding Mikey's reminiscences, I was keen to hurry through the next couple of decades to my own childhood. We hadn't yet reached the seventies, even, and there was a manic edge to his voice that, perhaps I imagined, meant a more watchful stare from the lurking Martin.

'Nah, then we went to 144 Piccadilly. That was famous, that one, because it was a mansion right on Hyde Park Corner. There was this group of homeless hippies around the statue of Eros that we used to call the "Dilly Dossers", who survived off fallen fruit in Covent Garden Market and the kindness of strangers. I think they started it by occupying the place. We used to drop with them sometimes. '69 this was, I remember because there were a bunch of Frenchies fresh from the '68 riots who turned up with a projector and showed us the footage. Anyway, so the main doors that faced the park were nailed shut, and we had this plywood drawbridge thing that we used to get in. It was massive in there, and there was no electricity or anything. Used a camping stove to eat, or else we liberated bread and milk from nearby doorsteps.

'We were only there for three weeks, before the dibble got us out, but it was great. One of the guys was in King Mob, I seem to remember ... '

'King Mob?'

'Anarchist group. They did this amazing graffiti in the early seventies, along the tube line from Westbourne Park. Famous it was. "SLEEP – TUBE – WORK – HOW MUCH MORE CAN YOU TAKE?" Something like that.'

'Oh yeah I think I've seen a photo of that.'

'We made loads of mates there, before the police tricked their way in by telling some kids standing guard there was a pregnant woman inside, giving birth. Fuckers. There was a media circus. They said we were spongers. Really it was a housing crisis, just like you kids have now. They were razing habitable buildings to the ground.'

Mikey lit another cigarette and I shivered as the sun slinked behind a cloud. I risked a quick glance at my phone for the time.

'Boring you am I? All right we'll wrap it up shall we? Need my meds anyway. You'll come again, though, yeah? Then I'll tell you the rest. That pretty much brings us up to Longhope Crescent, though I think there was another one, Prince of Wales Crescent, in Kentish Town, before then. That was a good one – had a treehouse and a paddling pool, and all. Not to mention one of the first ever health food shops. Mix your own muesli at Community Foods. There were three hundred of us squatting there, before they knocked it down. Council estate now.'

'Well it's been very informative,' I said. 'And I really hope you feel better soon.'

'Strange one, you are, girl.' Mikey did a smile that was almost a grimace. 'I'll be all right. I always am. Just need a few extended stays in the nuthouse, that's all. Tame the voices.'

'That must be tough,' I said, shifting on my feet and burying my fists in the front two pockets of my sundress. I nodded quickly and started to turn.

'Hold on a sec. Brought something for you.' Mikey delved into the pocket of his leather jacket and produced a round, green plastic ball. He handed it to me.

'A ball?'

'A *boule*,' he said, exaggerating the French. 'It's from 144 Piccadilly. There was a whole room of them, weirdly. In boxes. We used to use them to pelt the skinheads with when they tried to come in. It sounds stupid but it's always been a good luck thing for me. I mean, I've taken it everywhere. I want you to have it.'

'Why?'

Mikey tipped the peak of his hat at me and gestured to Martin that it was time to go. 'I feel like you need it more than me, babe.'

It was not a statement I took as a compliment.

Book

1 x copy 'The Water Babies – as told to the children' (Charles Kingsley & Amy Steadman), London and New York: T. C. and E. C. Jack, and E. P. Dutton (1905). 150 x 120 mm. 8 colour plates after Katherine Cameron. (Light spotting on the edges of the plates, several leaves torn.) Original cloth, gilt border and lettering.

A sign that I was feeling anxious, in those days, was when I took to searching for things. Looking back, I can see it was a kind of mania. My searching would take on an obsessional quality that made it difficult for me to eat, or leave the house, or do much of anything, really, except look. This time, I knew it was a bad patch because the nightmares became more frequent: there I would be as usual, wandering from room to room, as elsewhere in the house a telephone rang incessantly, unanswered. A tiny child standing in the cavernous hallway, looking up, up, up through the spirals of the staircase to the corniced plaster above, with its ceiling rose sculpted like ice cream from a van, a van whose eerie, tinkling melody could then be heard through illuminated open windows, a nursery song undulating on a breeze that caused the chandelier to swing back and forth, back and forth with a hoarse creak, as I stared up at it. And then, the sensation of running, but without my moving at all. I would feel a desperate urge to escape the house's darkened interior, a potent, numbing dread just at the point where I would wake as though suffocating, feeling every inch of my irritated ribcage as I gulped air into my lungs with tears in my eyes.

This time, the lost object in question was an early twentieth-century copy of the fairy tale *The Water Babies*, about six inches tall and cloth-bound, with beautiful coloured plates that when I was small I spent hours gazing at, running my fingers over their glossy surface. My favourite, on the inner facing page, showed a naked child kneeling next to a river bank, hands clasped together as though praying to a dragonfly. 'Oh! Come back, come back you beautiful creature,' read the inscription, 'I have no one to play with and I'm so lonely here.'

The book was one of the few things that I had been able to salvage from my childhood. It had belonged to my maternal grandmother, a kind, principled woman who, while not particularly warm, saw it as her respon-sibility to ensure I didn't end up completely feral. She read it to me every night before bed over warm cocoa and crackers, during those lengthy spells when I found myself palmed off, as Stella recuperated in San Francisco, Goa, or the Tuscan Buddhist community she had taken up with. When I had moved in I had had it with me, I was sure, a small box of childhood effects, now missing. The thought that I may have lost such a valued possession filled me with a feeling not unlike heartbreak, and I spent the daytimes before my night shifts ambling from room to room, searching in a desultory way for the sight of the familiar disintegrating spine.

This crisis was not helped by the fact that, as the summer progressed and our torpor increased, the flat had descended into complete chaos. The humidity of the conditions meant that the moths flourished and were

171

rising from the carpets in a flittering mass. As I tried to sleep I lay in bed listening to the sweeping of their dusty wings against the woodchip; the next day the evidence of their midnight snacks would be taken from my wardrobe and examined. Silk slip after silk slip pockmarked with holes. As the weeks passed and we drank more and cared less, the flat became a dumping ground for sticky mismatched crystal glasses and discarded takeaways; full ashtrays and light cotton garments shed like skin across sofas and chairs. Objects were witnesses to our disarray.

But despite this I looked, and looked. And when I did not find what I was looking for I looked again.

I was turning over the living room one morning when Lucia came in and flopped down onto the sofa. As was typical of Lou, she did not ask me what I was looking for nor remark on the piles of objects I had built during my systematic but frenzied hunting. Instead, she examined the beds of her nails and waited for me to stop what I was doing and turn around to look at her.

I turned around and looked at her.

'My mother has come to town,' said Lou, in a voice that implied these were not good tidings. She sighed. 'I'm to meet her in the Fumoir, at Claridge's. Will you come with me?'

'Why?' My nose ring was itching and I had the impulse to fiddle with it. 'I'm not very Claridge's, Lou.'

Lou did not disagree, saying simply, 'But I can't face her alone.'

'Fine,' I said. 'I'll go and get dressed.'

As I searched for something to wear, I reflected on how my brief years at university had taught me that it wasn't especially difficult to appear richer than you were, at least until you opened your mouth. As long as you didn't look as though you were trying too hard, like some keen out-of-towner down for a show, then people would usually fall for it. My mother had taught me that. While those who barely knew her were taken in by her professed egalitarianism, as her daughter I was aware of her bourgeois snobbishness. Hence her saying things like, 'Don't chew gum, it's common,' and 'Your Aunt Valerie married beneath her'. She was neither one lot nor the other, so looked down on the lower and privately aspired to the upper. She would never admit this.

That year high-heeled pumps with red soles were the thing, though not for much longer. Soon they would be regarded as cheap, though at over £400 a pair they were far from it. The designer, I had read, had been inspired by the shoes of cabaret dancers and prostitutes, those early twenty-first-century muses. I could not afford a pair, of course, but in my first year at university I had been invited to a friend's 21st birthday party at her large house in Belgravia, and had rustled up a decent imitation using a can of cherry red spray paint from the hardware shop. These I retrieved from the back of the cupboard and teamed with a loose, black silk slip. I left my nose ring in.

'Your collarbone looks gorgeous in that dress,' said Lou, who was wearing a pair of navy palazzo pants and a cream blouse made from the type of silk that forgives only the most budlike of breasts. 'We're not getting the tube in this heat. I'll call a cab.'

It was thirty degrees outside and, though the sky was a bright canvas of concentrated blue, the city air had a muggy quality. Steam seemed to rise from the pavements and mingle with exhaust fumes to form a noxious, greasy film upon the cool, clear oxygen we had craved for so long. Despite the lightness of my clothing, it had bonded itself to my skin. I wanted to peel it off like wallpaper.

As the driver pulled out of the crescent, I shifted about in an attempt to detach the moist pleather of the car seats from the backs of my thighs, thinking that there were many other things I would rather be doing today than going to meet Lou's mother, a woman she had never spoken about in the kindest of terms. Being in bed with Josh, as I had been almost every day since our first, was one such activity. His body made my insides fizz. It wasn't that sleeping with him was some transcendental revelation – I had had good sex before, the academic was proof of that – but there was a charge to it that made me feel vital, not just to him, but in the world.

We had not discussed the particulars of our relationship – he had merely slipped into bed with me one evening and that was that. I closed my eyes and remembered gripping his muscular shoulders as he hovered above me. I had forgotten to take my little beige pill.

The taxicab wove its way through the sunlit streets and looking out of the window I experienced a surging sense of unconditional love for the city. The pollution, the drills, the sirens, the gridlock, the fact that somewhere at that very moment, probably, someone was doing a murder: these were all defects that ceased to be of import. I watched a guy in a Rasta hat moonwalk along the line of a bus stop, a woman cooling her freckled shoulders against the glass façade of an office building, sunglasses towards reflected sky, cigarette in mouth. I saw a teenage boy in a kippah pulling his grandmother's shopping caddy behind him with a look of peaceful resignation, a lady shouting insults outside a supermarket as the unflustered folks of Camden strolled by oblivious, having seen it all before. The gutter punks, the paint-splattered builders crowding the pavement with their lunchtime pints, the gangs of teenage girls, all braids and trainers and unapologetic sass: the way these groups tessellated in this outlandish place seemed to me miraculous, and until we entered Mayfair and the crowds dispersed, I soared.

'Strange choice of venue, Mummy,' said Lou when we arrived at the bar, her cheek skimming that of her mother's. She eyed the art deco lines of the dark wood panelling. 'It's not very *summery*.'

'It's cool and dark and they do an excellent martini, which is all that matters to me,' said Lucia's mother, who, as soon as Lou had got close, had reached out to grasp the flesh on the underside of one of her arms and tutted. It was an act sufficient to silence her daughter.

'And who do we have here?' She turned to me, performing the subtle but arch visual appraisal of all mothers of a certain class, smiling warmly to show it was ironic in spirit. She had the blonde hair and pout of a much younger woman, but her skin was soft and unmeddled with, with deep laughter lines around her eyes. She wore an expensive-looking silk tunic.

'I'm Cecilia.'

'Lovely to meet you,' I said. I slid into the chair opposite while Lucia sat next to her mother, her bare arms lolling ostentatiously on the table, as if in protest.

'I suppose Lucia has told you a lot about me,' she said. 'All horrible, of course.'

'I —'

'Mother...' Lou exhaled. She looked tired already, sitting there. She seemed to shrink in her mother's presence, not from fear or shyness, but from sheer exhaustion.

Cecilia's laugh came out in a trill. 'Not to worry. It's what we pay that expensive therapist for. I assume you're

175

still seeing Dr Stein, darling? Daddy tells me he's certainly still paying for him.'

Lucia had told me several weeks previously that she thought Dr Stein was a crackpot and wanted to find another therapist, having recently cottoned on to the fact that the near-decade she had spent in his Highgate consulting rooms appeared to have been of extremely limited use. 'He keeps talking about how anxiety is my transitional object and how I have this untapped fury in my unconscious that supposedly stems from my lousy childhood,' Lou had said. 'It drives me absolutely berserk. There I am trying to deal with the trauma of this rape, or whatever it was' – she whispered the word beneath her breath in a hiss, although we were alone in the house – 'and he keeps asking about Mummy's drug use. The thing is, I have this strong suspicion it's all bunkum. So I told him, "But I don't feel angry, Reuben. I've tried ever so hard, I honestly have, but I can honestly say that I just don't." So then he said, get this, he said, "Well it's your unconscious, so by definition you wouldn't know what you are feeling." And I just thought, well isn't that terribly convenient for you? You can go around telling people what they are unconsciously feeling without any need to actually prove it, and if they query it you can just say they're repressed or in denial. I mean, honestly. So I said, "How do I go about releasing this untapped fury, then?" and he said, "Very slowly, over many sessions." I just thought, well isn't that just *perfect*.'

Lucia didn't explain any of this to Cecilia. She simply said, 'Of course I am, mother,' and ran a hand through the sleek black surface of her hair.

We ordered our £12 cocktails. I popped an olive in my mouth, suddenly starving.

'Our bohemian parenting has cost us dear,' said Cecilia, returning to the topic once our order had been placed. 'Lucia is evidence of that. Not just financially but emotionally, though, good God, the Priory was expensive. It's a good thing we had just sold the Notting Hill house ... '

'Is that where you grew up?' I said, in a mild sort of way.

I already knew this from my long talks with Lou, but her eyes were pleading with me to change the subject.

'Yes,' said Lou, with relief in her voice. 'In one of those houses that looks like a wedding cake. Mummy bought it for *nothing* in about 1967.'

'Notting Hill was a total slum in those days. Full of blacks and cockneys.' Cecilia said this in a volume particular to the posh. 'Now it's all Russians and Arabs of course.'

'Harmony's parents were real hippies,' said Lou, in what sounded like an almost-taunt. 'They were squatters.'

'Whereabouts? Quentin and I had some friends who were squatters, up on Freston Road. Heathcote, David. Some other people. They declared independence from the United Kingdom, actually. In 1979. The Republic of Frestonia. Had their own stamps. Though I don't believe the United Nations ever got back to them about becoming a member state.' Cecilia laughed.

'Mine were more North London,' I said, with a vagueness that I hoped would escape notice. 'Frestonia. Wow. What an incredible story.'

'It was the whole street,' said Lou, who looked suddenly animated. 'We've got loads of photos. I'll show you. Like a hundred people. The Clash recorded there. I'm really good friends with some of the grandchildren. They still live there. It's a housing co-op now.'

I looked from Lou to her mother, and considered the

strange trajectory of Cecilia's life, the rampant contradictions of it. Greenham Common Peace Camp followed by an anorexic daughter at boarding school. Separation, the drug overdose, the flogging of the mansion in Notting Hill, the retreat to a commune in Scotland. Now reunited, Lucia's parents lived platonically in a crumbling manor in Cornwall. Quentin painted and cultivated cannabis in the garden. Cecilia collected couture.

'Another round?'

'I'm going to step out for a cigarette,' I said. My heels were thunderous against the black and white tiles of the lobby.

Outside, I leaned against the red brick of the building and took several deep breaths as I watched Mayfair saunter by. The Rollses and the Bentleys glided past almost silently, a gaggle of Arab women in full burkas less so, the bright yellow of their Selfridges bags a shock against the black. The whole place felt like another world, a world to which, at least to an uncurious outsider catching sight of me through the windows of a taxicab, I was party. I didn't want to go back inside.

'Do you ever wish you had normal parents?' Lou appeared, cigarette poised, and waggled her fingers towards my lighter in a needing gesture.

'I used to,' I said. 'All the time. Dad in a suit, Mum working part-time, clean carpets, just like my friends. I used to envy their food when I went round for tea. Egg and chips and peas, five on the dot.'

'Before I was sent away to school, my parents used to seat me at their dinner parties,' said Lou, 'like I was their little pet. And all their druggy friends used to interrogate me and laugh at my responses.' She said this lightly, but with a wince.

'I would say that Cecilia seems nice, but it wouldn't be entirely true,' I said. 'What she said, about your mental health ...'

'I've learned to live with it.'

We were alerted, as if through telepathy, to the presence of a man. He was stout, balding and in black tie, in the process of lighting a cigar and appraising us from a distance. 'I hope you don't mind my saying ...' he began, in a strong Russian accent.

'We are having a conversation,' said Lou, who pretended that the frequent interruptions we encountered from men practically everywhere we went irritated her. I could already see that she was standing differently.

'I just wanted to compliment your friend on her taste in shoes,' the man said. 'Those are beautiful shoes for a very beautiful lady.'

I was tempted to compliment the old man on his taste in hardware store spray paint, but thought better of it.

'Thank you,' I said, stubbing out my cigarette. 'We have to get back in.'

'Let me give you my card,' said the old man. 'I will take you to lunch on my plane. Anywhere in the world, you choose.' He strode off before I had any time to reply.

'Oh my God, you have to go,' said Lou, as we re-entered the lobby. 'Imagine! All-expenses paid lunch in Venice. How incredible.'

'Lucia, you do realise that in order to attend said lunch I would have to have sex with the gentleman we both just met outside, don't you?' I said in a whispered hiss as the door to the bar was opened for us.

'Worth it,' she said. 'Mummy, some Russian oligarch just offered to take Harmony to lunch anywhere in the world.'

'You do realise, Harmony, that such things are of a purely transactional nature?' said Cecilia.

I nodded. I thought of the academic and his texts in the middle of the night, messages that would light up my face as Josh slept soundly beside me and I pressed delete, delete, delete. He had paid for lots of dinners.

'She's not going anyway, the bore. Plus she's sleeping with our flatmate,' said Lou, plucking another olive from the dish.

'As is her choice,' said Cecilia. 'It's not something to be sniffed at, choice. I remember a time before women had very much of it at all.'

'The swinging sixties? Please, mother. You were all sleeping around like nobody's business, men and women. Sometimes both at once.'

Cecilia raised an eyebrow. 'You say that, but for a movement called "sexual liberation", I didn't feel especially liberated. In fact, a lot of the time I felt rather used. But turning it down wasn't really the done thing. In fact, it was downright rude. Someone would crawl into your bed and if you were lucky they'd say, "fancy a shag?" before getting started, and well, that was that. You were meant to be eager and willing.'

'Did you not really get any enjoyment out of it?' I wasn't about to ask Lucia's mother explicitly whether she found it difficult to reach orgasm, but Cecilia caught my meaning.

'Sometimes. Rarely,' she said. 'Foreplay is a bit of a modern invention. What I remember most when I think back to that time – and bear in mind I was taking a lot of speed and other things – was looking at lots of cracks in ceilings. Peeling plaster and such like. I was at a party once where the entire ceiling collapsed. A man was almost impaled on a chandelier. But anyway, I found the whole thing rather tiresome after a while. There was always some hairy brute sliding under the covers with you, whether you liked it or not.'

'Why not just say no?'

'I did once and got called a frigid boring bitch. Like I said, it wasn't really done. Perhaps because it would have exposed the whole charade. We were supposed to be changing society, but really all that changed was that the sense of entitlement that men felt towards women's bodies became more obvious. To me, at least. It's why I joined the women's movement.'

'You never told me any of this before...' said Lucia in a tone I couldn't place. Her mother took a sip of her martini.

'You never asked. But there it is. So much for sexual freedom. I didn't feel very free at all. Maybe others did, I don't know. I remember feeling very sad and very sore. I quite envy you girls in many ways. You're so much more assertive than we were back then. Sleeping with whomever you want, whenever you want. Feeling entitled to an orgasm. Not experiencing sex with men as though you were some floppy rag doll to be bent about this way and that, or feeling like you had to do it because he had taken your picture. Things have really come on, thanks to the hard work of the women of my generation. You don't realise how lucky you are. Lucia, sweetheart... whatever is the matter?'

It was only then that I looked and saw Lou, head slightly bent, crying wordlessly.

Autumn 1987

The bairn's squalling wakes me and so, in darkness, I take her from the cot in their room, thinking she's hungry and could do with a bottle feed. Better, I decide, to let them sleep. Stella has not been well.

I become aware of the noise as I'm walking down the landing with the baby in my arms, a roaring that seems to shake the house at its foundations. No wonder she woke up.

I grope through the darkness in search of a light switch, fearing I will trip and drop her. I cup her head with one hand, the downy tuft of her hair tickling my palm as I use the other to reach for the switch. Nothing. The storm must have downed the power lines.

I put her down on my bed making soothing noises while I raid her father's shrine for candles. She's giving the storm a run for its money; I'm surprised the whole house is not awake. As the room fills with flickering light I hold her up to my face and kiss her, widening my eyes at the little face I can now see. She's keening now, is breathing heavily from the strain of all that howling.

We go over to the window. The other houses in the street all sit in darkness, the scene strangely rural seeming without the glare of the orange street light. As our eyes adjust we watch a tree float down the street as though made of hollow papier mâché. Others have been plucked effortlessly from the earth by an invisible hand, gnarled roots raw and exposed. Poor Mr Moore opposite. His brand new Honda Accord has been crushed. The bairn squeals with excitement as I bounce her on the windowsill.

We sit and watch until the sky lightens and the winds subside. We have no reason to expect any visitors. The fierceness with which Stella loves her baby daughter is being smothered by exhaustion. She walks around in stained nighties like a befuddled ghost, glazy-eyed, her face fastened up. Sometimes I see her looking at her baby with confusion, as though she is wondering how it turned up here. I have no reason to expect Bryn, either. He is trying to do his bit but he no longer climbs the stairs to my room or enters my bed. I do not mind this development. I'm not wanting for love.

She wakes up again, smiling and making a cooing noise. The sun is coming up. Daylight reveals a scene of chaos, smashed windscreens from falling roof tiles, a fallen plane tree blocking the road, rubbish everywhere. People will have died in the night, I am sure of it. And yet I find the carnage exciting, the suspension of normal rules a thrilling respite from the tedium of everyday life.

The incessant blaring of alarms is disturbing the baby, so we go away from the window and make our way downstairs to put a pot of coffee on. I experience a sudden, secret urge for a bacon sandwich, one of Mam's, dripping with fat and brown sauce. I take a banana from the fruit bowl.

Bryn's coat is missing from the hook near the door. Perhaps he has gone out to investigate the damage. I balance the bairn on my hip and carry a mug of hot coffee in my other hand, being careful to hold it at arm's length so as not to risk scalding her (another thing they never tell you – that holding a baby essentially disables you). We make our way slowly up the spiral stairs.

Their door is ajar, the cool light of morning a fissure in the floorboards. I push it open gently with my unoccupied hip.

'Good morning,' I say, my voice very quiet. 'Look who we have here.'

Stella is sitting up in bed, her hair tangled from a night of disrupted sleep. She puts her arms out in front of her, smiling weakly, and takes the baby from me.

'Have you seen outside?' she asks me.

'We watched it happen,' I said. 'Didn't we sweetheart?'

'Was there a horrible, horrible storm?' Stella directs her attention to the baby and switches to motherese. 'Were you very, very frightened? Were you? My poor darling.'

'She loved it,' I say, sliding into bed next to her, pulling the paisley duvet up over my cold arms and shivering. 'She'd have given it a standing ovation if she could.'

'She takes after her mother, then.'

We sit there with the baby happily between us, her legs in the air, goggling at us with her big inky eyes as we share the cup of coffee, passing it between us when the ceramic starts to scald our fingertips.

'Thanks for taking her,' says Stella. 'I really needed the sleep.'

'Don't mention it,' I say. 'We're in this together.' She smiles and nods, looking past me to the baby, picking her up and patting her over her right shoulder.

'Of course we are,' she says. But there's something in her voice, some small scrap of what feels like fear, which tells me she is not sure of this at all.

Cement

Plastic rubble bag containing miscellaneous cement shards.

My mother made myths like puff pastry; folding and tucking and smoothing and snipping, until her past was golden and fluffy and melt-in-the-mouth. She was a master pâtissière, spinning all her sorrows into sugar. Even as a young child I could tell this from the stories she told me, in which she would emerge as a fairy-tale mother figure, soft and kindly and protective. That is not to say she was ever cruel to me, just that her flightiness, and then later on her yawning sadness, had forged a gulf between us for as long as I could remember. Sometimes Stella seemed to me more like a slightly imbalanced aunt than a mother.

I was not particularly troubled about our relationship, having reached adulthood. We spoke on the phone occasionally, when she wasn't travelling, or on some retreat stipulating a technological detox. We rarely met, and I was happy with that. Despite having lived with her for most of my childhood, I hardly felt I knew much of her inner self at all. Her depression had been like a vortex, swallowing everything in the house, contracting only when a dubious man was spotted on the horizon. I was not bitter about this, just slightly sad. Seeing Lucia with her deeply eccentric mother and witnessing the way Cecilia had brushed the damp hair from her daughter's face and kissed her forehead as she stood by the open door of the cab made me crave the touch of my own. Throughout my life, Stella's manias had seen indifference giving way to flashes of extreme affection that I hoarded like marbles. I longed for more.

Lou was exhausted from seeing Cecilia, so I put her to bed and walked through to the kitchen. There I sat in the stifling quiet and smoked, picking at the end of a stale French stick and remembering how I used to hollow out the loaves of bread that my grandmother bought, rolling the white flesh between my fingers until it returned to little more than a ball of dough, at which point I would pop it in my mouth and suck, allowing it to disintegrate in my mouth. Josh was still at work, and I wasn't due at the pub until the evening, so I had very little with which to occupy myself.

Downstairs, Coral was playing Toots and the Maytals. It floated through the French windows into the garden below, which, I noticed, was looking remarkably bald. I stood at the sill stubbing out my cigarette, and several moments later saw Coral emerge in gardening gloves and dungarees. Her hair, in a parody of a woman undertaking menial work, was tied up in a scarf, and she was holding a can of Red Stripe.

'Need a hand?'

She looked up at me. 'Door's open'. I recognised in her that resolute sense of purpose that comes after a dark period, just as Stella's pull-your-socks-up determination to empty and thoroughly clean all the kitchen cupboards would manifest, like clockwork, after a long spell beneath the duvet. If you couldn't sort your life out, you could at the very least sort the pulses from the grains.

I went down. Coral had barely made a dent in the bramble jungle that was the yard, though she had been hacking away all morning. The tangle of vegetation reached almost to the tops of the high brick wall at the back of a long expanse of land, its tendrils reaching between cracks in the fences either side, intermingling with ivy and a mass of wild climbing roses like some tentacled creature made of weeds and dandelion fluff. Standing next to it on her skinny alcoholic's legs, Coral looked tiny.

'Got a letter from the council,' she said, in that hoarse voice. 'Neighbours have complained about all the fox crap. Say it's an environmental health hazard, that there might be rats. Obviously worried that it'll affect the value of their house ...' She took a swig. 'Give me a hand?'

I grabbed a pair of secateurs. The weeds and brambles came within six feet of the French windows, below which someone had tried to establish the semblance of a patio, but there were saving graces: the wildflowers I remembered from my childhood were in evidence, their heads poking through gaps in the thorny nest, dainty blossoms in white and yellow and blue set against the green. What's more, I detected a heady hint of honeysuckle; over in the corner I could spy what looked like the black wrought iron of a round table.

'Where's the motorbike grave?'

'I'm surprised you remember that,' said Coral, pointing at the split, pale stump of the lilac tree.

'I used to play here a lot, with Gabs. That time Stella and I left Bryn and came back again, I spent nearly the whole summer out here.'

A vivid image of the red-headed woman flitted past. Barefoot and in shorts, chasing me in circles as I laughed, her fingers tickling my tummy. And with her, the thought that that place would outlast all of those of us who had by chance wandered (or in Coral's case stumbled) momentarily through it, the musky sweet scents of the jasmine still clinging to the dusk long after we are gone.

'He was a beautiful boy, that Gabriel,' said Coral. 'Such lovely big brown eyes. Are you still in touch?'

'Mum and Vita speak sporadically, but I haven't seen them since I was eight or nine, when they came to visit us. He's not very well, I hear. Mentally I mean. They moved back to Brixton and he still lives with her there. It's been so long since we knew each other that I don't know how it would feel to meet him again.'

'So many casualties from this house. Just look at Mikey D.' She took another swig of her can, and, realising that she hadn't offered me my own, handed it to me and ducked into the darkness of the kitchen. I held it cool against my forehead, then drank.

Her voice floated through the windows. 'So how was he? I don't half miss the old bugger.'

'He seemed on fine form, though obviously I don't really know him. In fact he didn't seem crazy at all. He said I reminded him of my mum. Told me some stuff about him and my dad in the sixties, the parties they used to go to and the squats they lived in. I liked him.'

'Ah, he's not all that mad, most of the time. He just needs a rest sometimes. Wrecked that burning brain of his and had a great time doing it, but it came at a price.'

'Flashbacks?'

'More permanent than that. He sees auras around things.'

'That doesn't sound unpleasant'

'I don't think it is, in itself. But there are other things, like hearing voices, that probably don't have much to do with the drugs, but mix it all together and the world stops feeling real to him. He stops feeling real. And that's when he tries to hurt himself.'

I knew what she meant, the part about not feeling real.

'Poor Mikey. He gave me this.'

I pulled out the boule, shiny in the sunlight.

'He was always messing with that thing. He gave it to you? That's high praise, that is. He always loved you, from when you were a nipper.'

'I don't remember him,' I said.

'He was one of the originals. Came with your dad, right at the beginning. They'd been young tearaways together. Would have long chats in the kitchen about politics and religion and veganism and sex. Mostly sex. Your father quoting Bertrand Russell: "Love can flourish only as long as it is free and spontaneous." Most people had given up on that stuff by then. The sixties were finished, Vietnam was over. Joplin and Hendrix had died five years earlier, and punk was just getting started. In November of that year the Sex Pistols played their first gig.'

'Bryn would have been, what? Twenty-five?'

'About that. Mikey too. They had a lot of girls come through here. This was long before your mother.'

'Did you … ?'

'We all did. Don't look at me like that, love. It never meant anything. Plus, I had a fella for a lot of the time. Remember Andy? Fleur's dad?'

'I remember Fleur. She was a bit of a punk. She used to let me go upstairs with her when Rufus was doing his music. She was what, a teenager?'

'Born in 1970, the year we moved in. In what is your bedroom now, I do believe. Her mum was a Swedish girl whose name I can't remember, who did a runner, leaving them here.'

'What do they do now?'

'I don't know, Harmony.' Coral was pulling hard at an entrenched root which eventually gave, propelling her a couple of feet backwards. 'I could never keep track of all the people who passed through this house. I barely knew their surnames. We didn't have a phone in those days.'

'It's strange that you were with my dad.'

'Is it? I was one of many, I'll tell you that much.'

'Didn't that bother you? Didn't that bother Stella, when she moved in?'

'I was never that traditional. And yes, his past more than bothered her. She tried ever so hard not to let it, but she was always jealous. She married him on condition that he stop all that stuff, which he did, for a while at least. That was her biggest mistake, really. Thinking that she'd be enough. Then, after having you, thinking that you both would be enough, and taking you away, with no thought for anyone else, for how it might hurt them. Your dad didn't want to go, but she insisted. Predictable that it all ended in tears.'

'But how did it end in tears?' I threw down my rake. 'Stella won't tell me, Mikey won't tell me, Bryn won't tell me. Something happened here. A girl died. Didn't she? A young girl. And you blame Stella for it. Coral? Tell me, please. I need to know.'

'Calm yourself, girl. If you must know, I'll start from the beginning.'

She told me about the day Bryn brought Stella home, how young she had seemed, how Coral had raised various feminist objections to a teenager joining the commune, and how they had fallen on deaf ears. 'He'd been too dazzled by her,' she said. 'It was like there was a force inside her that dragged him away from us.'

We continued to work through the hottest part of the day, as Coral told me more about the commune and the people who passed through, of marijuana cultivation, meditation and squabbles over dietary requirements, and always, always, the washing up. It had been no utopia, she said, but it was home, where company was guaranteed and the music was good and loud and the drugs were free. There was an edge to her voice as she told me all this, because, I think, she knew that the questions about my parents would keep coming. How odd it was to speak to someone who viewed my mother, whose presence at the school gate had so embarrassed and thrilled me, as desperately conventional. She had always been so different from other mothers, but now I saw her attempts to force a stable family unit upon my father – all the while trying to maintain the persona of a free spirit – with renewed sympathy. She had tried to escape her Metroland upbringing of martini wines and tennis skirts, but had ended up trying to replicate the monogamy that had featured so strongly in it. I felt sad for her.

The afternoon drew on and the air cooled, the shadows in the garden lengthening. I had stopped after my fourth beer, mindful of the need to start work soon, but Coral was still going. There was something therapeutic about hacking and pulling at the brambles, listening to her disjointed remembrances, all recounted to me in that same, gravelly tremor. As she spoke, I began to feel part of a history that had previously eluded me, and the parents that I had known before, conceptually at least, and whose outlines I had so childishly worshipped, seemed to me to be strangers. That's not to say that their love for me felt suddenly false, merely that these caricatures I had created in the void of our family's shared history were now fleshed out. Flawed, yes, but also breathing.

My spade hit something solid. I had been digging up roots, and for a moment I assumed I had struck the rusted metal of the motorbike until I realised that the lilac tree was still some distance away. I continued to clear the earth and vegetation, vaguely excited that I may have made some valuable discovery, only for a largish patch of cement to reveal itself, no doubt another attempt to create a serviceable space free from weeds. It was only after frowning at it for several seconds that I realised that my name was staring back at me. 'HARMONY 1990', carved into the cement in a childlike script, as though with a stick, or the end of a paintbrush. Kneeling down, I traced it with my finger.

'Look Coral, I've found some of my juvenilia.' I was smiling, thrilled to look at those letters, in all their permanence. Coral's lack of surprise and excitement when she looked at them was deflating. For a few moments she said nothing, then she looked up at me carefully.

'Of course, they might not be yours,' she said. 'Someone else could have written them.'

'You mean the other Harmony? My namesake?'

Coral nodded.

'The name was your father's choice, though Stella seemed happy enough with it. A beautiful name, everyone said.'

'But she died before I was born. Of an asthma attack.'

'Did your mother tell you that?'

My face must have confirmed it for her, because I said nothing. Coral looked as though she was wrestling with herself.

'Harmony didn't die of an asthma attack before you

were born. She lived here, with you. Surely you must remember that?'

I said nothing.

'You had three parents, my love.'

An ice cream van turned the corner, tinkling out the incongruous strains of 'Yankee Doodle'. A neighbour's strimmer hummed. Somewhere through a distant window a woman laughed.

I continued to stare at the letters, but they no longer made any sense.

Sheets

Sheets featuring faded paisley pattern in pale green, circa 1970s.
220 × 260 cm. 100 per cent cotton.

I remember:

Standing in the dingy hall, in the late afternoon. The house seemed empty, but there was music playing some-where, cooking smells, footfall creaking. The sound of a dog barking. A clock ticking. I was playing with my bouncy ball, throwing it into the marked squares of the floor tiles: black, white, black. The noise echoed. The soles of my red Mary Janes squeaked.

The spiral of the staircase rose above me into darkness and then, right at the very top, disappeared in streams of light emanating for what seemed like miles above my head. The chandelier, always a source of anxiety, mocked me from above. I liked going up there, to the room at the very top. That might be where the grown-ups were hiding. Perhaps I'd go there now.

I am big enough for the stairs, but only just. I go up two at a time, to the first landing. It is gloomy, the window blinds are closed, as are both doors. I push one open and walk into the room, see bare floorboards. It's empty, so I take this chance to spin and spin in circles, my nose tilted up towards the meringue of the ceiling rose until I feel dizzy. I sit on the floor, wondering where my mum and dad are. I will try their room.

I mount the next flight of stairs. I am tired and grouchy, and clammy, even in the cool indoors. It's been very hot. I should be outside. Where is everyone?

I call for my mum, first in a small voice, then more loudly. I haul myself up onto the next landing, my bare knees hitting the rug of the second-floor landing, scratchy. I call for her again, the whine in my voice reverberating through the lonely house. I start to worry that they have all left me, that I am alone in the world.

Just as I start to cry, I hear the creak of the door to my parents' room, a shaft of light. In it stands one of the grown-ups. She is not wearing any clothes, and between her legs is orange and furry, like copper wire wool. I look at it in horror, but she smiles at me, and puts her fingers to her lips. Behind her, my father yawns. I glimpse him half uncovered by my parents' sheets – white, with a faded, mint-green paisley pattern (there are photographs of me lying on those sheets as a newborn). Harmony pulls the door to.

No, this is wrong, that is not how memories are at all. They are not neat narratives, but a series of shining flashes like those of a camera taking shots in quick succession, distinct from one another: there I am playing with the ball, climbing the stairs, calling for my mother, looking at the naked woman. One, two, three, four. That is all.

This is a memory I have always had. It was never repressed, just never dwelt upon. I grew up knowing it. That my father had other women Stella hardly kept a secret, nor was she especially forthcoming on the topic. It just was what it was, until it wasn't. To learn from Coral that in fact she had hated it, had wanted me, and him, all for herself, made me wonder how she had behaved towards anyone who got in the way. Harmony. My namesake. My other mother.

The chunk of my life during which my mother and father were apart was four times longer than the time they had been together, and yet somehow their relationship continued to loom large throughout my childhood. Stella had had innumerable boyfriends, Bryn fewer relationships, and for longer, but both spoke of their time at Longhope with a wistful longing – my mother in her good moments skimming over the less savoury details and recalling, above all else, the sense of camaraderie, the endless stream of kooky visitors, the togetherness of it. No wonder it seemed to her a golden time. The countryside, her depression, had isolated her, and she must have craved the companionship of the city. Though at her lowest points she appeared to blame Longhope bitterly for all the pain she suffered in her life, you only had to see her eyes blazing to know it was also the place where she had had the most fun.

Bryn was happier in the wilderness, but when asked would speak fondly of the thrill of rebellion and his various scrapes. As a squatter, he experienced a number of brushes with authority, the one I most remember him reminiscing about being the time when Longhope was raided by the police shortly after it was squatted. They broke the door down and the fifteen or so people staying in the house scattered. Bryn said he was in what was then the communal kitchen that was to become Coral's living room and kitchenette, and so bolted through the French windows into the garden and up a tree. 'I was up there for nearly twelve hours, freezing my bollocks off,' he told me, smiling.

To Bryn, Longhope prompted reflections no more profound than funny anecdotes. He was never one to live in the past, and that was part of his charm. He certainly never mentioned his other lovers, or 'your father's girl-friends' as Stella would darkly refer to them after several drinks. I remember there always being lots of women around, but my memory of the naked redhead in the doorway was the only concrete experience on which I could rely. There were other things I recalled about my time in the commune, of course, but it was and remains hard to distinguish between what had actually happened and what was the result of the legends created by my parents, or the few photographs I had seen. Did I remember the bathroom because I remembered it or because I had seen a picture of it? Were the faces of the residents masks that I had conjured or reflections of the people I had met?

I had always thought I remembered, for instance, playing in the garden. A rug would be put down for us under the lilac tree, and Gabs and I would lie on our backs and look at the sky through the leaves. Someone made a swing, and we pushed each other on it. Stella and Vita sat on deck chairs, watching. They gave us cubes of chopped-up mango, small enough to suck. They tasted of sunshine.

Another memory. Once, as I was being taken to bed, I looked out of the second-floor window below to see three of the grown-ups on the swing all at once, laughing. Another time I was trying to sleep but I couldn't because the music was so loud. The light from the kitchen glowed from the top of the stairs. When I stood on the threshold, there were people dancing.

Did she describe these things to me or did they leave a lasting imprint?

I knew I remembered the woman in the doorway. Before I returned to Longhope Crescent and my namesake began to sweep through my dreams, that was all I could be certain of, a series of scenes, as though imprinted on a negative. Returning, and meeting Coral, changed that, filling in some of the still-faint blanks. Harmony had picked up a spider that frightened us in the garden, she had held me when I tried to fly and instead fell, played with and tickled me, and, I felt with utmost certainty, loved me. According to Coral, this young woman wasn't just my father's lover but had been as much a parent to me as Bryn and Stella. Yet my parents – driven by motives which seemed to hint at mean and exploitative acts on their part – had told me she had died before I came to the world.

It is not that I couldn't countenance the idea that my parents might be cruel – I had been well aware from a young age how sadness can make a person unkind. Stella's warm love enveloped me with a depth of feeling I never doubted, but she was also brittle, taking even the mildest of comments as a profound criticism of her very being. In her mind, a minor mistake or upset was not simply a case of human error but a monument to her having failed as a mother, standing in testament to all her flaws and weaknesses. 'I might as well die,' she would say, sobbing, during some row or other when I had expressed myself as any teenager does, 'I'm a useless human being'. It was a tendency towards the dramatic that I also noted in Lucia – that automatic leap towards the worst-case scenario: yourself. And so I would comfort and reassure her and whatever small slight I had made would be forgotten as I swallowed my own grievances and held her to me like a baby.

Where Stella could be sensitive and prone to lashing out, my father Bryn seemed to run on indifference. As one of the calmest people I knew, it was a mystery to me how he had stayed for so long with my mother. He was perpetually unflustered, including by the fact he had a daughter, but again, I knew his love was under there, somewhere. The closest I can come to explaining it is that his affection was expressed in his treating me with respect. I was cocooned in the balmy comfort of his high regard. Even as a small child, he would speak to me as though I had the emotional and intellectual sophistication of another adult.

I was a child of whom grown-up feelings and grown-up conversation topics were expected, a legacy that came from having no siblings. There were other children in the house, of course, but they were to an extent expected to contribute to the commune as an adult would: by shelling broad beans, or pressing tofu, and entertaining them as they curled up on the sofa with their roll-ups and their home brews.

That day in the garden, when I unearthed the cement, was a shock, but confirmed a feeling that had always niggled about that summer, which is that things had gone horribly, awfully wrong and that no one, for reasons of guilt or estrangement or mistrust, would tell me what happened. And trying to remember it was like staring down into a murky garden pond: every now and again, at the corners of the shadow of your own reflection, you catch the shine of a fish scale in the light, and then it's gone.

I stared at the etching of our name. My thoughts were all white noise, cut through only by Coral's placing of her hand on my shoulder. Her skin was coarse against mine, like the palm of a girl I had known at school who lived on a farm and whose skin was cracked with criss-crossed lines, except Coral didn't work at all. But I did, and I needed to be at the pub soon.

199

'I think there are some things we need to talk about,' Coral was saying.

'Too right,' I said. Then, 'I can't believe Stella.'

'She had her reasons, though I can't say I agree with them. Hey, have you got any more beers upstairs? Might as well make the most of the rest of the sunlight while we talk.'

We had barely made a dent. I looked hopelessly at the remaining expanse of garden. It was hard to tell but it appeared to stretch out for over thirty feet. If you laid the house on its side, it would fit comfortably in the space.

'I don't think we're going to have time. I have to go,' I said. 'I have work.'

'Please yourself. Miss Curiosity the one minute, aren't you, and couldn't care less the next. Whatever, I'll amuse myself. Got a ten bag and a BBC4 documentary.' I tried to laugh. 'See you tomorrow.'

I ran upstairs. Josh was in his room dozing when I came in. He held his arm out to me, smiling, and tried to pull me down on top of him. 'I can't,' I said.

'What's wrong? You look odd. Are you ok?'

'I just found out that my dad was sleeping with this woman when I was a kid who I thought died before I was born. While he was with my mum. Which sounds weird and eccentric, but actually isn't all that surprising, except my mum lied to me which is why I thought she was dead, and I don't know why. Also she has the same name as me.'

And by the way, I added in my head, *we all used to live here.*

There was a pause. 'Ok,' said Josh. 'But are you all right?'

'I'm fine,' I said, in a way that I hoped sounded business-like. 'I have to go.' I kissed him, his chest hardening as

I reached up to stroke the hair at the nape of his neck. 'Wait up for me.'

'I will,' he said. 'I wanted to have a chat actually. I'm worried about Lucia. She's going a bit off the rails.'

I hadn't seen her, but it did not surprise me. 'Let's talk about it later.'

I descended the stairs just as Coral started screaming again. I really should plough through her gruff reticence and talk to her about that, I thought. I'm not proud that I hadn't, but the truth was that I was frightened to. But mostly I just thought what I always thought, whenever anyone of my parents' generation started behaving in their typically unfathomable way, like the time I visited my dad at his last place and they broke out the chanting with no forewarning. Which was, simply: *'Jesus Christ. These people.'*

Spring 1990

I wake to the sound of men's voices raised over mechanical churning. It is Saturday, and Bryn and Mikey are attempting to lay a patio outside. The little one cut her wrist open on broken glass there last week, and Stella put her foot down. 'She could have bled to death if we hadn't found her. We need a proper garden.'

I make my way down to the French doors, feeling clumsy and dreamy. I'm in dire need of a cup of tea. The kitchen is empty, so I walk over to see who is out back. Mikey's got his shirt off although it's only March, his brown chest peppered with a constellation of tattoos, his dreadlocks tied back in a stiff ponytail that makes him look goofy and innocent. Bryn is wearing a creased denim shirt covered in paint splatters, his eyes crinkling as he grins at some joke holding a trowel in one hand and using the other to push his hair back from his face. In a flash I realise again how handsome he is, and I stand there watching them unnoticed for a moment, thinking with a rush of love what a pair of daft buggers they are, but how they'd do anything for that little girl.

'Mony!' She spots me from the improvised swing and jumps off to toddle towards me. She's wearing a stripy long-sleeved T-shirt with dungarees that have a dinosaur embroidered on them, and a pair of high-top red booties that she likes to stamp in puddles. I hold out my arms.

'Watch the concrete!' Bryn shouts at her, and scoops her up into his arms before she can ruin all his hard work, before turning her upside down by her ankles and swinging her from side to side. Her screams and giggles fill the garden.

'Help! Mony!'

'Leave her alone, you ratbag,' I say, shaking my head, and his eyes meet mine as he puts her down and smiles at me. He's a kind man, I think, despite everything. A good father, warm. Not like mine.

'Either of you lads fancy a brew?' They nod, so I take the girl's hand and we go inside. 'Sit yourself at the table, pet,' I say, 'and I'll get you a banana.'

'Where's Mama?'

'Mama's upstairs sleeping. We'll see her later. What do you want to do today? We can go to the park if you like.'

She looks up at me with excitement, and I tickle her until she squeals before turning to make the tea. We've been out every day this week. The weather has been blustery, the cherry blossom swirling down the street like snow as she runs after it in her duffle coat. I could do this, I think, watching as she jumps from pavement stone to pavement stone. I'm already doing it.

We walk for hours, sometimes. It keeps her out of the house, so Stella can rest. The other kids are at school now, so she has no one to play with in the daytime. And the fresh air helps with the nausea I'm feeling. I know the signs, but I'm not ready to tell.

My little bean, I call it privately, because that's about how big it is. I wonder whether she'd prefer a brother or a sister, if she'll react with fierce protectiveness or petulance. She is possessive of me, I think because I am her constant. It's not like I'm working much, the odd bit of secretarial work. So I'm there almost every day to make FIMO models or paint pictures or read a bit of *The Water Babies* yet again. I sometimes wonder what I would have been, if I hadn't come here. A worker in a shop or factory, at most, but in truth eventually it would have been the same: this, but poorer and colder, and more alone.

I've told Stel to go to the doctors' but she keeps saying it'll pass. And it's true that it comes in waves; she'll lie in bed for days and then one morning I'll come down to start the bairn's breakfast and Stella will be standing in the hall, just as beautiful and alive as she has always been, doing up the little one's coat and announcing that they're off to the Natural History Museum. 'Thanks for helping,' she will say.

I'll tell her soon. Just her, at first. It was a one-off, I will explain. It's only been once, since the baby was born, and he didn't half plead. 'This is the last time,' I said to him, afterwards. 'She basically saw us at it.'

'Ah, kids that age don't understand what they're seeing,' he said. But I pressed the issue, saying that Stella was in a bad way, that this would be no good for her. What are the chances?

You'll have someone new to play with soon, I think, as we trudge back to the house. But I'll always love you the same. 'No one can replace you,' that's what I'll say to her. Besides, Bryn adores her. You can see it all over his face. I know he'll love our baby too.

The little one is singing as we skip up the path, those senseless tunes that children invent. I join in, my lalalas clashing, which delights her. As I reach into my patchwork bag for the keys on the doorstep, I bend down.

'Now, pet, we need to be quiet, because your mama

might still be sleeping. Can you do that? Can you be quiet for me?'

'Yes Mony.'

We slip in through the door having removed our coats outside, and I am placing them gently on the hook when I hear raised voices coming from the kitchen.

'It's just so conventional,' Bryn was saying. He didn't sound angry so much as exasperated. 'It doesn't seem like something we would do.'

Stella's voice was a hiss, the kind that is beyond shouting. 'I don't give a shit how conventional it is, or isn't. It's for the sake of my sanity.'

'What about Mony? How will they cope, being separated? You haven't thought this through. She's just as much a mother to her as you are.'

There was a charged silence. Little Harmony was looking up at me.

'Why are they shouting?'

I shush her, taking her sticky hand in mine. 'They're just playing, darling,' I say. 'They'll be quiet in a minute. Come, let's go to the sitting room and read a story, shall we?' I force a smile and shuffle her in the direction of the sofa, closing the door quietly behind us, feeling as though someone has taken an ice cream scoop to my insides.

Mirror

*Antique solid silver hand mirror. Very ornate (Art Nouveau)
decoration of flowers, leaves and swirls. 6" long and 3" across.
Weight 472 g. Good condition, with only slight staining and
tarnishing (please examine photographs carefully). I've seen
a great many of these as an antiques dealer and this is really
something special.*

It's tricky to determine what came next. To an extent the
ordering of things as I have presented them is arbitrary,
occurring as they did during a period of time that is
remembered not as a linear series of events but as a tangle
of incidents which, much like the brambles in Coral's
garden, it is necessary to hack away at and untwist. The
fact that, that year, we were blessed with endless summer
days does not help this process. Each of those months
merged into the next, and, like the cursive handwriting
you've just learnt at school by tracing joined-up letters
on a page with a metal nib, they appeared never to lift
or break.

Objects are easier. To think of that time is to see, vividly,
a glass sitting on the cracked paint of the windowsill –
white, but underneath a peppermint green, veined like
scales, losing its gloss. It is obvious from looking at it
that the night before, or indeed several hours before, in
the early drunkenness of the dawn, it contained red wine.
The dregs are clotted around the rim in a cherry tint. An

unseasonal choice of drink, but one that goes nicely with a smoke, the roachy remnants of which lie in the parched window box, drying up.

There was something thick and lifeless about those summer months, despite the drink and the drugs and the parties that went on all night, the quietly euphoric feeling of Josh's eyelashes against my cheeks and his fingers in my hair. My memories have the brightness of overexposed film but I felt a heavy pressure that is difficult to describe – like weights placed upon my chest. But of course it was fear; it's so obvious to me now.

As to what I was afraid of, it's hard to say. Unlike Lucia, whose room, in the weeks she spent mostly indoors, had become a squalid dump of overflowing ashtrays and dirty pairs of dark silk underwear streaked white as though with the shiny trails of slugs, I had not been attacked or violated. But it felt a horror of anticipation – something awful was going to happen, and the function of my dread was to prepare me for it. The only solution was to drink more.

Whatever the sequence of events, at some point, I went back to badger Coral. The discovery that my namesake had lived to know me as a child had conjured the momentary hope that she might still be alive. 'Perhaps I could write to her?' I said to Coral, one afternoon. I imagined her in a community of hippies somewhere exotic near the sea, receiving my letter and smiling fondly. She would send a photo of how she looked now, her hair faded to a strawberry blonde, her face lined but lovely, her figure lithe from early morning yoga. But Coral shook her head, sadly, and said the dead part was correct, it was just the whens and hows that were not.

She had come to the house from a pit village in County

Durham, Coral said, in 1984. The miners had been on strike for over a year, and the residents of Longhope had voted in favour of providing a couple of them with room and board as they marched on parliament that June. Harmony, my namesake, and the sister of a man called Mark, had come with them. She was just seventeen.

'History repeats itself,' said Coral. 'Your da' always did like the young ones.'

Everyone had been struck by her unusual beauty: her long, auburn hair, the fragility of her thin frame, especially Bryn. It's often said by those lacking in imagination that certain women look like china dolls, but according to Coral, Harmony truly did. Stella had moved in just a year earlier, and they were newly married. Though Stella had yet to assert her exclusive sexual rights to my father, she had dealt with any potential competition thus far by mocking him for his outdated utopian ideals, and then, in her clandestine way, making the atmosphere in the house as unpleasant as possible until the woman in question moved out. But Harmony was different: she seemed to mesmerise them both.

'The funny thing about when the miners came,' said Coral, 'was that even though they were suffering, their families starving, even, our lot looked like vagrants in comparison. We were of the same generation, remember. These guys, who came to stay, we were all barely a few years apart, but we were like foreigners to each other. There were Mikey D and Bryn, spouting their socialism and wearing garments that were more hole than jumper, while Mark and his mate stood there in their designer watches and smart clothes. You used to earn good money as a miner.'

Harmony had insisted on tagging along and was treated

by her brother as little more than a nuisance. She barely spoke but when she did it was softly and unobtrusively. That is not to say she was apologetic – she was far from being that. Coral said that, despite her serene composure, it was clear she had an inner core of wildfire. 'They underestimated her,' she said, 'but I knew.'

She quickly endeared herself to everyone, especially the children in the house, by helping with the cooking and playing with them. She won over the women, including my mother, almost immediately, simply by talking and listening to them, spending the long, early summer afternoons in the kitchen drinking mint tea. 'She was the focal point of any room, though whether this was from choice was always mysterious. People relished her attention. She had a clever way of making you feel as though she needed you. It flattered people.'

As Coral spoke, I revisited my meagre memories of that summer. My images of this woman smiling barefoot in the garden, and holding me in the living room as I wept into the curtain of her hair were, I was fairly sure, true recollections from that time.

'She was, I think, slightly in awe of your father. The others she treated as equals, you're supposed to in a co-op, after all. But she must have sensed that there was an unspoken hierarchy, seen how everyone looked to Bryn for decisions on group matters. She was exceptionally bright but had left school two years earlier, and was keen to see and learn more of the world.'

I suspect that this fulfilled a fantasy for my father, who, as my mother had said bitterly several times, could never find gainful full-time employment due to a persistent belief that his true calling lay in becoming a guru, if not in name, then at least in wisdom. A youthful and moon-eyed

Harmony provided an outlet for that. And, obviously, he really wanted to sleep with her.

'Your mother wasn't happy,' said Coral, 'but it was presented to her as a fait accompli one evening in the kitchen, and made clear that she had little say in the matter.'

In those short weeks after her brother went home, Harmony had succeeded in establishing a devoted friendship with my mother. Only a couple of years apart, they were always laughing and conspiring together, shopping for records down Camden Lock, making clothes with the sewing machine, drinking cheap red wine. I imagine that they had the shared intimacy of the youthful dropout. Both were running from something – Stella from her middle-class upbringing, and Harmony, it seemed, from a man who had never hit or hurt her, but who simply, because of a limited imagination, failed to inspire in her anything apart from the sensation of being suspended in aspic. Which is a different sort of violence. But you should know that this is all guesswork, and in all likelihood I've got her completely wrong.

And so, when the miners left, Harmony decided that she would not be returning with them. 'That's when I saw her fiery side,' said Coral. 'She would not be moved or cajoled. She had seen her future and it was in this house, with all of us, with Bryn and Stella.'

How strange, I thought. To fall in with a houseful of hippie throwbacks, who would have been viewed by so many as ludicrously crusty and out of date. But then that was the charisma of Bryn. My mother used to joke he would have made an excellent cult leader.

'She was a lovely girl. A joy to have around, and a wicked sense of humour. Very clever. She may have worshipped your dad, but she never stood for any bullshit. She was constantly questioning, analysing and challenging. Their late-night discussions were legendary. And I think for a while Stella appreciated the respite. She had wrapped so much of herself in him from such a young age that it gave her a chance to breathe a bit. I never remember Harmony doing anything that really inspired a passion in her, work-wise. She didn't need to work – odd jobs and dole payments brought enough in for us to live simply, and I think some of the others had money off their families. She did a series of temping jobs intended to bring money into the house, but she had been tipped for university when she was at school. She spent a lot of the time reading.'

'Was Stella jealous, of her and Bryn?'

'I'm not sure jealous is the right word for your ma. She knew herself too well for that. Say what you like about her, and I have, but she knew who she was. To her, Harmony was just a hiccup. I think the relationship bothered Stella more on an intellectual level than an emotional one – why should Bryn have two women? Why should she have to share him?'

'So she didn't have the option to see someone else too?'

'She had the option, but it was simple for her. She loved your father. She wanted to make it work, as a nice little family unit. Like normal people. And eventually she won. She got that ring on her finger, but that wasn't enough.'

Stella had told me that I had been my parents' impetus for moving out of Longhope to the cottage, but I knew very little about her pregnancy and the immediate aftermath. According to Coral, she had fallen pregnant about three years after Harmony first joined the household, by which point the two women and Bryn had established a sexual routine where he would move between rooms according

211

to some mysterious timetable at which the others could only guess. Meanwhile, my mother's unhappiness with the arrangement had, Stella later told me, begun to fester, so the pregnancy came as something of a relief: the baby growing inside her was an atavistic sign of possession. It was leverage.

'The balance of power changed as soon as your mother came back from the doctors',' said Coral, 'as of course it would. Suddenly your mother was carrying life, precious life, and it was almost as though Bryn began to see her anew. She went from hopelessly rigid and parochial in his eyes to a pagan fertility goddess in a peasant dress. He used to pick wildflowers from the garden and weave them into her hair, and cook her macrobiotic meals.'

If Harmony was jealous, she didn't show it. 'She embraced your mother's pregnancy, viewing it as her role to help as much as she could. She knew the dynamic had shifted. The thing about Harmony was that she projected this powerful sense of unconditional gratitude towards the world, for the privilege of existing. I've never seen anything like it before.'

'Are there any photographs of her?'

'Tell you what, I think there might be.' Coral shuffled over to a darkened corner of the room and reached under a chair, pulling out a peeling suitcase on whose dusty surface her shaking fingers left a smeary patina. 'Do me a favour and get me a can will you? There's years' worth of junk in here.'

We sat on the floor sorting through the photographs, pausing occasionally to take gulps of lager, over the course of many hours. Because what Coral had in that tatty suitcase amounted to a history, an archive of alternative London seen through her own lens, ranging from the late sixties to the early nineties, a mishmash of quaintly-sized, white bordered instamatic oblongs and Polaroids and glossy black and white prints that she had developed in a dark room in the cellar. Most had been taken in the building in which we sat, Woodstock being one notable exception (so she had been there), a set I found remarkable not just in its historical value but because of how not a single semi-clad festivalgoer appears to be overweight. How slender and tanned they all looked, with their post-war portions.

Coral had taken portraits of practically all those who had passed through the house, some fleetingly – 'He crashed here on the way to Berlin'; 'She was ANC'; 'They had some strange religious ideas and eventually joined a sect out in Wiltshire' – and some longer term, all young and good-looking and exuding a bemused cool, holding cigarettes and spliffs and beers and mismatched glasses. There were punks and anarchists and hippies and new romantics, and girls dressed like fairy brides in pale lace. There were men in make-up and dangly earrings made of paste, and women in boiler suits. I saw Fleur in her teenage goth phase, arm in arm with a grinning Rufus, his T-shirt much too big for him. In one photograph, my mother and father sit side by side on the batik sofa. My father is reading a slim paperback, and my mother is asleep, her head on his shoulder, the ink of her hair a spill down the front of his cheesecloth shirt. There are group shots, too: one shows fifteen or so adults – hair long and corduroy shabby – at the turning to Longhope Crescent with its dilapidated terraced houses with windowless facades, sometime in the late seventies, all blinking in the sun as they hold up the various toddlers and babies of the house to face the camera. A family.

213

As I examined the prints, tracing my fingers across their patent surfaces, skimming the faces of strangers whose names I would never know, I experienced a swell of pride in my parents. I had always felt a slight sense of embarrassment at how invested I felt in their past, the extent to which, like much of my generation, I idolised their lifestyle by copying their music and the clothes they had worn. But here was the proof that that life had been in many ways magnificent, and how the supreme loss of it had felt, to Stella, a tragedy. This woman, who had come to hope for a smaller, more settled life, only to find when she achieved it that it revolted her, was made palpable to me for the first time.

And there was the Harmony of my memories, in greyscale and technicolour, smiling out at me across the decades, ageless in her cut-off shorts against the wildness of the backyard, laughing as she sits cross-legged on the Turkish rug, always barefoot (those pale, opal feet) and, most arrestingly, lying on a screen-printed bedspread the colour of tiger lilies, a baby in the boney crook of her arm. 'Is that … ?'

'You,' said Coral, turning her face away. 'She loved you so much. She was heartbroken when they took you away. I don't think she ever recovered. She was like a mother to you. It was cruel of Stella, considering what Harmony had been through.'

'You mean watching my parents bond over me as a baby?'

'That, and basically raising you, once Stella's depression kicked in. She had you most of the time, you know, from when you were a few months old. You probably don't remember, but you used to call her Mony. That was your first word. Not Mummy. Mony. Stella didn't like that, I can tell you. I think that was when she started to think about going. Well. And then, when you were four, Harmony got pregnant.'

I stared at her, waiting for her to continue.

'She was so happy, thinking you'd all be a family. Your mother was the only person she told. Didn't want to excite Bryn before the three-month mark. And when Harmony miscarried, less than a month later, it was your ma who found her crying in the bathroom upstairs and put her to bed, who cleaned the blood off the floor.'

'That's awful.'

'Bryn didn't know. Stella took you both away less than a week later. She was never the same after that.'

There had been no secrecy; we left in daylight. She had stood at the door as they had packed up the car. Coral said she could barely watch, that when Stella gently prised me away from her arms and carried me to the car that Harmony fell to the floor and howled.

She handed me another photograph. This time, we are sitting in an armchair, backlit by the bay window, framed in incongruously opulent heavy gold brocade curtains. From the composition, you would think Madonna and child. I am very small and gazing up at her in wonder as she smiles down at me in partial shadow. On her lap rests a silver hand mirror, its handle a knot of art nouveau swirls.

'You didn't have a christening, obviously. But we had a little party, where we all gave presents, after you came back from the hospital.'

'I have that mirror upstairs', I said, crying, 'on my dressing table. I never knew it came from her.'

'Doesn't surprise me. Far as I can tell, Stella's barely told you anything about her. Guilt, probably.'

'How did they cause her death? You can tell me.'

'It's not that. I'm not saying they're murderers or anything. We were hardly the Manson family. But something you learn over time, you see, is that there's more than one way to kill a person. That's the trouble of it.'

Butterflies

*STUNNING VINTAGE RETRO SHABBY CHIC FRAMED
BUTTERFLY TAXIDERMY*
*4 x framed butterflies in gold frame (38 cm x 32.5 cm), mounted
on white cotton. Real specimens, domestic species (Western
Europe).*

There are men that I have slept with, whose naked bodies I have pressed to mine, whose names and faces I can barely remember. My reasons for coming across them, for choosing them to be the ones to take me home, are lost in the maelstrom of my punch-drunk twenties, but what I can always remember from these episodes, in vivid microdetail, is the clothes that these men removed from my body. So while I couldn't tell you, for instance, the name of the young man who scooped me off a Soho curb at 3am one November with the words, 'Alright, girl', I could tell you that I was in a black taffeta cocktail dress and ankle boots, and that I kept those clothes but never wore them again.

My wardrobe was full of these past versions of myself. The larvae of the moths spent that humid summer solidly chewing through this collection I had curated until the cloth reached the point of disintegration. My attachment to these clothes, cut-price items I had shed like a second skin reflected in the dilated pupils of total strangers, was altogether typical of my tendency to distil my emotions into material objects. The men I cared little for; the clothes they had pawed were heavy with smoke and meaning.

The final time I saw the academic, I was wearing cut-off denim shorts, and a semi-sheer, seventies-style floral blouse, which I had tied together at the front to expose my stomach. No bra; plain black cotton pants. On my feet I wore white patent leather sandals that gave me blisters, so the back straps had a tendency to smear pink with blood.

These are the clothes he removed from my body as we lay on his bed in a room that had the appearance of belonging to a boy my age, not a man of nearly forty. In the six months he had lived there, he had barely unpacked. Cardboard boxes filled with hundreds of books lay open on the floor, his dirty clothes a pile in the corner. 'When the bills mount too high, I simply move out,' he had told me, at the beginning, and I had found this somehow impressive, a sign of his nomadic spirit, rather than what it was – the peripatetic existence of a middle-aged man whose life was slowly unravelling.

I had not seen him since he had taken me to a hotel and told me that he loved me. 'You don't,' I had said, 'and that is fine.' Afterwards (broderie anglaise sundress, no underwear, converse trainers) I had got up and left, assuming his interest in me would slowly peter out as I spent my nights in Josh's bed, the phone vibrating, ignored, in the other room. But the messages continued, and so after several weeks of this I decided to meet him. I told myself it was to throw him over, but there was another impulse lurking there too. One more time, I told myself, and I'll make sure to feel every second of it. Then I'll file it all away, forgotten.

'I know you have a child,' I said, when I first walked into the room (his flatmate had let me in). He was sitting in the bay window, and if nothing else confirmed the truth of this, his look did, then.

'How did you know?'

'I just guessed. I knew you didn't just walk into my life without a past, I'm not a fool. I knew there was a wife somewhere.'

'Not wife, girlfriend. Ex.'

'How old is he? Your little boy?' I knew it couldn't be a girl.

'He's two. David.'

'David.'

The child, or rather his lack of honesty about the child, made it easier to leave him, but I didn't blame him for it all that much. I knew barely anything about this man or his life, and I had made very little effort to find out. I had met only one of his friends, a slightly podgy writer with spectacles who, unlike the academic, looked his age and treated me with a leering offhand resentment that I found all too transparent. I would stay true to my word, would not see the academic again after leaving his room that day, but weeks later, as the warm weather tailed off and the beer garden and the punters switched from rosé back to red, this writer sidled up to me as I worked in the pub, having slipped away from his boozy lunch.

'You know he had a wife—.' His opening gambit.

I looked at him. 'I'm working.'

The writer swayed slightly. 'Don't think you were special,' he said. 'What man his age wouldn't want a twenty-four-year-old body in his bed ... ?'

I pushed past him, sighing audibly. He wobbled after me, his voice a hiss.

'There's a lot you don't know about him. He's done smack, you know.'

'None of this matters to me. You know we stopped seeing each other.'

'He shot a Palestinian child when he was in Israel.' His voice rose. I turned to wipe a table down, only to almost crash into him.

'Come for a drink with me when I finish.'

'You're pathetic.'

I doubt, as I doubted then, that my academic lover had ever harmed a child, but I can't deny that there were other things that hinted at an underlying malice, that had occasionally manifested themselves over the course of our time together: his sexual dominance; his strange messages. The only picture in his barely lived-in room had been a giant tableau of butterfly taxidermy, containing twenty or so pinned creatures in vivid colours. I could identify them because of a book I had once had, names I would repeat in a whisper under my breath like a mantra: ringlet, brimstone, peacock, bramble hairstreak, mournful dusky wing, comma. Fender's blue.

'How can you find something so cruel, so pretty?' I asked him, the first time I went back to his house, and he told me how every summer he was dispatched to see his father on the other side of the continent, and how that man, a poacher, would take him out to catch butterflies with a net.

'You net it, and then you stun it by pinching the thorax between your thumb and forefinger,' he said. 'Then you put it in a jar, with mothballs,' he said. 'Or you freeze it. Then you relax it and pin it. We did all of those.'

'Did you know that they only live for a day?'

'That's a myth.'

I had had something similar, once, when I was in my early teens. Given to me by my grandmother as a birthday present, were four butterflies in a gilt frame. In a fit of adolescent self-righteousness regarding animal cruelty, I had thrown them away. Though she died long before I reached my twenties, I had felt guilty about it ever since.

When I told him I couldn't see him anymore, and that it wasn't because of the kid, he had simply nodded. We both knew we'd have sex before I left – there was so little left to say – and when he walked over and kissed me I felt only familiarity, never regret. In many ways he had been like the Prozac of relationships: being with him dulled many of the negative emotions that I often felt without ever offering that exquisite serotonin high that Josh had taught me to need. When he was on top of me, or me him, I felt outside myself.

Our sex had always been fun, experimental and unhampered by self-consciousness, but still, I was surprised when he put his hands around my neck as we lay naked on top of his sheets for that final time. The first thought that crossed my mind as he did it was that it must have been something that he had seen in porn. It was at that time that we young women were starting to notice a shift in men and their demands, a desire to degrade that had not been there before. Certainly it didn't feel as though he was trying to hurt me; when I looked up into his face his eyes implied that he was elsewhere, as though his hands on my throat were absent-minded, almost. His breaths were deep and heavy as he moved inside me, while, as my panic increased, mine became rapid and shallow. I could barely breathe, and when I tried to cry out all I could discern was a gargling noise at the back of my throat. At the same time, the edges of my vision became crowded with an encroaching blackness, the movement of which reminded me of iron filings drawn towards the magnet in a child's toy. I was losing consciousness. Then – I was elsewhere.

There is no other way that I can describe it: I was transported. I was standing in the darkness of the hall of the house in Longhope Crescent, the warm air of the mid-morning motionless in the swelter, and I was looking for someone.

It was not déjà vu. I did not feel that I had already experienced the situation I was in, but that it was happening to me for the first and only time. I was there, it was now.

I was standing in the hall, calling out in the small anxious voice of a child when I looked up towards the ceiling and the only real source of natural light. The first thing I saw were the pale pink puckered soles of Harmony's feet. How odd, I thought (for we so rarely see the undersides of people's feet); I did not understand what they were doing there, far above me, swaying, casting a long shadow across the floor. I called her name but the arid air stayed silent, so I painstakingly mounted the stairs, two feet on each tread, continuing up until I was almost level with her face, which was blank and dipped off at a strange angle, like the head of an empty hand puppet. It was only then that it dawned on me she was hanging by a rope from the chandelier high above us.

I was screaming as I ran back down the stairs, stumbling, to find Gabs at the bottom, his eyes wide and glassy. He reached out for my hand, and together we sat on the cold cool tiles and wept, as Harmony's dead body swung back and forth above our heads and the chandelier creaked and jingled.

And that is how they found us, three hours later, when the rest of the adults came back to the house.

Summer 1991

Coral wasn't best pleased, when they came back. 'We'd be within our rights to send them packing,' she said, but she knew I'd never turn them away. When she phoned me crying from the service station, I wanted more than anything to comfort her. 'Of course you must come,' I said. 'We'll look after you.'

I couldn't believe how much the bairn has grown – like a little person now, full of questions, babbling away to Gabriel as they play pirates and mermaids in the paddling pools. I lie on a blanket on the grass, ignoring my book in favour of watching them. I spend every day counting my lucky stars that she is here with me, again.

I may have lost my baby, the pain of that will never go. But at least I have her, will watch her grow from this sweet little sprite into a spirited, clever young woman – how could she not, with us all for parents? She'll be released into the world with all the boldness of one who has been loved unconditionally, and it will answer sweetly back with opportunities and adventure. I want to freeze her in time here, now, but I also cannot wait to see what she does, who she will become.

Look at me, talking like a grandmother, when I'm barely halfway through my twenties. But that's what caring does to you, I think. It ages you. I don't mean physically, though of course the labour of it is tiring: the

223

crying in the night and the arse wiping and the feeding and the comforting. The nuts and bolts of loving someone helpless. That's all knackering. But I'm talking about a less visible metamorphosis, a maturity that comes from being schooled in a love that is verging on painful. It's like when you bump into one of the girls in your class who, a year ago was doing pivots in a gymslip, laughing at a blow-job joke, and now is wrestling with a pushchair, sniffling kid in tow. It's not the dark circles and the worn-down demeanour that strike you, it's something else. She has learned the brutal lesson of loving that much: you are now forever vulnerable. There is no longer 'I' – the self-centeredness of childhood has crumbled, and there's a knowing in her manner now. As though she's had an extra dimension added. I used to watch these women – my mam, my aunties, my friends – in awe. The scars they carry. Now I think I'm one of them.

Stella stays mostly in her room. The split has been tough for her. She tried so hard to make it work. But I know that after several weeks she'll be back to her old self. It's home to her. And once she's back to normal, we'll be a family again. Harmony will be starting school in September. Perhaps I'll even get a job, a proper one. I'd quite like to work in a library. I can see myself doing that. All those books.

All these grand plans. Maybe I'm running away with myself. But I can't help feeling that things will be better without Bryn here. He means well, but he's not good at taking care of people. Me, it's what I'm best at. How lonely she was in that house, staring out at miles of sky and sea, with barely anyone to talk to. I'll make sure she's never that sad again. That's what it's for, family. We pick each other up, dress each other's wounds. That is what it means.

Note

Suicide note on one side lined exercise book paper, faded. Blue ink. Author unknown.

Stella, Bryn

I'm sorry. All I can say is that I hope the children do not see me afterwards, or that if they do that they soon forget. It was my only chance while you were all out, and I was worried that if I did it with pills it wouldn't be enough and I would go on living which is something I just cannot do anymore.

I was so happy when you both came home, Stella. I even thought we could make it work; you, me and the little one. I know you haven't been feeling well. I could have taken care of you both.

This is the only home I've known, and I want to say thank you for opening it up to me, for sharing with me what is yours, for as long as you could. I know it wasn't easy. And for giving her my name. It has meant everything to me.

Bryn, when you came back to get your girls last night I knew I couldn't face them being taken from me again. I lost two babies. I know our child would have been beautiful. I know that if you had your way things would have been different.

Tell her I love her, and that she is the most precious thing alive. I know she will grow to be brave and clever and good, like her parents. And know yourselves that I forgive you for hurting me. I wanted a family but I looked in the wrong place. It's my fault.

Don't let her forget me, even if you do.

Blackberry Wine

Empty glass bottle (circa 1970s) with handwritten label reading 'Stella and Harmony's Blackberry Wine' in black biro.

That silence, before the line connects. You're not sure if the words you speak are reaching anyone or just dissipating, unheard through the crackly ether. And so you call out, hello, hello, hello, as the person at the other end does the same in that slightly comical way, until finally the sounds from your mouth and the vibrating of your eardrums converge, and vice versa. Breakthrough.

All I said, when she answered, was one word: 'Mama'. I hadn't called her that for years; she was always Stella, even when I was really little, because that is how she asked me to refer to her (one of those parents). When friends at school said, 'my mum' or 'my mummy' I felt envious of the loving closeness it implied, like being tucked in. To say 'my mother' or 'Stella' conveyed not only an obvious distance, but a precociousness that mystified children and scorned adults.

'Mama,' I said, and then took one of those awful rasping breaths that make you sound as though you have been drowning.

The fear in her voice was almost a balm. 'Harmony, my darling. Tell me what's happened.'

Without going into detail about how the flashback came about, I told her in a hysterical staccato that I remembered everything.

'I suppose I always knew this would happen eventually,' said my mother. 'Please, breathe for a moment. Take a deep breath. There. Another one. I had better come and explain.'

'I'm at Longhope. Have been for a couple of months. I didn't want to tell you because I thought it might set you off.'

'You must hate me. You'd be right to hate me.'

'I don't hate you. I mean, the whole thing is completely messed up, but I don't hate you. I don't understand. Coral's been filling me in a bit ... she still lives here, downstairs, though she's a complete mess.'

Stella swore, was quiet for a moment, then said, in a businesslike tone that was barely familiar, that she would be there soon. If there was a hint of defensiveness in her voice then I didn't notice it; for my part, I felt too grief-stricken to be angry that she had lied to me. All I felt was that I needed her, in a way that I hadn't since I was a child.

I had left the academic's house in a state of extreme distress, deaf to his pleas that I stay with him a while until I became calm again (for his part, having a girl start screaming in terror while you are in bed together would leave anyone shaken, his poorly-signposted experiments in sexual strangulation notwithstanding).

'You could at least have fucking warned me,' I shouted, as I bent over the bed hyperventilating.

I didn't start crying until I was several hundred feet clear of his flat, but once I did it was in that ugly, insuppressible way that never seems to afflict female characters in Hollywood movies: huge, guttural honks of sheer despair that pay no heed to decorum or attractiveness. I sobbed like this standing up on a busy, bendy 29 bus all the way home, and, it being London and not some other city, no one cared to bother me or to enquire after my well-being. I have female friends who have cried all over town, in tube trains and restaurants and under the bright lights of the supermarket, and they say to me in bitter tones that not once, not once did anyone approach them to offer sympathy or assistance. One friend sat sobbing on the statue of Eros at Piccadilly Circus for an entire Saturday afternoon, and no one even thought to stare. The indifference of Londoners was infamous, but that afternoon I felt meekly thankful for it.

The word 'trauma', in Japanese, takes the form of two characters, one meaning 'outside' and one meaning 'injury'. To be traumatised is to sport a visible wound, a pain that can be seen and perceived by others. But this was not the case for me. The trauma that I had suffered when, aged five, I had found myself shut in a house with the hanging corpse of a young woman was apparent, in hindsight, in a million barely perceptible ways. By coming back to the house I had forced a reckoning, had worried at the scab in the same way as I had with the childhood flea bites on my legs, the scars now bleached white against the tan of my shins.

Stella got the first train up from Cornwall, and turned up on the doorstep at around 9pm that evening with her arms spread outwards in preparation for our emotional embrace. I sidestepped this and beckoned her inside, where she stood in the hall for a moment with her face tilted upwards, inhaling the house and all its histories. 'The old place still smells the same,' she said. 'Like a church.'

I tried to smile.

'Christ. I never thought I'd be back here. So which one's Coral's?'

I gestured towards the door. 'We can go and say hello

229

if you like, I'm sure you both have a lot of catching up to do.'

'Perhaps not quite yet.'

We went up to the kitchen, where I immediately poured us two large gins, in that way you do when there's a crisis, like someone dying, and your grief grants you permission, tells you, 'You may smoke all twenty of those cigarettes.'

I had been crying for hours, but now I sat quietly at the table, my sorrow having given way to something more dense and simmering. I was struggling with the guilty anger I felt towards her, a legacy borne from years of tiptoeing around her vulnerability as though I was its captive. That's what happens when you're a child but there's an adult competing with you for the role, pre-empting all your lines so that, instead of being the precious thing they worry about, your fear for them becomes a familiar hum, as prosaic and unnoticed as the drone of the fridge. It was perverse, after everything that had happened, but my main concern was for her well-being.

'Are you sure you feel strong enough to talk about this?' I said, but to my surprise instead of picking up this familiar, extenuating thread, she put down her glass and looked me in the face.

'I want you to know, Harmony, that the consensus at the time was that if you forgot completely about what had happened, then so much the better.' She reached a hand across the table, and to my surprise her eyes were wet. 'Though we weren't sure how much you had understood about what you saw, you wouldn't sleep alone for months afterwards, and you had real separation anxiety. It was as though suddenly the world was set with traps that would take me away from you as well. You would follow me around the house – you and I moved to that place in Bristol, do you remember? – from room to room, because you were frightened, and you kept asking where she was, and why she had looked so poorly, and why we had come away. But then one day you stopped asking, and we thought it best to not remind you.'

'We?'

'Me and Bryn.'

Towards the end of the summer, my father had followed us back to London, turning up on the doorstep in the middle of the night, begging for us to try again.

'It was Harmony who answered the door,' said Stella. 'And I think she knew we would patch things up. In fact, the day ... it ... happened, we had gone out for crisis talks. He said he would do anything; give me the monogamy I wanted, be a better father, live like a normal family. Grow vegetables to make perfect salads. And I probably would have gone, had it not been for her death.'

'So you left him for good?'

'It wasn't easy,' Stella downed the dregs of her glass. 'After Harmony died, I just couldn't cope any more. I'd been feeling down for months, but this was different. I was helpless. I thought about ending things myself. But I had you to think about.'

Stella, poured herself another gin. And so we sat in the fading light, and she told me all the things I had never asked but always subtly known: how young she had been when she had met my father at the protest, and the fascinating lure of his charisma and intelligence to an unschooled teenager from an all-girls grammar who had barely left the manicured enclosures of the London suburbs. 'I romanticised him, of course, as only a girl can. And his desire for me felt like a stamp of approval, like getting the little row of As on my school report.'

She became, in some ways, his follower, or at least that is how her parents would have put it. They saw his radical politics and his Eastern-influenced philosophies, his strange girlish clothes, and essentially came to the conclusion that their young daughter had joined a cult. Where others were revelling in Thatcherism, the delights of marketing and money, Longhope remained steeped in the gauzy residue of the hippie era, a house in which barely anyone worked, and when they did the cash was pooled. They had come once or twice to try and get her back, but Stella was resolute. She had found her place.

'I never imagined myself in an open relationship, and we never really described it in those terms,' she said. 'It was just a natural consequence of our stance on ownership. Why should another human being belong to you? Who are you to limit their bodily pleasures? That's what your dad said anyway, and I wasn't sophisticated enough to contradict him, until I got involved with the women's movement, that is. And then I started putting my foot down.'

She had joined a women's group, which I already knew, though I didn't know the role it was to play in their relationship. By the time Harmony moved into the house, she had started to assert herself about Bryn's other women. His extracurricular activities had dwindled to one or two a year, and Stella had begun to dream of having a child. Then Harmony arrived.

'Coral said you got on well with her, that you didn't mind her sleeping with Dad.'

'I didn't really, at first. It was quite nice to have a break. He could drone on for hours, Bryn, as you well know. Having her there allowed me to focus on myself for a bit. And she was a lovely girl, a great friend, so caring and generous, which is why I felt so guilty about my jealousy of her. She never meant anyone any harm, and was so fragile. I was closer in age to her than I was to Bryn, and I felt a need to protect her. In this I failed, obviously. Sometimes I wonder if she might have been as much in love with me; we were very close, always cooking and drinking together. Would wear each other's clothes and sometimes all shared a bed. She was very attractive in a striking sort of way, you know, that beauty that you want to bask in, regardless of whether you like men or women.'

They had only kissed once, Stella said. One autumn they had made blackberry wine from the brambles in the garden, and the following August it was ready to drink. 'I'm not sure where your father was,' said Stella. 'We were in the house alone.' They had sunk several bottles while listening to soul records, she said. 'Harmony used to roll these incredibly thin, elegant little joints, but they were very potent.'

They were both dreamily high and very drunk when they stood up from where they had been sitting on the rug to dance, and that was when it had happened. Just one small, soft kiss that was open to interpretation: a declaration of intent, or nothing at all.

'There were never any threesomes or anything like that,' she said, and I believed her, though it didn't really matter to me either way.

'Why does Coral blame you for Harmony's death?'

Stella exhaled slowly. 'Did she say that?'

'Not in so many words. She's very cagey, she wouldn't tell me everything. She liked Harmony, didn't she? I could tell she was fond of her. She told me about the miscarriage.'

'I handled that badly.'

'How could you do that to someone?'

Stella gave a shamefaced shrug.

'And I was happy for her. I was. Though I did worry how it would all pan out for our unconventional little family. To be honest, I'm embarrassed to say that I don't think I gave it much thought. Perhaps on some level I thought I was saving her. From us, from her attachment to you. You could see it was hurting her. She had her whole life ahead of her. There was so much she could have done. I imagine Coral feels like we sucked a young, relatively naïve girl into our fucked-up relationship, and there was an element of that, yes.'

'She seems fairly fucked up herself.' I was in the process of explaining about the screams when, as if it had been engineered from above, Coral's bizarre, feline wailing forced itself through the open window.

'What on earth?'

'It's her,' I said, and explained how Josh had told me what was happening to Coral.

'And you've just sat by and listened? None of you has thought to knock on the door, or call the police?'

I shrugged. Coral had never seemed exactly balanced, but neither had I been overly concerned. Coral had never given the impression that she needed my help and made it quite apparent that, had she been in trouble, the last person she would have asked for assistance was the daughter of a woman she hated who lived in the upstairs flat. Or perhaps I am being disingenuous, a selfish child caught up so much in finding the truth of her own story that she failed to take notice of someone else's.

'She seemed ok to me,' I said. Stella was already heading out of the door.

Sosmix

Empty Sosmix (vegetarian sausage mix, 350 g) box from the early-1990s. Cardboard (cream & purple). Reads: 'Vegan & Vegetarian – Cruelty Free & Meat Free, Free From: dairy, egg, lactose, GMO.
Easy to use to make: Veggie sausages, burgers, pies, kievs, sausage rolls, breakfasts and more, just add water and herbs/ spices. Ingredients: Vegetable Oil, Rusk [Wheatflour, Salt, Raising Agent (E503)], Textured Soya Protein [Soya Flour, Zinc Oxide, Niacinamide, Ferrous Sulphate, Copper Gluconate, Vitamin A, Calcium Pantothenate, Thiamine Mononitrate (B-1), Pyridoxine Hydrochloride (B-6), Riboflavin (B-2), Cyanocobalamin (B-12)], Salt, Stabiliser (Methyl Cellulose), Rice Flour, Soya Flour, Modified Potato Starch, Flavourings (contain Wheat), Hydrolyzed Vegetable Protein, Colour (Beetroot Powder), Wheat Flour, Yeast Extract, Spices.
Nutritional Information per 100 g: Energy 1949 kJ / 467 kcal, Protein 18.5 g, Carbohydrate 33 g, Fat 29 g.'

'The funeral was awful,' Stella said, as we all sat on Coral's floor, twilight noises floating through the open doors. 'It was the worst day of my life. And what a setting. The grey Hartlepool docks, the dense lead clouds, her parents standing there, looking so old, stumbling as though every slight move pained them in an indescribable way. Mark's cool fury. I will never forget it.'

'They blamed you.'

'They blamed all of us,' said Coral. 'But I blamed you, for leaving that poor girl at her most vulnerable, after she had lost her baby – all of yours' baby, really – and then toying with her like she was just some ... *thing* to be picked up when you felt like it and then chucked out on the dump. All your toing and froing. You went and gave her hope. She loved you all to death.' She said this simply, with no anger left in her tone. The dusk was drawing in, and the raised voices had long lulled, the tears dried in sticky streaks across the older women's faces. Now they sat, side by side on moth-eaten velvet cushions on the floor, necking from a dusty bottle of brandy. Not friends, exactly, but two people unpicking their shared history after decades of discrepancy, and attempting to re-stitch it in a way that forged some sort of peace.

When Stella had gone downstairs, she had tried banging loudly on Coral's door, and even threw herself against it as I watched with nervous detachment. I had spent the past few months skirting the periphery of Coral's life in the way a child dips the very tips of her toes in the lapping edges of a forbidden pond, taking from her the information I needed while staying enough outside her destructive orbit that I didn't get sucked in. I never asked about her circumstances, or the pain behind her cries. In some ways I considered her squalid existence a natural consequence of the person she was: a poor, washed-up alcoholic who frequented dodgy pubs and even worse men, and who had never worked a day in her life. I created a picture of Coral's life in the same way Josh had, because of the comfort offered by a known, familiar narrative. We were both wrong.

I doubted Coral even heard Stella's attempts to break her door down, so loud was the demented howling that came from within. 'There's a side gate,' I said. 'She never closes her French doors.' We went around the back, negotiating the brambles until we made our way to her cracked patio, the glare from the sunlight so vivid that we could perceive only darkness within.

'Where is he?' I had an old brick in one hand, and was ready to brain him if necessary. I expected Stella to echo my demand, but instead she just stood there and started to laugh. Coral was alone in the middle of the room, wearing a pair of paisley silk harem pants and a greying bra that revealed a sagging belly, her fingertips outstretched at her sides and her pallid face tilted upwards. She was still screaming. No one else was there.

'I can't believe you're still engaging with that bullshit,' said Stella.

Coral said nothing. She didn't even look surprised to see my mother, she just stared.

'What's going on?' I placed the brick gingerly on the floor and stepped towards them. Coral inhaled. My mother turned to me.

'Primal therapy. She used to do it years ago. I can't believe I forgot.' Stella was still laughing. 'Thinks having a good old scream lets all the childhood trauma out. Utterly ridiculous of course, and long discredited.'

I was open-mouthed, 'I thought you were...' I began to laugh too.

'I see you're still the same stuck-up bitch you always were,' said Coral. Then, 'You have two minutes to get the hell out of here before I do you damage.'

Stella stayed where she was, still in the dimness of the near-empty room as I waited for something to happen near the relative safety of the French windows. It was in the flatness of that moment that I saw the room as it had

237

once been: our kitchen, with its sacks of lentils on the floor and the cats sleeping on an old batik cushion beneath the large wooden table as I lay by their side stroking their fur. Instead of curtains, an orange Indian bedspread muted the incoming sunlight; in the dark corners of the room the dust-coated spider plants loomed like monsters. I was seeing it all as though from below; up there on the counter stood several boxes of Sosmix, a substance I had long forgotten but which somehow more than any other foodstuff seemed to sum up the tragedy of my childhood. I could even taste its salty, granular texture all those years later, the artificiality of it that made it both moreish and faintly sickening. I used to stand on a chair next to a bowl on the top and roll it between my chubby palms into cigar shapes, ready for one of the adults to fry, afterwards sucking the pink crumbs from my fingers.

Stacked up next to the sink were piles of cracked, floral pottery. Plates I recalled eating endless lentil curries from, bowls we used to mix interminable nut roasts. The air was thick with the scent of patchouli joss sticks, the dresser littered with poetry periodicals and copies of *The Ecologist*. But I was too big to hide underneath that kitchen table now.

The sound of Coral slapping Stella around the face brought me back. My mother was rubbing her cheek with a mild look, but I could tell she was afraid by the wildness in the other woman's face. Coral was speaking in a low hiss. 'You killed that poor girl. She needed you.'

'She did it to herself,' Stella said, but she had started to cry now. Coral moved her face closer.

'Good. I'm glad you're crying. You should be crying. He should too.'

'No.'

'You left her, still bleeding. What kind of person does that, Stella? You're heartless.'

'I loved him. I loved my child. I just wanted peace. We didn't know she was ill. We didn't know.'

'You knew. How could you not know? You killed her. I have thought about that night we found her every day of my life since. Her hanging there. You don't get a picture like that out of your head. Not ever. And then your daughter moves in and starts asking questions when I'm just trying to live my life.'

Coral had built up some momentum now, and as the words tumbled out, Stella stood and sobbed harder. I felt sorry for her, then. It was a feeling that was unfamiliar to me. I had spent so many years scornful of her inept mothering that I did not know how to comfort her; the physical expressions of compassion seemed alien, as though they were a foreign language. Should I walk over to her, lay my palm on her arm? I did not want to draw Coral's eyes in my direction in case I became the focus of her rage, and so in the end I stood and watched as though it were playing out on a stage, as though afterwards I could rise from my seat, push open the fire door and stride into the cool darkness of the night away from it all.

'I think about it every day too. I couldn't function. Believe me, you can never blame me as much as I blame myself.'

'Bullshit.'

I don't know how long I stood there as Coral berated my mother and she cried, her only retaliation coming in the form of frantic bouts of nodding to indicate that yes, she accepted the blame, but eventually Coral paused and stood exhaling heavily, as though unsure what to do next. Stella was pale and shaking, so I went upstairs to our kitchen to fetch her a brandy, noticing only vaguely as I was up there that the sky had darkened and the rooms were all lit up.

'I thought I had better bring the bottle,' I said. So we sat down, and I listened to them talking of the past, of Bryn and Mikey and that Swedish groupie (what was her name?) and all the other souls who had passed through that house over the years, refusing to accept that the revolution had not happened, that the others had laid down arms, rejoined the 'straight world', and were looking forward to full pensions. Apart from one young girl who never got the chance.

'I hated you,' said Coral. 'I felt like you'd destroyed all that was good about this place, the dream that we could all live together in a haven free from our desire to possess things. But as time has gone on I see that it would have all gone wrong whether you were here or not, because if not you, then it would have been somebody else. We were naïve.'

It all seemed so idealistic. An experiment designed to fail. How could they have failed to acknowledge the inherent graspingness of romantic love? Did they really think that you could simply choose not to feel? But when I thought about my own experiments, the men who had wandered fecklessly in and out of my bed and I theirs as though we were all on our way to somewhere else, I saw that I had been trying to do exactly that. We all were. You learn from the best.

After a while I left them talking. There would be time to go over it all again, to try and scratch out some accord with Stella. Could I blame her for wanting what she had been taught to want? They were careless, but neither of them could have known the inner workings of that poor girl's wretched heart. How could anyone?

It was late by the time I went upstairs, and Josh seemed to have gone out, so I was surprised the lights were all still on. It was only when I walked through the kitchen and the living room that I noticed that Lucia's door, which had been closed for weeks, was wide open, revealing the chaotic squalor of the pit she had been living in. The other two bedroom doors were also open; only the bathroom's was closed.

'Lou?' I tapped lightly. I heard a groan, and then a retching. Then, a low guttural 'shit'.

'Lou darling. Can you open the door?'

There was a hoarse croak in reply, then the sound of a body pulling itself across the linoleum and reaching up to trip the lock.

Bear

Get well soon teddy bear (bought from gift shop in the Whittington Hospital, Archway, N. London. This 20.5 cm (5") teddy bear is made of soft shaggy gold fur and has a blue nose and patches on his head and body. He wears plasters on his head and holds a green felt first aid case printed with the greeting 'Get Well Soon'.

Lucia's face was a pale, waxy mask looking up at me from the floor. She looked horrid, her skin visibly clammy. The toilet wasn't just full of vomit but also surrounded by it. The smell burned the back of my throat.

'Oh darling,' I said, wiping her matted hair from her fringe. 'We've all done it. Let's get you into bed.' I put my hands under her armpits and tried to haul her up, but she was a deadweight, a rag doll stuffed with lead. Her eyes were rolling back in her head. Just how much had she had to drink?

'You're going to have to help me here sweetheart. Come on.'

Lou retched again, and was sick all down her front. Her gaze was objectless, unfocused. 'How much have you had to drink?' She wouldn't look at me, and had closed her eyes, so I slapped her lightly on the cheek.

'Not ... drunk,' she eventually said, in a vague slur. 'Ambulance.'

'Lou. What did you take? You need to tell me now. Coke? MD? 2CB? What was it?'

I grasped her by the shoulders and shook her. 'Lou, you need to tell me. Now.'

'Panadol extra.' She was crying now, and the words were coming out in painstaking gulps. 'I just... didn't want to feel any more. I just wanted it to be dark, and quiet, and nothing. I wanted nothing. I thought I was done.'

'You're not done, Lou. You are very much not fucking done. I'm going to call an ambulance, ok? And we are going to go to hospital, and they are going to sort you out. And you are going to be fine. I promise. You are going to be fine.'

I ran into the kitchen and grabbed my phone, but first I shouted down to Stella. 'Mum!' I brought out the word after years of neglect, and far from sounding childlike and pleading it sounded right. 'Coral! Help!'

Stella stood at the bottom of the stairs. 'What's wrong? What's going on?'

'My flatmate has taken an overdose. She tried to kill herself. She needs an ambulance, now.'

'Is that her car outside?'

'Yes, but I don't know where the keys are.'

'Find them. There's no time. Let's take her up the Whittington. Coral,' she shouted into the doorway, 'we're going to need your help moving her. Let's go. I'm not letting another young girl die in this house.'

We were lucky that the keys were next to Lou's bed, as were several empty packets of paracetamol, and a note that I pocketed. After getting her down the stairs, we laid her along the slightly damp back seat of the 2CV. She was conscious, but not really with us. All that was left when she retched was fluid.

It was only a ten-minute journey, but in that old banger,

which barely went above forty miles an hour, it felt like forever. As always in that car, you had the disturbing sensation that all that was separating your feet from the tarmac was a piece of carpet. Stella, who didn't have a car and had never driven much, stalled several times on the Junction Road, swearing. But eventually, she pulled in with a screech to the ambulance bay and we rushed into A&E.

'She's taken an overdose of paracetamol,' I was shouting. The woman in scrubs looked barely older than me. 'She needs her stomach pumped *now*.'

'We don't do that anymore,' said the doctor. 'What's her name? Lucia, can you hear me? What time did you take the paracetamol? How much did you take?'

'I changed my mind. I changed my mind,' said Lou. 'Stupid. I'm. So. Stupid.'

'It must have been in the last hour or two,' I said. 'She wasn't in when I went upstairs at around ten.'

'That's good news. Right, let's get you sorted out. We're going to measure her levels. If you could stay in the waiting area, we'll come and find you when we know more. Are you family? No. You need to get in touch with them if you can.'

We waited. At some point, Josh joined us in the greyness of the A&E lobby, but we didn't speak after the initial retelling of events. Stella was frantic, moving and twitching constantly. I welcomed the stillness of him, pressing my face into his chest, its solidity grounding me when the urge was to float away. Who knows where, somewhere happier, I suppose, somewhere where Lucia's pain was not etched on her face. I wondered if there was something I could have done to help her, rather than leaving her to suffocate under the weight of her sadness alone in the sultry chaos of her room as I moaned and pirouetted next door, Josh turning my body this way and that.

Another doctor came in and told us that Lou's levels were dangerously high and that she would need to be put on an IV drip containing a reversal agent for forty-eight hours. Stella started to cry, but when I returned from getting coffee Josh had his hand on her shoulder and she was smiling weakly, and I saw that his gruff, northern tenderness had charmed her. 'She'll be all right,' he said, 'just you see.'

'You've got a good one there,' she said, sotto voce.

Hours passed. He fell asleep and I sat there, counting his eyelashes, wondering what Lou was thinking, if she was thinking at all. They wouldn't let us see her. Quentin and Cecilia arrived, the latter fraught. I noted Stella's empathy when comforting her and, when Lou's parents went in to talk to the consultant, I hugged her tight. Odd though it may be for an adult to admit, but the softness of her breasts against my cheek felt like a homecoming.

Eventually, they let us in to see her. She thanked Stella weakly. 'You gave us all a fright,' she said, brushing Lou's sweaty fringe from her face in a maternal fashion.

We brought her a bear, from the gift shop, the sticking plaster above its eye a cheap pastiche of illness that made her laugh, us all thinking if only things were so simple.

'They're sending over the psych team,' said Lucia, after Stella had left the room. 'Perhaps they'll put me in a straitjacket and bundle me into the back of a van.'

An odd picture of my ex clutching a giant butterfly net flitted through my mind, and I smiled. No one could ever mothball Lou and put her in a case.

'I feel like a complete twat,' she said. 'It hasn't worked out at all'.

'The killing yourself part?'

'Well, obviously that. Don't hate me, but I wanted it to be glamorous. You'd come home and find me draped across the bed like a leggy fashion model, and my note, an empty bottle of red, and a Leonard Cohen record playing. Instead I took it all and then thought, oh shit. I don't want to die. Rookie mistake, when you're trying to kill yourself, bottling it. Almost as amateur as cutting horizontally. What a fool.'

All I said was, 'Lou.'

'Sorry, it's too soon to joke, isn't it? No wonder they think I'm a headcase.'

'It's me who should be sorry. I should have noticed how bad things have got, instead of being so wrapped up in my new boyfriend.'

She reached for my hand. 'You're in love. It's spectacular to see. I'd like that for myself, one day. But all the men I ever seem to meet are bores, or rapists.'

We were silent, both aware of the significance, the naming of it.

'I'm so angry with him, Harmony. I loved sex, it was what I did best. I loved the feeling of new skin, and lips, and hair. New bodies against mine. The fucker took that away from me.'

'You'll get it back.'

'Who knows if I will? You know, sometimes I felt like I only existed when I was being looked at. I liked to be wanted, by women, but especially by men. There was power in their wanting. Until that moment, in bed, when I realised that actually I hadn't any power at all, that his wanting was a tyrant, and I this bleak, broken thing for him to use.'

She choked.

'I hate it. I hate them. A victim. It doesn't suit me.'

'They'll get you the help that you need, I'm sure of it. You'll see. They'll mend your head just as they did the bear.'

She laughed, her fingertips pressing into the side of my hand.

'Thank you for helping me,' she said. 'I'm glad you found me. Really. I didn't want to die, not even a little bit. Not when it came down to it.'

She came home two days later, undeterred by pleas from her parents that she go to live with them for a while ('I'm already mad enough'). As a compromise, they forked out for a new Harley Street therapist, whom she began seeing immediately, three times a week. She had the frail look of someone who has just wandered dazed from a bomb site and is clutching the side of a building to steady themselves, but she was joking more, and sleeping less, which meant a marked improvement.

Several days later – or at least I think that's how long it was, it is hard to tell because of the cloud of booze and drugs that engulfed us in those days – Amy died. I know it was not long after Lou's botched overdose, because we were nagged by the unpleasant feeling that it so easily could have been another girl from only slightly further up the Kentish Town Road, with amazing hair and a set of problems of her own. But it wasn't, it was Amy.

Lucia was the one who broke it to me, walking into the lounge the morning after. 'Amy Winehouse is dead.' She was crying, for the snuffed-out sparkler that was Amy, of course, but also for her own lucky escape. It felt personal, this death, not only because we knew the words of this woman's heartache as though we had written them ourselves, but because it took us back to a time, five or six years earlier. We didn't know each other then, but it turns out we were both slumming it around Camden, and were loosely part of the same scene. You'd see Amy a lot back then, hanging around the pool table of the Good Mixer on Inverness Street, a hole of a pub that probably isn't even open any more, though if it were it would smell of shit as much as ever. Or she'd be there, stumbling out of the Hawley Arms with a man in skinny jeans, skipping down the high street. She was famous already, but that didn't stop her being Camden's girl. You'd see her bleeding in the *Sun* one moment and having a fag on the corner the next, as though she had stepped out of the pages and been made real. It was a similar feeling when I saw Pete Doherty queuing in a branch of the Camden NatWest around the same time. I'd assumed he kept his money in his mattress.

We didn't know her, this was not our tragedy, but nonetheless we went down to the square where her fans had gathered outside her house, and held each other and wept at the awful sadness of it as people laid flowers and lit candles and did all those things that you do because you can't bear to think of the nothingness of it. Some people had left fags and glasses of wine, a bottle of Smirnoff vodka, a can of Carlsberg. Tasteless perhaps, but who were we to judge? These were the offerings of those who had also been attendant at the party – whether with her, or near her. It didn't matter.

We gave our alms and scrawled our names, along with many others, on the covered street sign, ducking under the police sign, and left, walking home through the dusk, reminiscing about our younger years. We were older now, and Camden, with its Spanish teenagers and its sunglasses in cheap neon, had lost its sheen for us; it was all about the East.

It's funny how the mind creates patterns in retrospect, so tempting and easy to say tritely that Amy's death for us meant the party was finally over, that the lights had come up, and we didn't like what we saw. But it wasn't like that; we carried on drinking, and smoking, and snorting, though perhaps with less carelessness than before. It had occurred to me that Lou might not be the only one who needed help. The nightmares and flashbacks had stopped since hearing of Harmony's death and my presence at it, but I was left with a residual feeling of nausea. I had begged Stella not to disclose my past at Longhope, feeling that I needed to tell Josh and Lou without her there, and she had kept her promise and treated the place with the deference of a guest.

She and Coral had not made amends, exactly, but they parted with Coral hating her a little less. Like it or not their pasts were entwined, and their time at the commune, or co-op, or however you want to categorise that odd assortment of hippies and misfits and grubby-faced children who had spun their lives around that house, had created the lost older women they were today. Both had failed to inhabit any of the roles society had stood ready for them with: as mothers, as employees, as wives or girlfriends. Stella told me once that after she married Bryn, something she had been desperate to do, she had heard someone refer to her as his wife and had physically recoiled. But she had fought for a traditional set-up, dragging Bryn far away from Harmony and any other potential lovers, and so was required to make it work. That's the thing about nuclear families: they leave you nowhere to hide.

Card

Card showing rainbow, clouds and sun with face. Holes where a badge would have been affixed (missing). Reverse of card shows number 4081, reads: 'Nickel City Buttons, Printed by Sunrise Publications under licence to Nickel City Buttons Inc. © 1986.'

Some things my father likes:

> Eastern religions
> Macrobiotic cookery
> *The I-Ching*
> Foucault
> The Isle of Wight Festival
> Anarchism
> Marijuana
> Lentil curry
> Shamanism
> Statues of the Buddha
> The *Guardian*
> Spider plants
> Vegetable gardening
> Folk music
> Chunky knitwear
> *The Ecologist*
> Chairman Mao Tse-tung's *Little Red Book*, the inner flyleaf of which contains a sheet of rice paper the ideal dimensions for the rolling of a joint

Patchouli
Yoruba beads
The Tibetan Book of the Dead
The Kabbalah
Drumming
Jam

I took the train north, and then waited near the border as a diesel engine was affixed to the front of the train, which pootled at its own pace along the coast until the scenery turned from green to grey. That day the sea was flat and still like molten silver, but I imagined it could be wild, that the spray could splash the windows leaving a salty residue that made them hazy and blurred as the carriages jerked and wheezed. I don't know what I thought about, if anything at all. I know that I felt a sense of relief following the conversation I had had with Josh and Lucia that morning.

'I'm just going to come out and say this', I said, taking a big breath, 'and I know you're both going to think I am completely unhinged. But I lived here before, as a child. With my parents. And a lot of other people. You see, it was this commune…'

Of course they were surprised, and a little alarmed, but both admitted that my reticence had been a source of curiosity, and on Josh's face, there was a flickering of understanding. 'I wondered why you were spending so much time with her downstairs,' he said. 'I thought it was odd, and you were so secretive about it, but I could sometimes hear you going in and out.'

When I told them about Coral's primal screaming, they both just stared. Then I explained about Harmony's suicide, and Lucia came over and put her arms around my neck.

'How awful for you,' she said. 'How traumatic. You were just a baby.'

'You could have told me,' Josh said, quietly. 'I could have helped.'

'The thing is,' I said. 'I didn't really know myself. Or rather, I knew there was something: the nightmares, and feeling sad. This weird feeling of dislocation from the world, sometimes, like I was separate. But I just thought maybe it would go away on its own.'

It hadn't. And it wouldn't. Such things take time, if you can ever really get over them. But I knew that a part of trying involved having to go and see my father, with whom I'd barely had any contact from one year to the next. I had lost his telephone number, Stella hadn't spoken to him for over a decade, my grandparents were dead and his sister estranged, but I knew the name of the closest village to where he lived, and figured that, as it was so small and rural, someone would be able to direct me from there.

The station was shabby, looking more as though it belonged in the former USSR than a coastal town in Wales. The ticket office was closed, the paint on its hatch peeling. A few wilted hanging baskets were the only nod towards aesthetics. As I walked outside my cheeks were misted with rain. The air was damp and cool. After weeks of clear blue skies it felt very much like another country.

I took a small green bus from outside the station, whose route seemed to incorporate every village in the surrounding area whether it was easily accessible or not. I was the only passenger, and very unsure of where I was. The roads were narrow and winding, bordered by overgrown hedgerows. We stopped several times for sheep. Every time we began to mount steadily into the drizzle, I would wonder if we had nearly arrived, only for us to reach a dead end where we would turn around and descend, down past the curved-up mountainsides, pocked with giant holes spewing out mounds of purplish slate hundreds of feet high. This happened four or five times in an hour, until the white dots of cottages and the solemn grey spires of isolated chapels became denser, and we passed signs of more close-knit habitation: a red telephone box, a church yard, a village post office, though boarded up. There was a static, depressed air to the place. It seemed abandoned except for kids in baseball caps on bikes, and the odd elderly lady shuffling up the street with a shopping bag. Perhaps it was the weather; I could see the place was beautiful.

The driver came to a halt at the edge of a narrow road that had no bus-stop sign, not a usual stopping place. When I had got on, I had haltingly pronounced the name of the place, and he had corrected my pronunciation gruffly but kindly. 'Just down there,' he nodded now towards a single dirt track bordered by bent over trees, 'for about a mile'.

Within seconds, I was wet through with the rain. There was little in the way of scenery to keep me occupied, just trees and fields, though the lie of the land, it's sharp drops and curves, made me aware that I was in a forest on the edge of one of the mountains. About halfway along I passed an old abandoned car through which a mass of weeds grew. They poked through the windows and around the bonnet like tentacles, and with a start I realised that it was the old yellow Datsun, the one Stella had put me in when she drove us away from him and back to Longhope. I wondered how long it had been there, whether her tape would somehow magically still be in the slot of the cassette player, her Afghan coat draped across the back seat so I could use it as a blanket, as though we'd only just popped out for twenty minutes, not twenty years.

At the end of the track I came to a typical stone Welsh cottage, squat but sprawling, with many additional outbuildings dotted around a garden of drenched wall-flowers. I took a deep breath, and knocked on the door.

'Harmony.' It was Mokomo who answered the door, and she did not look best pleased. Her arms were crossed around herself defensively as she held the silk dressing gown she was wearing close to her body, but nonetheless it was clear that she was naked underneath. When she used one hand to trip the latch I saw a glimpse of a full, pale breast, almost perfectly round, like in a drawing. She can't have been more than four years older than me, so it was difficult to treat her with the deference of a stepdaughter and impossible to approach her with the warm familiarity of a friend. In the end I settled for a light kiss on the cheek.

'Why didn't you call?'

'Lost the number,' I said. 'Do you mind if I sit down? I'm knackered. Where's Dad?'

'Bryn's just meditating in the yurt,' said Mokomo, with a straight face, as she beckoned me into the kitchen to fetch a floral teapot and fill an old-fashioned metal kettle for the hob. It was so chilly in there, with its slate floor tiles and its bare stone walls, that they had a fire burning in the grate. 'Best not to disturb him. He'll be in in half an hour or so. I wish we had known you were coming. I would have tidied up. Though as you know with your father that's a losing battle.'

She was not wrong. Bryn's hoarding problem – a neurosis he had developed as he got older – seemed to be as bad as ever. Every single surface was piled with books, papers and miscellaneous objects. While Stella moved from place to place shedding material things like dead skin, Bryn would bed down somewhere for several years and, somewhat ironically for someone who sought to free himself from the binds created by possessions, spent that time accumulating. It wasn't a mental illness as such, but it was a problem. You struggled to get him to throw anything out, including things like old newspapers and broken ornaments and used train tickets. Everything that had passed through his house was imbued with a powerful but inexplicable sentimentality that was exasperating for those around him, and none of us had ever known what to do about it. So more stuff piled up.

I made stilted small talk with Mokomo as the kettle hissed on the stove, the steam rising towards the bare beams of the ceiling, the windows becoming misty with condensation and the room filling with that smell of warm, wet fabric as it dried off. I had resorted to asking her about her yoga teaching by the time Bryn walked into the room, his face breaking out into a big smile when he saw me.

'Darling,' he said, his arms outstretched. I hugged him, feeling like a little girl again, as I always did whenever he was close, wanting so powerfully for him to approve of me. As we embraced and I breathed in his earthy cloth smell, I found myself wondering if this was how the other Harmony felt, whether her desire to be loved by him outweighed the value of her own self to such an extent that she only felt she existed when he was there, lending her tangibility with the prize of his approval.

We sat and talked as Mokomo prepared dinner in the background. We discussed the current state of politics, the anti-austerity protests of the previous autumn and the death of the counter-culture, the coalition government, London and its smirking, constantly changing face. I say discussed, but mostly he talked and my eyes flickered around the room, taking in the Eastern art and marijuana plants and back copies of the *Guardian*, and wondering if he knew he was a cliché or thought his way of living renegade and unique. I explained my departure from university, and he looked momentarily disappointed before joshing about having brought me up with a healthy disrespect for structure and authority. I've been anxious and depressed, I said. He replied that this was a rational response to late-stage advanced capitalism.

'No, Daddy,' I said, putting a hand on his arm. 'I went back to Longhope, after leaving,' and he raised his eyes to mine and shook his head almost imperceptibly to mean, later, not while she is here.

We were able to talk freely only after our dinner of homemade pizza (toppings foraged from the garden, naturally) and a big fat joint that saw Mokomo retire to their bedroom, bidding us goodnight. We sat in what he called his study, though what exactly it was he studied and to what ends had always been a mystery to me. He poured us some elderflower champagne that he had made and began rolling us another spliff. I watched the expert movements of his fingers as he wetted the Rizla and rolled that breed of three-skin joint that no one knew how to make any more, thanks to the introduction of king-size papers, an innovation that my father had always regarded as cheating.

'I know about Harmony's death,' I said, as he twisted the end and handed it to me to light (he always let me do this, even though he always rolled). I inhaled sharply, three times. 'I remembered it. And Coral and Mum confirmed it.'

Bryn coughed to hide his surprise, then shifted in his seat, looking embarrassed.

'Hiding it from me wasn't exactly the best way forward. I've been having nightmares, panic attacks...if I hadn't met Coral I might never have realised why it was happening.'

'Coral is still there? Blimey.'

'She's in a bad way. Drink.'

'That's sad.'

'Not as sad as what happened to Harmony,' I said. 'Why didn't you tell me?'

'We haven't exactly had a close relationship in recent years,' said Bryn. 'Plus, I let your mother decide what to do about all that.'

'You used her,' I spat, hot smoke burning the back of my throat. 'Aren't you embarrassed?'

'With all due respect, Harmony, you don't have a clue what you are talking about.' He frowned at me. 'What have Stella and Coral been saying, exactly?'

'Just the truth. About your whole free love bullshit, which was, by the way, about twenty years out of date even in the eighties. Nice work keeping up with the times.'

He was shocked into silence.

'Very convenient philosophy that, isn't it? Allowing you to have sex with much younger women, not caring when you knock them up. Leaving Harmony to suffer alone.'

He looked pained. 'I didn't know she was pregnant, or that she had miscarried. I only found out at the funeral. I'll never forget the look Coral gave me when she told me, as we walked away from the church yard.'

His eyes were watery. I actually thought he was going to cry. The only time I had seen him do that before was when the cat died.

'And if by free love, you mean the fact that I don't believe in monogamy, then yes, you'd be correct. But everyone involved was consenting. You can't really understand unless you were there. When we moved in, in the early seventies, we wanted to form a new type of community. A new way of living, and loving, and bringing up children, communally. Which includes you, by the way. You had a house full of parents, don't you feel lucky to have had that?'

I didn't say anything.

I knew what he meant, in a way. There were always people in the house, and they cared for me, certainly. But most of the adults were around only as vague, shadowy presences – they cooked your dinner and they put you to bed, but it wasn't the same as the bond I shared with Stella, Bryn and Harmony. A child can only take in so much, after all.

'I don't remember Stella saying that you changed any nappies.'

Bryn sighed, and reached out and stroked my cheek with his thumb.

'You're my only daughter and I love you very much, but I've never been good with children. Or at least, I was never made to feel as though I was. I always tried to show you that I loved you, and to treat you as an equal, give you the respect that you deserve as an intelligent being.'

'But that's the thing, *Dad,*' the last word as loaded as one of his bongs, 'we're not equals. I'm the child. I. Am. The. Child.'

I was shouting now, despite feeling slightly ridiculous.

'Harmony, you are not a child. You are twenty-five.'

'You're a misogynist.'

'I beg your pardon?'

'With all your women. It's pathetic. It was all free love for you. But not them, oh no.'

'That was their choice.'

'Of course. Of course it was their choice.'

'I'm not a misogynist. Do you think Mokomo – a feminist – would be with me if I were?'

'I doubt Mokomo can even spell the word feminist, to be honest.'

'Don't talk about her like that.'

I was standing now, while he remained seated. I felt a fury that was foreign to me, but at the same time there was a pleasurable electricity to it. I felt alive with livid possibility.

'Why couldn't you just be normal parents? Why couldn't we just live in a normal house, with you in normal jobs, doing what parents are supposed to fucking do rather than all this insane hippy bullshit that has by the way totally messed me up, not that you give a shit. You're too busy following your sainted 'principles' to care about anyone around you. And someone ended up dead, because you just couldn't help yourself. You had to go and seduce her.'

Bryn spoke in a measured tone. 'I did not seduce her. The thought of having a family seduced her. She was a lost soul.'

'Bullshit.'

'It's true. And I loved her very much. She was a wonderful young woman, and particularly great with you. She mother-ed you more than Stella, in the early years. That's what she couldn't stand, actually, it wasn't just about losing Stella and me, it was about losing you, too, it was about the break-up of the house. For us, it was the natural end of an era. We were sad, but in many ways it was time to grow up and take some responsibility. She didn't feel the same. That house had become everything to her.'

'So it's my fault.'

'I'm not saying that. But you have to understand, it was a different time. We gave it a go but after having you we quickly realised that we wanted something more private, more stable. I wanted to make your mother happy. I don't see what's so misogynistic about that. I resent that accusation, in fact. We used to take in lots of single mothers, actually, with their children, who had left their violent partners. Bit of an occupational hazard with communes – you end up with people who have nowhere to go. But we could never say no, we always tried to help them. Harmony had been through the ringer, what with the strike. And Longhope made her happy, but it had to come to an end.'

'Why?'

'A multitude of reasons. I think – and I hope you don't find this patronising and if you do I really don't mean to be – but you've always glamorised Longhope a bit. I know you have problems with the way we brought you up but I can see secretly you're quite proud of it. It gives you a touch of bohemianism perhaps, and sets you apart from your peers ...'

'Oh, please.'

'Hear me out. You need to realise that it wasn't like that. We had to have a cleaning rota. There would be furious arguments about whether or not we should be vegan or vegetarian or macrobiotic or whatever. No one ever did the washing up, or if they did they demanded a parade afterwards. Once one of the mothers blew a gasket because Harmony gave you all beans and fish fingers for tea. We had to ask her to leave. Mikey D was off his face on drugs all the time and sometimes used to leave them around within reach of you all. Fleur had furious arguments with her boyfriend where she threw things across the room. And there were always, always people there. Never any privacy at all. Most of them we didn't even know where they had bloody come from. It was like a temporary holding pen for the lost and directionless.'

I didn't say anything.

'Why do you think I live with Mokomo now? Just the two of us? Yes, we have people come and stay for retreats and storytelling workshops, but I just couldn't run a commune full-time. It didn't work.' He took another toke and gestured to me, and I sat down again. 'And by the way, I don't believe that humans are meant to be monogamous. That's never been a line of thinking that has held much sway with me, and it's why it never really worked with your mother. It's not really in our nature. But what I will say is that it is a hell of a damn sight easier.'

I laughed, but he wasn't joking.

'For what it's worth, sweetheart, I am sorry that Harmony died. And I'm sorry that your mother and I weren't honest with you about it. We blamed each other, and that was difficult. And most of all, I'm so sorry that we left you alone with her and that you had to see her ... doing that. I'll never forgive myself for that.'

I reached out a hand and put it on his shoulder. There's something about seeing your dad cry, even if he hasn't been all that good a father. But there he was, in front of me: my rubbish dad, and I didn't have another one.

We stayed up for the rest of the night talking, not amicably, exactly, in fact the whole exchange was fairly challenging, but with a newfound comradeship. He saw me, and I started to see him, not as a hero or a villain in a children's story as I had had it, or as the prisoner of uncontrollable events he was in his version, but as a man with flaws. He had disappointed me, and I loved him. The two would have to coexist.

He drove me to the station the next day in his beat up old van. I didn't want to hang around. For a start the weather was atrocious, but I was also keen to get back to Josh, a man who didn't look at me with an expression that implied I was some strange unidentifiable creature, but with a soft familiarity coupled with a healthy helping of wry scepticism. I suppose what you need the most in that other person, if you are fortunate enough to find him or her, is an ability to cut through the mythology you have created around yourself and really see you.

Bryn walked me onto the platform and we hugged goodbye.

'You really should sort out that house of yours,' I said. 'Or else one day they'll find you crushed beneath a mountain of stuff.'

'I think we know that is never going to happen,' he said. 'But speaking of stuff, I thought you'd like to have this.'

He handed over a large brown envelope that was stuffed almost to bursting.

Once I had found my seat, I emptied it out onto the folding table in front of me. Letters. One for each day that Stella and I had been away from him. Letters pleading for us to come home, saying how much he missed us. Messages he posted to me and saved from the house, written in childspeak, saying Daddy loves you, Daddy will see you soon. I spent the rest of the journey reading them, and cried properly and hideously and without shame, almost all the way to London.

Then, at the bottom of the pile, a small, rather kitsch card with a rainbow set against a blue sky peppered with cartoon clouds, and a small smiling yellow sun not unlike the one on the side of that old squat that I had loved so much when I was little. It read: 'You are my sunshine', and inside, in a childlike hand, was written 'Gabriel', and three kisses.

It wasn't difficult to find him. Stella passed on Vita's phone number, and as soon as I arrived back in London I called her from a payphone and took the underground down to Brixton. I hadn't been watching the news, and my phone had run out of battery several days before, so when I emerged from the train and was met with the eerie silence of the station I was completely unaware of the chaos that had already begun to sweep the city. 'You should probably get yourself home, love,' said the solitary member of TFL staff hovering by the ticket machines. 'Take care.'

The absence of any music struck me as strange. There was always music at Brixton station. The year before I had watched smiling as three beautiful teenage girls clutching cans of beer danced to the beat of a steel drum, laughing as their skinny limbs flailed carelessly, and the gathered crowd applauded in the drawing dusk. All I heard this time as I mounted the stairs were the sounds of smashing glass and police sirens. As I came out of the exit, something lobbed from the other side of the street made contact with the window of the adjacent Sainsbury's, and I jumped. There were no cars on the high street, just groups of teenagers in dark clothing clustered in groups, their faces covered. Half the shop windows had been smashed up, the pavement and road iced with broken glass that crunched beneath feet as a couple of kids rushed to help themselves to the stock. Towards the Ritzy cinema I saw what seemed to be a large bonfire, framed by dark figures flickering. A few people stood back, watching from the relative shelter of the station, but apart from the looters running back and forth the street was mostly deserted.

And there, in the middle of this war zone, was Gabs, in jeans, white trainers and a Grandmaster Flash T-Shirt. Two decades later and I'd have known those eyes and those smooth, chubby cheeks anywhere. His face broke out in a massive smile when he saw me walking over. When I reached him, I threw myself upon him, feeling the lithe tightness of his muscles beneath the cotton as his arms enveloped me. I was crying hard, and it was only after several minutes of this that I noticed that he was crying too, and that we should probably get out of the way or else we would be hit by the car that was pulling out, its boot loaded up with half the stock of Curry's.

'Let's head to mine,' he said. 'Can't stay here. They'll arrest me. Though to be honest I could do with some new trainers.'

'Those look pretty box fresh to me,' I said, and he grinned.

As we walked, he explained that a man had been shot by police, and that there were riots all over the city. 'But to be honest, it was only a matter of time. It's been bubbling for a while.'

I had never seen London looking like this, lawless, anarchy crackling in the air. The sirens were deafening, but I didn't feel frightened. Gabs and I had seen worse than this.

Vita enveloped me in her bosom as soon as she opened the door of the flat. 'I told him not to go and fetch you,' she said. 'I didn't want him getting stopped and hassled, or arrested' – a silent 'again' – 'but the boy wouldn't listen, he never would. Come here, let me look at you. I can't believe how big you are.'

We sat in the small living room as Vita busied herself in the kitchen, the stern cadence of BBC news announcers booming from the radio. 'You'll have to stay the night,' she shouted through the hatch. 'I'm not letting you back out there darling. Your mum would kill me.'

'You can stay in my room, with me,' he said, and we exchanged a look.

We talked of many things that night, Gabs and I, of that summer together, of what we had been doing since. Gabs was a student at Camberwell, but had struggled with depression on and off since his teens.

'What happened was never a secret in this house,' said Vita, as we sat around the tiny table, her hands clutching one each of ours as though in a circle of prayer. 'We talked about it whenever you raised the subject, didn't we darling?'

'Yeah. And maybe it helped. I dunno. I spend months in my room, sometimes. At school ... didn't want to see my mates, or chase after girls. Smoked a lot.'

Vita clicked her tongue against her teeth.

'When I get that way, it's like there's a part of me missing. Some vital organ. I'm not sure if our way of handling it was better or worse.'

'Just different,' I said. 'I was never depressed, but I felt separate from everyone. It's only now that I can see how lonely that was.'

Vita squeezed my hand. 'And what will you do now? Gabs is teaching drawing, one day a week.'

'They wanted to put me on workfare. Make me stack shelves at Poundland for my benefit.'

'I don't know,' I said, in answer to her question. 'Go somewhere abroad, maybe. Get some sun. Have an adventure. I can't just be a waitress forever. And London feels harsh to me now.' I nodded towards the window.

'It's not the same city,' said Vita. A siren somewhere outside blared as if in response.

'By the way, I've got something to show you.' It was the card he had given me. Vita roared with laughter and said he had always been a smooth talker. 'Your first girlfriend,' she goaded. 'The first of many.'

I couldn't keep my eyes away from his face, and he could barely speak for smiling, and so eventually long after midnight she left us like that, bathed in the warm light of the kitchen, speaking softly to one another, drunk on our pasts and several cans of Red Stripe, until the fingers of sleep engulfed us and we curled, fully dressed, into one another on the faded sofa.

Coral died that autumn, her liver packing up as she had always said it would. Josh and I were the ones who found her, slumped in her armchair as though asleep, the door ajar: a hint that she had known and wanted to be found in good time. As I stood there, looking around her decrepit flat, anywhere but at her bloated face, I felt glad that she died knowing someone was around. She may have been a rude, cantankerous addict, but I had grown fond of her.

Her death came as a surprise to no one. What did, however, were the details of her estate. She left the house in Longhope Crescent entirely to me. I discovered shortly after the funeral that she had owned the entire building – bought for £50,000 from Islington Council in 1993 – and had amassed a not-insubstantial fortune as a result of the income from tenants. 'That dark horse,' said Josh, in a low whistle. 'You think you've got the measure of someone.'

'You told me a housing association owned it,' I said.

'I thought it did,' said Josh, a look of wonder on his face. 'The agency dealt with everything.'

'I'm not surprised she employed them, actually. She barely knew what day of the week it was, bless her.'

One misty day in late October, after a short memorial service, we scattered Coral's ashes beneath a tree on Hampstead Heath. 'She would have preferred Stonehenge during the solstice,' sighed Stella, and Mikey D, who looked dishevelled even in his smart funeral suit which happened to be red, let out a loud hoot of laughter. There was only a small group of mourners: Me and Josh, Lucia, Fleur, grown with two boys now, though no longer with Rufus, Bryn and Mokomo, Gabs and Vita, and Harmony's brother, who, it emerged when we looked through her papers, had stayed in touch with Coral throughout their lives. We tried to give her a good send-off. Mikey, who greeted Bryn with a slap on the back that almost knocked him off his feet, played 'Spirit in the Sky' on the mandolin, and as we clutched handfuls of her ashes and released them in finger starbursts we all sang 'Blowin' In The Wind', accompanied by Bryn on the harmonica and laughing through our tears.

'She'd have liked that,' said Stella back at the house, sipping on a glass of red, her dangly earrings chiming metallically as she spoke. Her mascara had run and she hadn't bothered to clean it up, but otherwise, she looked wonderful in the bell-sleeved floral dress she had dug out in tribute. None of us wore black.

'She would have liked it to see us all together again.' Bryn clinked his mug of green tea against our glasses and put his arm around me. 'I can't believe the old girl was still here.'

'I don't think she ever really moved on,' I said.

'It was a colossal mess at the end, but we had some great times in this place.' My parents smiled at each other, a temporary intimacy restored. Their initial meeting had been polite and stilted, with both taking refuge in other people's presence. As I walked away, I heard my dad turn to her and say, 'hey, remember when ...'. After reaching a polite distance, I turned and saw Stella raise her eyes to his and laugh at some anecdote or other that I couldn't have made out, and my throat caught and my nose tingled as it struck me that one day they too would cease to be, and that all those 'remember whens' they'd shared, all those trips and parties and rows and mornings would fade to nothing, and I felt glad to have had the chance, just to see them standing there together, once.

Then came the job of clearing her flat, a doddle considering she owned barely anything, save for a few boxfuls of photographs that I was happy to inherit. We burned Harmony's suicide note, which Coral had folded into eighths and kept in a carved wooden box. There was no need for it now. I knew that she had loved me; and by telling me her story Coral had fulfilled her final wishes: I would remember her. I'm not one for hippie bullshit, but keeping the note felt like bad energy.

I'd asked Mikey if he wanted anything but he told me to have it all. He was living in a maisonette in Hackney now and had set up an online group called 'Longhope Crescent Commune 1970–1992'. 'You should join,' he said. 'You might find out some more stuff.' I declined the offer. I felt I had had enough reminiscing for a lifetime, though I hear that Bryn and Stella both remain active members.

Josh, Lucia and I planned to remain in the flat, but when I finally got around to having a survey done it was found to be structurally unsound and I was told that the whole building would need to be demolished. Coral's final joke. 'If anyone was going to inherit a condemned building, then it was going to be you,' said Josh, patting me on the shoulder. But nevertheless, the sale of the land would be enough to set up comfortably somewhere else.

In early spring of the following year, we decided to leave London. An ageing photographer with links to my old department was looking for an archivist to come and sort through the chaotic back catalogue he had amassed in his house in Italy, so I volunteered myself, and Josh decided to come with me. Lucia, who had offered to stay behind in the building until the sale went through, helped me fill an entire skip, a process that was agonising at the time. All those lost things, all that history, off to the dump. Letting it go was a wrench, but afterwards I felt a lightness, and I haven't thought of a single one of those objects since.

The day before we loaded up the car and drove away from Longhope I took one last walk along the Regent's Canal. It was a boiling hot afternoon, unseasonably so, and I felt drunk with love for the city and the people in it. I passed the Muslim families filing into Central Mosque and smiled at the furious cockney objections of a small boy dawdling in full traditional dress, 'We've been walking for ages, Dad' as his sister, in a headscarf, clipped him around the ear. Around the back of the zoo I marvelled at the caged

270

exotic birds and wondered whether sometimes they forget where they are and take flight, only to hit a mesh threshold thousands of metres short of where they want to be. The manicured lawns of the opulent houses around Regent's Park spoke to me of hidden lives, lives which even Lucia – privileged though she was – had only brushed past some gilded cocktail evening. On the approach to Camden Town I saw a woman in a baggy denim shirt painting an enormous canvas, an abstract view of the scene that was vivid with colour; I pointed two lost tourists from Yorkshire in the direction of the lock, and skipped past a barge dweller swearing at his pit bull – 'scuse my French, love'. There were the people on the bench smoking conspiratorially, their intimacy unbreachable despite the looseness of the mood, and, under a bridge, a begging hippie in a patchwork jacket, stinking of pot. As I reached Camden the crowd got thicker, the Rastas mixing with the tour groups, who sat with their containers of dodgy street food, their legs dangling along the edge of the canal and joggers wove in and out, doing their best to avoid the swarms of people jostling for the perfect photograph next to graffiti that politely read, 'Can we have the revolution yet, please?'.

I would be sad to leave this city, but it wasn't what it once was. It certainly wasn't the place my parents had found when they had come here; it wasn't even the place that I had found, and no doubt, for some stranger who arrived with a suitcase the day that we left – one in, one out, because that's how it always goes – it is now no longer the place that they first found, either.

But as we drove away from Longhope for the last time, giddy with the freedom of movement that would take us somewhere warmer, cheaper, lighter, I gazed out of the window at the sunlit streets, and all of the Londons of the past seemed to shimmer and converge, with each house and open window and pedestrian springing from a different era as the film of the air flickered and constricted. It felt as though the city, smelling as it did of a mixture of pie and mash and weed and jerk chicken and rubbish and expensive cologne, had become, momentarily, a projection screen for all its histories, reaching back, far back into the past of its people, the hippies and punks and migrants and rappers, city workers and career politicians, cabbies and dealers and hookers, the gypsies in the underpass at Marble Arch, the woman in a mobility scooter outside the chippy, the addict grasping at remnants of scratchcards on the pavement, and Bryn and Stella and Lucia and Coral and Mikey and Josh and Gabs, and Harmony, and me. All of us just passing through.

www.sandstonepress.com

 facebook.com/SandstonePress/

 @SandstonePress